R. G

BIDDING FAREWELL

Already preparing to come to Brenda's rescue, Cody McCloud paused to see if the three strangers were going to agree to leave. When it became apparent that they had no intention to do so, he glanced at Jug, who nodded his silent confirmation. Splitting up, they both drew their revolvers. "I expect you'd best put that gun away," Jug said, eyeing Blackie with a look that promised serious consequences if the suggestion was ignored.

Blackie hesitated, not sure of his chances. Jug's pistol was pointed straight at his head. He glanced nervously at his partner, John Crocker, who had Cody's gun aimed at him. "Let the lady go," Cody said to Burdette.

Burdette was smart enough to see they had reached a standoff and he didn't like the odds that he could release the girl's wrist and draw his own weapon before getting shot. Reluctantly, Burdette fashioned an exaggerated smile and let Brenda go.

With guns still drawn, Jug and Cody followed them out to make sure they got on their horses and left. "It's a good thing you fellers had us outgunned, biggun," Crocker snarled. "I mighta enjoyed kickin' your ass."

Never one to shy away from a good scrap, Jug responded with a laugh, "Sorry to disappoint you. Now get on that horse and get outta here."

Crocker deliberately took his time putting a foot in the stirrup and pulling himself up in the saddle, still smiling defiantly at Jug the whole time. "Maybe I'll see you again sometime," he snarled.

"Maybe," Jug said, "but it better not be around here, or I'll shoot you on sight."

THUNDER OVER LOLO PASS

Charles G. West

A SIGNET BOOK

SIGNET
Published by New American Library, a division of
Penguin Group (USA) Inc., 375 Hudson Street,
New York, New York 10014, USA
Penguin Group (Canada), 90 Eglinton Avenue East, Suite 700, Toronto,
Ontario M4P 2Y3, Canada (a division of Pearson Penguin Canada Inc.)
Penguin Books Ltd., 80 Strand, London WC2R 0RL, England
Penguin Ireland, 25 St. Stephen's Green, Dublin 2,
Ireland (a division of Penguin Books Ltd.)
Penguin Group (Australia), 250 Camberwell Road, Camberwell, Victoria 3124,
Australia (a division of Pearson Australia Group Pty. Ltd.)
Penguin Books India Pvt. Ltd., 11 Community Centre, Panchsheel Park,
New Delhi - 110 017, India
Penguin Group (NZ), 67 Apollo Drive, Rosedale, North Shore 0632,
New Zealand (a division of Pearson New Zealand Ltd.)
Penguin Books (South Africa) (Pty.) Ltd., 24 Sturdee Avenue,
Rosebank, Johannesburg 2196, South Africa

Penguin Books Ltd., Registered Offices:
80 Strand, London WC2R 0RL, England

First published by Signet, an imprint of New American Library,
a division of Penguin Group (USA) Inc.

First Printing, April 2011
10 9 8 7 6 5 4 3 2 1

Ⓢ REGISTERED TRADEMARK—MARCA REGISTRADA

Printed in the United States of America

For Ronda

Chapter 1

"Damn, lookee there, Jug," Cody McCloud exclaimed. "There's a new saloon gone up since we've been back in town." It was one of several new businesses in the settlement, no doubt attracted by the recent establishment of Fort Missoula in Montana. Cody, youngest of the three McCloud brothers, and by far the most adventurous, was always ready to follow a new trail. "Whaddaya say we have a look inside? I could use a little drink about now."

Jug, the middle McCloud brother, and two years older than Cody, was more interested in getting something to eat. Largest of the brothers, Jug seldom allowed his mind to be complicated with thoughts more serious than finding the next meal. Gifted with an oversized and powerful body, he was, however, of a peaceful nature, requiring considerable agitation to ignite the fearsome violence he was capable of. "That suits me," he said in answer to Cody's suggestion. "Maybe they've got a little somethin' to eat, too." The gentle giant's real name was

Ryan, but everybody had called him Jug ever since he was twelve years old. His eldest brother had pinned the nickname on him after he sneaked a full jug of cider their father had cooling in the spring box and drank over half of it. Afterward, he had been too ill to refill the jug with water as he had planned. He got the licking his father had promised, but the terrible sick stomach he suffered had been the greater punishment. The nickname stuck and in time replaced his given name.

Having just delivered twenty cattle to the new fort to feed the recently arrived detachment of soldiers, the brothers were in a mood for a mild celebration before riding back up the valley to the M Bar C Ranch. Already advised of the portion of the money they could spend on food and drink by their father, they were determined to spend the limit, so they tied their horses at the hitching rail alongside a half dozen others and went inside.

Before going directly to the bar, they stopped to look the place over. Generous in size, the new board building featured a long bar across one end of the open room with about a dozen tables filling the rest of the space, except for a small area in between that appeared to be a dance floor. There was a piano up against the wall. About half of the tables were occupied. The thing that caught Cody's eye, however, was the dark-haired woman with a bored expression, sitting with four soldiers at the rearmost table. "Don't even think about it," Jug warned. "Let's just get us a drink and be on our way. We've got a long ride home." From experience, he knew the workings of his younger brother's mind, and more times than not, it ended up with him in a fight. It never seemed to matter if the woman was young and pretty, or seasoned with time. As long as she was not sporting gray hair and a toothless grin, she was worthy of Cody's attention.

Cody flashed a mischievous grin in Jug's direction. "Now, brother, you know it doesn't hurt to look. She don't look all that bad from here. I could tell more if she would stand up."

"Well, she's obviously with those soldier boys," Jug said, "so it don't make no difference to you." He took hold of Cody's arm and started him in the direction of the bar. "Let's get us that drink, so we can get started back home."

"I swear, you're gettin' more and more like Cullen every day," Cody complained, but offered no resistance to Jug's prodding. The reference was to their older brother, who was four years senior to Jug and had always employed a quiet authority over the younger two. It was never resented or contested by Jug or Cody. It seemed the natural order of their family. In fact, they were both proud of their older brother. Cody's only concern for him was the fact that he seemed too serious at times, and he wished Cullen would find a woman to lighten his somber moods. On occasions like the present, Cody always preferred to partner with Jug. Even though Jug complained some, he always went along with whatever Cody wanted to do.

"What can I do for you fellers?" Roy, the bartender, asked.

"A couple of shots of whiskey," Cody replied, greeting the bartender with a friendly smile.

"And a couple of them eggs," Jug added, causing Cody to scrunch his face up in disgust. Jug had been eyeing the large jar of pickled eggs ever since he stood in the doorway.

"You're gonna have to eat both of 'em," Cody said, still making a face.

"I figured," Jug replied with a smile.

After another shot of Roy's whiskey, Cody seemed content and he turned around to look the room over again. Someone called out something to Roy and the bartender went down to the end of the room to a door leading to the rooms in the back. When he came back into the room, he was followed by a thin, bald man with heavy gray sideburns. Roy returned to the bar while the bald man shuffled wearily toward the piano and sat down. In a few minutes, the sounds of the old piano echoed off the wall in a spirited arrangement of an old hymn. None among Roy's clientele was qualified to identify the tune as a religious selection, especially since it was rendered up-tempo, and after a few seconds, one of the soldiers pulled the woman from her chair and led her to the dance floor.

"She ain't half bad," Cody commented as he watched the woman dance with first one, then a second soldier. He was content to be no more than a spectator, since Jug was persistent in reminding him that they should get started toward home. "One more little drink," he said, "and then we'll go."

"If you didn't buy at least one more," Roy felt obliged to comment, "I was gonna have to charge ol' biggun there for eatin' all my pickled eggs."

Cody laughed and replied, "I'm fixin' to take him outta here before he starts gnawin' on the corner of the bar."

Roy laughed with him and was about to offer Jug another egg when a startled cry was heard from the woman, causing them to turn to look toward the dance floor again. A third soldier—a husky brute, almost as big as Jug, wearing corporal's stripes on his sleeve— had cut in to dance with her. It was apparent that his idea of dancing was to physically maul the helpless woman. As they watched, she tried to pull away from his unsolicited advances, a sharp tongue her only defensive weapon. The more she cursed him, the bolder he became until it appeared the corporal was going to have his way with her right there in the saloon.

"Now, that just ain't right," Cody said. "Even a whore don't deserve to be treated like that." He turned to Roy. "What's her name?"

"Mae," the bartender replied, showing little concern for the woman or the table of soldiers.

"All right, then," Cody said, and walked toward the arguing couple. "Hello, Mae," he greeted her cheerfully. "I'm sorry I'm late for our appointment, but I'm here now." Addressing the startled corporal then, he said, "Thanks for entertainin' her till I got here, soldier. You can let her go now." He took her hand and pulled her toward him. The surly corporal was too astonished to hold on to her and she had scurried to safety behind Cody by the time his whiskey-soaked brain realized what had just happened. "Enjoy your drinks, boys," Cody called to the corporal's three companions at the table who obviously didn't know what to make of the intrusion upon their fun and were slow in deciding if there should be any action on their part.

"Your appointment?" The corporal sneered. "What the hell are you talkin' about, you little asshole? The woman's with us, and I'll bust your head for you if you don't get the hell outta here."

Cody shook his head as if perplexed. "There, now see, you had to go and get rowdy about it when it was all just a simple misunderstandin' between the lady and yourself." He glanced at the woman. "Mae, do you want to go with the soldier, or come with me?"

"Hell no, I don't wanna go with the son of a bitch," Mae spat in anger as she examined the abrasions left on her wrists by the corporal's rough hands.

Cody looked back at the corporal and shrugged. "Well, there you go. I reckon that clears everythin' up."

"Why, you little bastard," the corporal cursed.

"Sic him, Jarvis," one of the soldiers still seated at the table goaded.

"Jarvis," Cody responded. "Is that your name?" There was no verbal response to the question, but the corporal's eyes looked capable of igniting a fire, as he appeared to brace himself to launch an attack on the brash young man. Ignoring the threat, Cody continued. "Well, Jarvis, let me give you some advice. I know what you're thinkin' and it's the wrong thing. It's only gonna cause you pain you don't need, so why don't you sit down with your friends there and finish that bottle, and forget about Mae until you sober up a little?"

Knowing full well what was about to follow, Jug unstrapped his gun belt and, emitting a tired sigh, handed it to Roy to hold, since it was obvious that the soldiers were not armed. "I shoulda known we had no business stoppin' for a drink," he muttered as he sidled up to the end of the bar. "Ma'am," he offered politely to the still infuriated woman when she moved past him on her way to sanctuary behind the bar.

Back in the center of the tiny dance floor, Corporal Jarvis was sizing up his opponent after a standoff, astonished at Cody's emotionless approach. With his anger rising, he took a threatening step forward, his fists raised in pugilistic fashion, causing another of his companions to exclaim in enthusiastic anticipation of the contest, "You'd better get on your horse and get your ass on outta here, cowboy, 'cause you just picked a fight with the regimental heavyweight boxing champion!"

"Is that so?" Cody replied while keeping a steady eye on the formidable figure of a man now slowly moving toward him with nothing save mayhem in his gaze. "Well, if this is gonna be a boxin' match, then I guess we need some rules."

"Rules?" Jarvis bleated, dumbfounded and eager to administer the beating he had in mind.

"Yeah, rules," Cody replied, stepping aside to avoid the wild charge launched at that instant. Drawing his Colt .44, he cracked Jarvis squarely across the bridge of his nose with the barrel as the bully lumbered drunkenly by. "Like none of that," he said. The blow sent the larger man reeling clumsily to keep his feet. "And no kickin' in the balls," Cody said as he brought the toe of his boot sharply up between the corporal's legs. Completely helpless, Jarvis bent over in agony. "And no hittin' behind the head," Cody added as he slammed the pistol barrel down solidly on the back of Jarvis' skull. In that brief space of time, the match was over and Jarvis lay, out cold, on the floor.

It had happened so fast that the corporal's friends were still seated, staring in stunned disbelief at their champion lying in a heap on the floor. Finally one of them thought to react. Kicking his chair back, he charged over the table only to be met with Jug McCloud's fist, which stopped his head while his legs ran out from under him, causing him to land on his back, unconscious. The third soldier, instantly wiser after seeing his friend finished with one blow from a fist that looked the size of an anvil, scrambled around the table and jumped on Jug's back just as Jug aimed a kick at the fourth soldier, who had sense enough to run for the door. Left then with the one soldier clinging to his back like a parasite, Jug twisted left and right in an effort to get a grip on the desperate man. His antics proved highly amusing to his brother, who stood by enjoying the spectacle of Jug bucking like an unbroken mustang while the soldier hung on for dear life, afraid to let go.

Finally Jug grew tired of the contest. "Get him the hell off my back!" he roared.

Roy, who had been a silent spectator to the whole performance, casually handed Cody a broom and Cody began whipping the soldier across the back with it until he finally released his death hold on Jug and dropped to the floor. As soon as he landed, he started scrambling on his hands and knees across the floor and out the door, the sound of Cody's laughter ringing in his ears. "Well, I swear, that was some fight, wasn't it?"

Cody exclaimed, grinning at Jug as his brother picked up the table and set the chairs right side up. "That was downright lively." Turning to Roy, he said, "Don't nothin' appear to be broke."

"I reckon not," Roy replied, "but it might be a good idea for you boys to get on your way. Them other two soldiers might be back here with half their company to get those two." He nodded to the two casualties who were just beginning to show signs of life.

"I expect you're right," Cody said. "I apologize for runnin' off four of your customers."

"Don't matter," Roy said. "They'd done spent all their money, anyway. Besides, I might sell some whiskey to their friends when they come back lookin' for you two."

"What about me?" Mae piped up, an astonished spectator up to that point. "You mighta cost me money."

"Oh yeah," Cody said. In the heat of the action, he had forgotten what started the altercation. "How much do you charge?"

"Three dollars for a straight ride without no extras," she replied.

"Fair enough," Cody said, and dug into his pocket. "Here's three dollars and a dollar extra."

She looked surprised. "You want it now?"

"I ain't got time now, lady, but I figure I owe you for one. I'll settle for a kiss." He planted one on the startled prostitute and then sang out, "Let's go, Jug, before the whole damn army shows up." He paused a moment while Jug got his gun belt from Roy and then started for the door after his brother.

Outside, they wasted no time. Stepping up in the

saddle, they turned their horses toward the trail to Stevensville. "You gonna tell Pa you gave a whore four dollars of that money we got for the horses?" Jug asked.

"Hell no," Cody answered with a chuckle. "I'm gonna tell him you ate four dollars' worth of pickled eggs. He'll believe that."

Chapter 2

Donovan McCloud was coming from the barn when he was startled to see a pretty young woman ride into the yard. It was late in the season on an unusually warm day for the first of June in the Bitterroot Valley. She rode in on a strawberry roan mare—not sidesaddle, but astraddle the horse like a man, dressed in her denim split riding skirt. It was the first such skirt that Donovan had ever seen, a sight pretty unusual in the valley. Mule Sibley's wife, Rena, rode straddle-legged, but she always wore a pair of men's trousers—one size larger than her husband wore. Even more unusual on this day was the fact that the woman was riding unescorted a half day's ride from the closest town, less than a week after the Bailey ranch next to Donovan's had reported some cattle stolen. Elwood Bailey suspected it the work of a band of outlaw Salish Indians that had hit a couple of other ranches after crossing over on the Lost Trail Pass and working their way up the valley. Of even greater concern for most of the folks in the valley was the recent news of the trouble with the Nez Perce over in Idaho Territory. This particular threat had been of no concern to Donovan, for he and his three sons were friends of the peaceful Nez Perce.

McCloud's cattle had not been struck, as far as he knew. Why the Salish raiders had skipped his spread was anybody's guess. Maybe it was because Donovan McCloud had also been a friend to the Salish as well as the Nez Perce since he first built his simple log cabin as a young man in 1847, three years before Fort Owen was built. Or maybe it was because of the respect for Donovan's three sons and their proficiency with the Winchester '73s that each carried—plus the knowledge that one or all three would most likely be on their trail before they had time to disappear into the mountains. In any case, it did not seem fitting for a young woman to be riding in the valley alone, even if there had been no recent hostile activity.

When the woman spotted him at the barn, she turned the roan to meet him. Donovan stopped and waited for her to approach. Seeing his apparent astonishment, she favored him with a warm smile and asked, "Are you Mr. McCloud?"

"I am, miss," Donovan answered, making no effort to hide his frank appraisal of the young woman. He didn't think to help her dismount, instead looking beyond her to see if there was anyone with her while she stepped down from the horse. "Where did you come from?" he asked; then before she could answer, he said, "Where's the rest of your party?"

"There's just me," she replied cheerfully, her smile

still in place. "They told me in Stevensville that you would be the man to see."

"About what?" Donovan asked.

"They said that nobody in the valley knew the Bitterroot Mountains as well as Donovan McCloud and his three sons," she replied.

Donovan stroked his chin as he thought about it. "Well, I s'pose that's a fact. I don't reckon there's many places in the mountains that my boys ain't seen—Cody more'n his two brothers. I expect he'd never come outta there if I didn't need him to help on the ranch."

She affected a demure smile then. "Why, I assumed you to be one of the sons," she said. "You don't look old enough to be the father of three grown men."

Well aware that the lady was teasing him, Donovan chuckled and replied, "You just might be in need of some spectacles." It had been a long time since any female had graced the McCloud spread, especially one as young and handsome as this smiling lady. "Miss, it ain't none of my business, but it sure don't seem smart for a woman like yourself to be ridin' down here without some protection."

She responded with a confident laugh. "I brought some protection with me," she said, and pulled a Colt revolver just far enough out of her saddlebag for him to see.

Donovan shook his head, astonished. After a brief pause while he continued to search his surprise visitor's face, he finally said, "Didn't nobody in Stevensville tell you everybody in the valley is worried about the Nez Perce?" When she nodded, he shook his head, astounded. "Well, I reckon you've got some spunk. I'll have to give you that. So, why were you lookin' for me?" Then before she could answer, he interrupted, "Excuse my manners, miss, but it's been one helluva long time since there's been a young woman on the place, and I reckon I'm a little rusty when it comes to lady visitors. Let me take your horse. No sense in us standin' out here in the yard to talk. Come on to the house. You must be thirsty. I'll get you a cool drink of water."

"Why, thank you, sir," she responded, and followed him as he led her horse to a hitching rail in front of the house.

The unlikely appearance of this mysterious woman was still stirring confusion in Donovan's brain as he looped the roan's reins over the rail, then motioned for her to take a seat in one of the rocking chairs on the wide porch. Most everyone else in the Bitterroot Valley had been nervous since news that Chief Joseph had refused to go to the reservation when ordered by the army. There had already been fighting in the Idaho Territory on the western side of the Bitterroots, with reports that the Nez Perce had whipped General Oliver Howard's troops at White Bird Canyon. Donovan's eldest son, Cullen, had just returned from Fort Missoula with news that the Nez Perce band had crossed over the Lolo Trail into the Bitterroot Valley. Surely someone would have advised the lady of the potential risk. Everybody up and down the valley was bewailing the massacre bound to come if the Nez Perce moved through the valley, even though they had been at peace with the white settlers from the beginning. As far as he was concerned, Chief Joseph was a friend, so he agreed with

Cullen and discounted any talk of attacks from the Nez Perce.

After the lady settled herself, he walked over to the front door, opened it partway, and yelled, "Smoke!" Then he returned to sit in a rocker facing her to once again ask her purpose in coming to see him.

"I need help in finding someone," she started to explain, only to be interrupted again when a gnarly-looking little man stuck his bald head out the door.

"What are you yellin' about?" Smoke Butterworth asked. Then seeing that Donovan had company, he came out on the porch to get a better look. Like Donovan, he immediately looked around, expecting to find others. When he discovered none, he remarked, "You musta dropped right outta the sky. Ain't you a pretty thing, though?" He grinned openly at her in frank appraisal.

Donovan smiled patiently at his surprise guest. "Don't mind Smoke. He ain't got good sense when it comes to meetin' proper ladies." Then to the grinning man, he said, "Get the lady a drink of cool water. She's been ridin' all the way from Stevensville."

"By herself?" Smoke responded. "Maybe she'd like some coffee. I just made a pot."

"That sounds even better," the young lady said.

"Bring us both a cup," Donovan said, then added, "You must be hungry. Would you like somethin' to eat with it?"

"Oh, I wouldn't think to put you to the trouble," she replied.

"Ain't no trouble," Smoke volunteered before Donovan had a chance to respond. "Matter of fact, I was gettin' ready to fix supper. If you're real hungry, I'll have steak and potatoes ready in a few minutes. We could stand to see a pretty face around the supper table for a change."

She glanced at Donovan, who was nodding in agreement. "If you're sure it won't be an imposition," she said.

"Not at all," Donovan replied. "We'd be glad to have you. Smoke's right. It'd be nice to have some gentle company at the table." Then it occurred to him. "It's too late for you to start back to Stevensville this evenin', anyhow. You're gonna need to stay over. We'll fix you up with a place to stay for the night."

"Oh, I couldn't impose upon you," she protested. "I can find my way back."

"Ma'am, I wouldn't hear of it. That ain't no ride for a lady alone in the daytime, much less at night," Donovan insisted. "We've got plenty of room. You can have a room to yourself. Why, my late wife would come back to haunt me if I let you ride off by yourself."

"Well, if you insist," she replied sweetly. "You are most gracious to offer. I was a teeny bit concerned about riding all that way at night."

"We'll be pleased to have your company," Donovan said. "Like I said, it's been a while since we've entertained a pretty young thing like you around here, with just me and Smoke and my three boys." He took on a fatherly expression for a moment or two then. "I'll have one of the boys escort you back in the mornin', though. It ain't fittin' for a lady to be travelin' alone out here."

"It's sweet of you to be concerned," the woman said, "but I'm hoping not to be going back to Stevensville if you can help me."

He had forgotten for the moment that he still didn't know why she had landed on his doorstep, so he started to ask the purpose for her visit again, but paused once more when he spotted a rider approaching from the north pasture. "Here comes my oldest boy now," he said, and she turned to follow his gaze.

Seeing the roan tied at the porch rail, Cullen McCloud guided his horse in that direction instead of going directly to the barn. He pulled up before the house just as Smoke came out the door carrying two cups of coffee. As surprised to discover a young woman visitor as his father and Smoke had been, he was naturally curious to learn why she happened to be there. "I could sure use a cup of that coffee myself," he said as he dismounted.

"Well, you know where the pot is," Smoke replied, his hospitality reserved for attractive young women.

Accustomed to Smoke's ornery disposition, Cullen ignored the rebuke, stepped up on the porch, and waited to be introduced. "This is my son Cullen," Donovan said. Turning to Cullen then, he said, "Son, this here is Miss . . ." He paused. "I don't believe you ever said your name."

"No, I didn't," she replied with a warm smile for the tall young man. "I'm Roberta Morris," she said, and extended her hand.

"I'm pleased to meet you, ma'am," Cullen said as he took her hand. "What brings you to the M Bar C?"

"As I was about to tell your father, I came here at the suggestion of the deputy sheriff in Stevensville on a rather troubling matter." Seeing that she had the rapt attention of all three men, she went on to explain. "My uncle is somewhere in the Bitterroot Mountains searching for gold, and it's been almost a year since Aunt Edna has heard from him. He sent word at that time that he would return home to Butte this past spring and we fear he has come to some harm. The deputy said you might know where to find him. I didn't think there was any way, since he could be anywhere in the Bitterroot Mountains, but his message came from Stevensville. So I had to at least try."

"That's that Thompson boy," Smoke interrupted, as if it was necessary to remind them who the deputy sheriff was. His comment was ignored by Cullen and his father.

"You came all the way from Butte to look for your uncle?" Cullen asked. "Alone?"

"There wasn't anyone else," she replied, causing Cullen to exchange puzzled glances with his father. Like Donovan, Cullen found it surprising that no one in town had advised her against riding down the valley without escort, considering the present concern about trouble with the Indians. He supposed it could be explained by the fact that she had been given directions by Charley Thompson, Sheriff Tyler's not so bright deputy.

"What's your uncle's name?" Cullen asked.

"Gabriel Morris. Do you know him?"

Cullen took a moment to think before he answered. "Gabe," he replied. "I expect you're talkin' about ol' Gabe. I didn't know his last name. I doubt if anybody in this part of the valley does. I never thought about it, but I guess his name is probably Gabriel." He looked at his father for confirmation, but Donovan merely shrugged, so he went on. "Jug and Cody oughta be back any time now from Missoula. If anybody knows where your uncle is, it would be Cody. That is, if he's still in the Bitterroots or the Sapphire Mountains."

"That's a fact," Smoke chimed in as he remained standing close over the lady's chair. "That boy's half Injun, I swear. I expect he knows ever' rat hole and game trail between here and the Selway River."

Aware then of the cook's hovering over their guest, Cullen said, "I guess if we've invited Miss Morris to supper, you'd best be getting about fixing it, Smoke."

"I guess," Smoke snorted, and backed up a step. "Ain't nobody else around here likely to fix it." He bent close to Roberta's ear again and confided, "They'd starve to death if I didn't take care of 'em." She smiled discreetly and he nodded as if the two of them had a secret not shared by the others.

Cullen followed him inside, still looking for that cup of coffee. When they had gone, Donovan said, "You'll have to excuse Smoke. Ever since my Charlotte died, he thinks he's the boss of the house, but he's pretty much harmless."

Still smiling, she said, "I suspected as much."

"And he's a good cook," Donovan added.

A moment later, Cullen returned with his coffee. After Roberta rejected an offer for a warm-up on hers, he sat down to enjoy it. While he sipped the hot black liquid, he cast a casual eye on Roberta's horse. "I expect your horse could use some grain and water. I'll take it along to the barn with mine," he said. "I'll bring your saddlebags in for you." Then he commented, "Don't believe

I've ever seen a lady travel with less baggage than you've got on that horse."

"I travel light," she replied, then laughed. "To tell you the truth, I was hoping I'd get an invitation to stop over with you folks." Guessing then that Donovan and his son must be forming opinions of her as a rather bold and reckless woman, she sought to explain her circumstances. "I'm afraid you might think me excessive in my actions—certainly unladylike, I must confess. But Aunt Edna is in poor health and I'm afraid she may soon be failing. There was no one but me to come searching for Uncle Gabriel, so I had little choice but to come on my own."

"We're sorry to hear your aunt's doing poorly," Cullen said. He could not help admiring the woman's determination to help her aunt and uncle. "Of course we'll try to help you if we can." He glanced at his father, who nodded in accord. "Why don't we get you settled in the house and then we'll have some supper? Jug and Cody should be here by then, and we'll decide what to do."

"Yeah," Donovan said, "they oughta be here any minute. Jug can smell supper cookin' from halfway across the valley."

"I swear, Cody," Jug McCloud complained, "we ain't got time to stop now. It's past suppertime and I'm 'bout to starve to death." He had been thinking about supper all the way back from Stevensville, their last stop on their way back from Missoula.

"I just wanna pick up some smokin' tobacco," Cody

said. "Won't take but a couple minutes, and it ain't that far out of the way to Sibley's."

"Hell," Jug replied, "you coulda bought tobacco back at Stevensville. I'll give you some of mine 'cause I know you got plenty back at the house. You just wanna see if Sibley's daughter is hangin' around the saloon."

"Well, now, I hadn't thought about that," Cody lied, "but now that you mention it, it would be nice to just say hello if she *is* there." Cody realized he wasn't fooling his brother. Jug knew he was kind of sweet on Brenda, the fiery raven-haired daughter of Mule Sibley, owner of the small trading post/saloon on the Bitterroot River only two miles from the M Bar C. A fact that Cody was sure his brother didn't know, however, was the occasional rendezvous between himself and Brenda at a little spot among the towering cottonwoods and pines on the river below the trading post. It was a secluded glen surrounded by large ponderosa pines, a place where the trees bore old scars left by Nez Perce Indians where they had stripped the bark back to extract the chewy sweet cambium. It was here that Cody had first been introduced to the joys of lovemaking free of obligation. Some might have criticized the rakish younger brother of Cullen and Jug for wantonly using Mule's daughter for his selfish pleasures. Truth be told, however, they were using each other and both were satisfied with the arrangement.

Cheerfully ignoring Jug's protests, Cody turned down the narrow trail that led through the trees to the river's edge and Sibley's trading post. There were four horses tied in front of the log building when they pulled up, three with saddles, and one carrying packs. Jug and Cody tied their horses at the corner of the narrow porch and stepped inside the dark, smoky building. Sibley's business fronted his living quarters and was composed of one long room with his store at one end and the saloon at the other. They paused to let their eyes adjust to the dimly lit room before walking up to the counter to exchange "Howdys" with Mule. "I need a little smokin' tobacco," Cody said while looking around the room to see if Brenda was there. She was nowhere in sight. Mule's wife, Rena was tending bar, as she often did. Disappointed, he resigned himself to passing the news of the day with Mule, who asked right away if they had heard anything new about the Nez Perce problem.

"Well, they finally got some soldiers posted at Fort Missoula," Jug said. "But it didn't do any good when it came to stoppin' the Indians. Cullen said Joseph and his people are already over in the valley without a shot fired by the army. They'll be passin' through here, no doubt about it."

"When they do," Cody said, "we're gonna have about eight hundred Nez Perce Indians with a couple thousand horses movin' through the valley."

Sibley shook his head, a worried frown on his face. "We ain't never had no trouble with the Nez Perce," he said, "but now that they're already fightin' the army, they might attack any whites they run into." He was momentarily distracted by a sudden rise in the conversation from the three strangers down at the saloon end of the building.

Noticing the look of concern on Mule's face, Jug asked, "Who are those fellers?"

"I don't know," Mule replied. "They rode in here a little while ago, and didn't waste no time on conversation—just wanted to set down at the table and drink. Rena's already set 'em up with two bottles. I reckon they'll move on when they've had enough."

Jug nodded. "Most likely," he said. He understood Mule's concern, since his wife was working the bar at the moment. They were a pretty rough-looking bunch—didn't look like trappers, farmers, miners, or anything else respectable—but it was none of Jug's business. They didn't seem to be inclined to cause any trouble, he decided. He was soon proven wrong, however, when the door to Mule's dwelling opened a second later and Brenda Sibley walked in. Giving the three seated at the table no more than a brief glance, she started around the end of the bar on her way to the front of the store when she spotted Cody.

"Now, that's more like it," one of the men said when the saucy girl swept by her mother. "He reached out and grabbed her wrist, almost jerking her to the floor. "You can set down here with us, honey, and have a little drink."

Brenda regained her balance and tried to pull free of the leering man, but his grip was too strong on her wrist. "Let her go," Rena demanded, and started around the bar after her daughter.

Quick to join in the fun, the man's two partners jumped up to block the angry mother's attempt to come to her daughter's aid. Laughing lasciviously, they each grabbed one of Rena's arms and held her back. Realizing what was going on, Mule grabbed a shotgun from under the counter and ran to his family's rescue. Seeing a .44

drawn and pressed against Rena's side caused him to stop before he reached the table. "I expect you'd better slow down, old man," the gunman, a wiry little man with dark bushy eyebrows, warned. "Put that shotgun down before I put an air hole right through your old lady."

Mule had little choice but to comply. He placed the shotgun down on the floor, but still attempted to reason with the three men. "You fellers have had enough to drink. There ain't no call to get rowdy with my wife and daughter, so I think it best if you just take the rest of that bottle and be on your way."

Already preparing to come to Brenda's rescue, Cody paused for only a moment to see if the three strangers were going to agree to leave. When it became apparent that they had no intention of doing so, he glanced at Jug, who nodded his silent confirmation. There was no hesitation to respond. Unlike the barroom brawl they had had with the soldiers in Missoula, these men were clearly dangerous and had already drawn a gun. The two brothers moved deliberately toward that end of the building. Splitting up, they both drew their revolvers. "I expect you'd best put that gun away," Jug said, eyeing the wiry man with the .44. His expression promised serious consequences if the suggestion was ignored.

The man hesitated, not sure of his chances. Jug's pistol was pointed straight at his head. He glanced nervously at his partner, a big brute who was holding Rena's other arm, and had Cody's gun aimed at him. "Let the lady go," Cody said to the man holding Brenda.

The man was smart enough to see they had reached a standoff and he didn't like the odds that he could release the girl's wrist and draw his own weapon before getting shot. To further lower his chances, Mule had quickly picked up his shotgun again. There followed a brief period of total silence as all parties considered the possible outcome if the first trigger was pulled. Reluctantly, he fashioned an exaggerated smile and let Brenda go. "Put it away, Blackie. Let her go, Big John," he ordered. Turning his attention back to the two brothers, he said, "There ain't no need to get into a tangle over this. We was all just havin' a little fun. We ain't lookin' for trouble. Hell, let's all have a drink, and no hard feelin's."

"Like her father said," Cody replied as Brenda moved quickly behind him, "you and your friends have had enough to drink. It's time you were sayin' good-bye."

As soon as Blackie removed his pistol from Rena's side, she jerked free of the two men and retreated behind the bar to retrieve another shotgun from under the counter. "By God," she roared, "I think I'll blow your head off for sticking that gun in my ribs!"

"Whoa, lady!" the one who had started it all when he grabbed Brenda exclaimed. "We're leavin'. Come on, boys. I believe we've worn out our welcome here." He got up and left some money on the table to pay for the whiskey, then led his partners toward the front door.

With guns still drawn, Jug and Cody followed them out to make sure they got on their horses and left. The largest of the three, the one called Big John, paused before stepping up in the saddle to glower at Jug, who was about the same size. He was not accustomed to backing down to any man, and it was eating away at his pride to do so now. Consequently, he couldn't resist baiting Jug. "It's a good thing you fellers had us out-gunned, big'un," he snarled. "I mighta enjoyed kickin' your ass."

Never one to shy away from a good scrap, Jug responded with a laugh, "Sorry to disappoint you. Now get on that horse and get outta here."

Big John deliberately took his time putting a foot in the stirrup and pulling himself up in the saddle, still smiling defiantly at Jug the whole time. "Maybe I'll see you again sometime," he snarled.

"Maybe," Jug said, "but it better not be around here, or I'll shoot you on sight."

They all stood outside and watched until the three disappeared into the trees where the trail turned up-river. "Whew," Mule exhaled. "We ain't had trouble-makers like them three in here for a long time. I'm just glad you boys showed up when you did."

"You never saw 'em before?" Cody asked again.

"Nope," Mule answered. "They ain't ever been in here before. They said they was just passin' through the valley, but they didn't act like they was in any particular hurry."

"Well, maybe you've seen the last of 'em," Jug said. "Might not be a bad idea to keep those shotguns handy. You never can tell about men like that." That said, he turned quickly to his brother. "We'd best be on our way, Cody, if we're gonna be home before Smoke throws the chuck out." The recent conflict had done nothing to discourage his appetite.

"We could stick around for a while if you're worried about those three comin' back," Cody suggested, causing a frown on his brother's face and the hint of a smile on Brenda's.

"'Preciate it, Cody," Mule said, "but I'll be ready for 'em if they show up around here again. I've been dealin' with men like them three for over twenty years and we're still here. I'da been ready for 'em this time, but I swear, they didn't seem to want nothin' but a bottle of whiskey."

Cody shrugged and replied, "Whatever you say. Come on, Jug, I reckon we'll be leavin'." He glanced at Brenda, and she acknowledged his gaze with a twinkle in her eye and a shy smile. "I'll most likely be goin' huntin' for elk soon," he said. "Maybe I'll bring you a haunch."

"That'ud be good," Rena piped up. "That last you brought was mighty fine eatin'." She was always happy to get the fresh meat, even though she knew the real reason behind Cody's thoughtfulness had strictly to do with Brenda. Rena was not at all blind to her daughter's occasional walks down by the river, but she was confident that Brenda was smart enough to handle the situation—and they could always use the meat. It was her thinking that a matchup between Brenda and one of the McCloud boys might be advantageous to both parties, especially the Sibleys.

Back in the saddle, the two McCloud brothers turned their horses away from the porch and started for the M Bar C. When they were out of earshot of the three people watching them leave, Jug chided his brother. "I saw those sheep eyes you were throwin' at Brenda. You're wastin' your time. That gal ain't got time for your non-sense. Besides, Rena would use that shotgun on you if she caught you foolin' around with her daughter."

"Maybe you're right, brother," Cody replied while smiling to himself and already contemplating the possibility of another visit to the shady glen by the river. "I reckon I ain't got a chance at that."

"There they go," Blackie Cruz said when he saw Cody and Jug ride out the trail from Sibley's store and turn to the south. "Looks to me like they're headin' toward the M Bar C."

"I had a feelin' them two might be McCloud's boys," Burdette, the man who started the fight, said. He reached over and gave Crocker a playful kick with his boot. "One of 'em was big as you, Big John." He knew the confrontation was eating away at Crocker's peace of mind.

"Yeah, well, he was lucky he had a gun on me," Crocker snorted, "else I'da broke his back for him." He threw a stick down that he had been fiddling with while the three of them waited for the two riders to leave Sibley's. "Why don't we settle up with those two bastards right now?"

"'Cause if they are the McCloud boys," Burdette patiently explained, "they just might be the ones to lead us to what we're after. And I don't wanna risk shootin' the only ones who might know where that old son of a bitch's camp is."

"How do we know we ain't just wastin' our time followin' that woman all the way over here from Butte, anyway?" Blackie asked. "That old man might not'a found a damn ounce of pay dirt. I ain't heard tell of anybody else strikin' it rich in them mountains."

"Maybe he ain't," Burdette replied, still patient. "But she must be sure as hell he's struck it rich. Why else would she risk goin' to find him in a country full of Flatheads and Nez Perce?"

"Hell, the Flatheads ain't bothered nobody in this valley for a month or so," Blackie said, having no knowledge of the recent cattle rustling. "And the word we've been hearin' all summer is that Chief Joseph and the Nez Perce are tryin' to get away from the army. They ain't got time to worry about nobody ridin' up in the Bitterroots lookin' for a crazy old man."

"Maybe so," Burdette conceded, "but that don't mean the Flatheads have gone peaceful, and all the Nez Perce ain't gone with Chief Joseph. There's still some parties ready to raid and plunder—she's still takin' a helluva chance, so she must be pretty damn sure it's worth the risk. We don't wanna cause any trouble this close to McCloud's spread to let folks know we're here." He got up then and went to his horse. Stepping up in the saddle, he said, "Now let's just follow these boys and see if they don't lead right to the M Bar C."

As Burdette predicted, the two men who had spoiled their fun back at Sibley's rode straight to the sizable ranch house with a gatepost out front that proclaimed it to be the M Bar C. "Looks like you're right," Blackie said, "they must be two of them McCloud boys." He grinned at Crocker and added, "If the woman talks 'em into guidin' her, you might get a chance to settle up with that big'un. Maybe that would get that burr outta your ass."

"Maybe I oughta stick that burr up your scrawny little ass," Crocker replied, still fuming from the humiliation over having to back down to Jug McCloud.

"Maybe you oughta try," Blackie said with a grin. "See how you'd look with a bullet hole between your eyes."

Impatient with the meaningless banter, Burdette said, "You two weary my ass. Let's find a place to camp where we can keep an eye on 'em." They backtracked then until reaching a suitable place by a stream, far enough from the house where a campfire would not be spotted— the same spot from which they had watched Roberta Morris approach the ranch house earlier. "There ain't no use in watchin' the house till mornin'," Burdette said. "They ain't gonna start out nowhere this close to dark." They settled in for the night.

Supper was on the table when Jug and Cody filed into the kitchen after taking care of their horses. Stopped at once by the sight of an attractive woman seated to the right of their father, they were speechless for a moment before Cullen introduced them. "Meet the part of the family we don't brag about," Cullen joked. "These are my brothers, Jug and Cody. Boys, say hello to Miss Morris."

"Please, call me Roberta," she said to Cullen, then turning back to bestow a warm smile on the two brothers, she said, "I'm so pleased to meet you both. I've heard some good things about you."

Always a hair quicker than Jug with a gun or a quip, Cody replied, "That would most likely be me, ma'am," he said with a wide grin. "There ain't nothin' good you coulda heard about Jug."

Not ready with an immediate comeback, Jug favored his brother with an exaggerated sigh before saying, "Didn't take long to hear from Cody's biggest admirer, did it?" He turned back to Roberta and tipped his hat. "I'm pleased to meet you, ma'am."

Roberta laughed delightedly. From the expressions on his sons' faces, Donovan McCloud could judge that she had wasted little time in charming all three. He had to admit, the lady had a way about her, and not just her looks. Supper that night took about a half hour longer than usual as they talked about their guest's quest to find her uncle. "Well," Cody told them, "I know where ol' Gabe's camp was for the most part of a year, but I ain't been in that part of the mountains for a month or more. It was the longest he's stayed in one spot since I've seen him—musta found somethin' to keep him there that long." He gazed at Roberta then and smiled. "I reckon you were right in lookin' for help, 'cause if you don't know those mountains, a man would be mighty hard to find, especially if he didn't necessarily wanna be found—and the Flatheads ain't been too friendly to most white folks ever since the soldiers opened Fort Owen."

"Can you take me to his camp?" Roberta pressed.

Cody hesitated before answering. "Yes, ma'am, I can find it again. I just don't know if it wouldn't be better for you to wait here and let me go look for Gabe."

Seeing a hint of concern on Roberta's face, Cullen stepped in to explain. "What Cody's worried about is the country we'd have to travel. That part of the Bitterroots is some of the roughest country you'll likely find anywhere. It's nothing but one high ridge after another that drops off into rock-walled canyons that go straight up. It's hardly a place most ladies would care to travel."

Roberta favored him with a sweet smile. "I'm not most ladies."

"I guess I can see that," Cullen replied.

"How soon can we get started?" Roberta asked.

Cullen and Cody exchanged uncertain glances, both feeling as if they needed a little time to think about it first. "Well," Cody said, "speakin' for myself, I can go tomorrow mornin', if Pa can spare me for about a week." He paused to explain. "Where I last saw Gabe was in a narrow gulch about a day's ride up the creek that runs through Blodgett Canyon."

"Blodgett Canyon?" Roberta responded, somewhat surprised.

Cody went on to explain. "There're about two dozen or more canyons like that running through the Bitterroots, but old man Lyman Blodgett named that one for himself. He took up homesteadin' on a piece of land in the valley about ten years ago at the mouth of that canyon and I reckon he thought the creek and the canyon oughta be named after him. Most everybody calls it that now. It's rough country, but a horse can follow the creek all right."

After much discussion, none of which seemed to discourage the lady's determination to be part of the search party, Donovan decided that all three of his sons should go. "I've never had much trouble with the Salish ever since I first came here," he said. "But others have, and I expect it'd be a good idea to take a couple of extra rifles with you." His decision obviously pleased Roberta, but Cody displayed a hint of irritation. Donovan expected his reaction and commented, "I know you're thinkin' that you ride those mountains all the time by yourself, Cody. But it ain't the same when you've got Miss Morris to worry about. You run into a Flathead or Nez Perce huntin' party and you'll be glad to have your brothers there."

Cullen and Jug looked at each other and grinned, both aware that Cody had already been speculating on the possibility of being alone with the young lady for several days in the mountains.

"What about you, Pa?" Cody protested. "You're gonna need help with the cattle."

"Not for the little while you boys will be gone," Donovan replied. "If Miss Morris don't mind, I'll have you wait till day after tomorrow, so you can move the horses to the other side of the river. If I need help after you're gone, I can get Jesse and Howard to give me a hand." Elwood Bailey's two sons had helped before on occasion. The last time was with the spring branding.

"Of course I don't mind," Roberta replied at once. "I'm just so grateful for your help, especially for the services of your three sons. I know I'll feel a whole lot safer. I just hope I'm not causing you a problem to have them gone."

Unable to resist the opportunity to tease, Jug said, "Don't worry, little brother. Cullen and I will be there to look after you."

Cullen detected a twinkle of amusement in Roberta's

eye. She glanced in his direction in time to catch him gazing at her, and favored him with a smile. Embarrassed, he looked quickly away. Turning to his father, he voiced his concern about the rumors of Chief Joseph's flight through the valley. "I don't know how long we'd be gone," he said, "and you might need us here."

"I ain't worried about the Nez Perce. I've been friends with Chief Joseph for a long time." Donovan smiled reassuringly. "We've bought a lot of horses from his folks."

"I reckon," Cullen said.

Supper had been a great deal more enjoyable with the presence of Roberta at the table. Donovan could not help noticing a marked improvement in the boys' manners, starting with the removal of their hats when they filed into the dining room—all voluntarily with the exception of Jug, who had to be reminded by Cody. Roberta had even volunteered to help Smoke when he placed a platter of steaks on the table, but of course he refused, replying, "No such thing, you're our guest. Besides, with you here, I feel like I'm fixin' for a civilized family, instead of sloppin' a bunch of hogs."

Roberta once again had been gently rebuked when she started to help Smoke clear away the dishes. "You go on out and set on the porch," he said, "and I'll have some fresh coffee made in a few minutes." So she joined the men on the porch to witness the sunset.

Taking a chair next to Cullen, she sat back to enjoy the evening. "I feel guilty for having come here to ask for your help, and to be treated so elegantly," she said.

"I must admit that I expected far less, and you and your father and brothers have made me feel so welcome."

"Believe me, it's our pleasure," Cullen said. "I'm glad you came to us."

She smiled in reply. The evening passed so quickly. All the McCloud men took part in the conversation, but it almost seemed there were only the two of them sitting there. When Cullen asked about her aunt Edna, Roberta's eyes seemed to turn misty as she talked about the long-suffering wife of an incurable gold prospector. "Poor Aunt Edna," she said. "Uncle Gabriel promised this was his last trek off into the wilderness, looking for the gold that everyone told him was not there." She recalled that she was Aunt Edna's favorite from the time she had been a small tyke, visiting her uncle's house. Then she told Cullen of the hardship left upon her aunt when Uncle Gabriel failed to return as he had promised. "I'm afraid Aunt Edna isn't going to make it," she said sadly. "That's why I've come looking for him."

Cullen could sense the closeness Roberta felt to her aunt, and he only hoped they would be successful in finding the old prospector. Not many folks knew much about ol' Gabe. Some thought he was no more than a myth, but Cody had seen him and talked to him. If anyone could find the old man, Cullen knew that Cody would. "If your uncle is still in the Bitterroots, I know Cody will find him. He's the best tracker I've ever seen, and I hope for your aunt's sake that he's all right."

"You're so kind," she said, her words soft and sincere. "I'm so glad I met you, Cullen." She paused. "And your brothers," she added, but her words seemed to be meant only for him.

Bright and early the following morning, the boys were in the saddle and riding out to drive the large herd of horses to new grazing on the other side of the river. Up almost as early as the men, Roberta was on the front porch to wave good-bye as the three brothers wheeled their horses and loped off toward the meadows east of the ranch house. Cullen wondered if Jug and Cody noticed the way the morning sunbeams seemed to dance in the lady's long dark hair as she stood there smiling at them. They would ride him mercilessly if they suspected he had such thoughts.

By the time the men returned at the end of the day, Roberta had succeeded in melting the heart of the crusty old cook. She had spent part of the afternoon helping Smoke in the kitchen, causing him to forget his cynical view of the world in general for a little while. The transformation was enough to make Donovan wonder if his houseguest was in fact a saint. Smoke even went so far as to share his recipe for sausage corn bread with her. Supper that night was a thoroughly enjoyable affair with thoughts of the serious cause for her visit forgotten for most of the evening. Like the evening before, after supper was over, and Roberta was shooed away from the kitchen again, she joined Cullen and Cody on the porch.

"What a glorious evening," she exclaimed as she stepped to the edge of the porch and turned her face up to the starry night. Then she turned, just then remembering the journey planned for the morning. "I feel I have no right to be this content. I hope Aunt Edna will forgive me."

"I'm sure she will," Cullen said. "I suspect she's grateful for what you're trying to do."

She walked back beside his rocker and placed her hand on his shoulder. "Thank you. I pray you're right. I don't know what I'll do if we can't find Uncle Gabriel."

"We'll find him," Cullen said. "Won't we, Cody?"

"We'll do our best to," Cody replied, a faint grin on his face as he watched his elder brother's reaction to the young lady's hand on his shoulder. *He won't move an inch as long as her hand is there*, he thought. *Ol' Cullen might be in deep over his head.*

Chapter 3

The morning broke with a light frost, unusual considering the recent warm days, but not unheard of for this time of year in the valley. After a hearty breakfast of steak and eggs, served up by Smoke, who was back to his usual cheerless self now that Roberta was leaving, the search party was ready to ride. At Donovan's insistence, Roberta went through a trunk filled with the late Charlotte McCloud's clothes in order to find wear more suitable to the rough country she would be passing through. In further consideration for the lady's comfort, he also made sure they took a packhorse with cooking utensils and a coffee grinder, along with ample supplies of flour, elk jerky, and dried beans. As Cody stood by shaking his head in amazement, Donovan reminded his son that not everyone was content to live like a wild Indian. Smoke walked out to the porch to watch their departure. Moving up beside Cullen, he said, "Find that old coot fast and get on back here. I ain't as trustin' of them Injuns as your pa."

Overhearing, Donovan grinned as he stood and watched while the party rode out to the south on the western side of the river. He was not the only one watching their departure.

Hesitating for a few moments to be sure, Blackie Cruz climbed on his horse and hurried back to the ravine where his companions were waiting. "They're ridin'," he said as he pulled up before them. "Just like you said, them two fellers is with her and one more, and they're headin' out to the south."

"Three of 'em, huh?" Frank Burdette replied. "Well, there're three of us." He kicked some dirt over the fire and headed for his horse. "Let's get started. We don't wanna lose 'em."

Moving at a comfortable pace to accommodate the lady, the party consumed much of the afternoon to cover the twelve miles or so to the entrance to Blodgett Canyon, which was easily identified by the steep rock wall that loomed up as a warning to casual travelers. As Cullen explained to Roberta, anyone could find Blodgett Canyon. The difficult job was to find the gulch where Gabe had made his camp. They skirted Lyman Blodgett's farm and followed the creek up the canyon. Cody led them along the rapidly flowing water into a wilderness of fir, larch, and lodgepole pine forest on the lower slopes that gave way to spruce and white bark pine higher up. Above the tree line, the barren rocky spires stood like giant spears thrusting into the blue sky.

Nighttime came early in the steep-walled canyon, so they decided to make camp after riding only a mile or so up Blodgett Creek. Cody and Jug unsaddled the horses and hobbled them while Cullen helped Roberta gather wood for a fire. Once it was going, she insisted that they should all keep out of her way while she made supper. "I might not be as good a cook as Smoke," she offered cheerfully, "but I've never had any complaints before."

"I don't know about that," Cody said, "but I'd a-heap rather watch you fix it."

"Why, thank you, sir," Roberta replied sweetly.

"I'll make the coffee for you," Cullen volunteered, "since you're doing the cooking."

She rewarded him with one of her warm smiles and thanked him. Over by the water's edge, Jug remarked softly to Cody, "I wonder if she does cook as good as she looks. I'm already hungry enough to eat the south end of a northbound mule."

"I believe ol' Cullen has noticed that she's better to look at than Smoke," Cody said with a chuckle. Both brothers had already noticed that most of her lingering smiles were cast upon their older brother. There was no sense of competition for the lady's attention. Jug was more interested in her skills as a cook. As for Cody, he was as fond of the opposite sex as any man, but he had no interest in a serious relationship—and Roberta Morris looked to him like a very classy lady who might even attend church occasionally. He was actually pleased to see her apparent interest in Cullen. His tall, quiet brother needed some nice woman to break through that somber shell that he seemed to dwell in.

After proving her skills with the simple fare she had to work with, Roberta made herself comfortable near the fire where she could study the brothers more closely. All three seemed highly capable of handling themselves in a tight spot, so she felt no apprehension regarding Indian trouble. She couldn't help being amused by Cody's playful swagger, but she felt he was harmless. Jug seemed to be content with whatever came his way, and she wondered if the young giant had ever had a worrisome moment—as long as supper was on time. She reserved her more serious thoughts for Cullen. Tall and lean, he carried himself with an air of confidence that suggested he was more than ready for any sudden danger, Indian or highwayman. Roberta had been drawn to him from the first. In the event of trouble, Cullen would be the one to take charge. Those thoughts stirred her curiosity and prompted her desire to learn more about the man. So she got up and followed him when he left the campfire to check on the horses.

"It just now occurred to me that you may be looking for privacy," she remarked when he turned to see her following him. "I beg your pardon if that's the case."

He smiled and replied, "No, I'm just gonna take a look at the right front hoof of my horse. I'm not sure, but he kinda acted like he was favorin' it a little just before we decided to make camp." He paused until she caught up to him. "Is there somethin' you need?" he asked. "Is anything wrong?"

"No, everything's fine," she was quick to reassure him. "I guess I'm just worried about Uncle Gabriel— up in these mountains all alone." She looked around her then, gazing at the sheer walls of granite rising hundreds of feet on both sides of the creek. "We should have heard from him long before this. I just so fear what we may find. This country looks so threatening." Realizing then that she had not given him any reason for following him to the creek, she said, "You just seem so much in control, I guess I just wanted some word of confidence that we'll find Uncle Gabriel."

"I wish I could guarantee that for you, but I can't," he replied. "But I can guarantee that Cody will find the camp that your uncle had in this canyon. He knows every part of these mountains, and if your uncle is not there, then we'll keep lookin' till we do find him. All right?"

She placed her hand on his arm and gazed up into his face. "I guess I also wanted to let you know how grateful I am to you for coming with me to look for my uncle."

Very much aware of her hand on his arm, his brain was immediately flooded with conflicting thoughts, for she left it there for several long moments. "Why, we're glad to help you, ma'am," he managed.

She affected an impish smile for him then. "Cullen McCloud," she playfully scolded, "we're going to have some serious trouble if you don't stop calling me ma'am. You make me feel like I'm your aunt or something."

He grinned. "All right, Roberta, I'll try to remember."

"See that you do," she said, and gave his arm a gentle squeeze before releasing him and returning to the fire.

It was no more than a little squeeze, but the sensation remained long after she had gone. He lifted his horse's front foot to inspect it, but his mind lingered on the past few minutes as he traced the bay's hoof with his fingers. Afraid that he was probably reading something more into Roberta's manner than she actually intended, he reprimanded himself for being a fool. *She is a fine-looking woman, though,* he thought as he released the horse's fetlock, having found nothing that would indicate a problem. When he returned to the fire to join the others, he found Cody helping Roberta make her bed. *I should have done that before I checked on my horse,* he thought. As soon as he thought it, he realized she had already reduced him to thinking like a schoolboy, competing for the affections of a little girl. He could imagine what fun Cody and Jug would make of it if they had any notion. He had to remind himself then that this was no picnic they had embarked upon. Roberta's uncle was long overdue and there were considerable odds that he might have come upon some bad luck, either in the form of Indians or the steep cliffs themselves.

Just before it was time to turn in for the night, Roberta excused herself to move away from the circle of firelight and walked downstream to attend to her private needs. Cullen took advantage of the opportunity to talk to Cody. "You sure you can find that camp again? All these damn gulches look pretty much the same, and I practically guaranteed her that you could find the right one."

"Oh, hell yeah," Cody replied confidently, then backed off a little. "It's been a while, and you're right—they do all look pretty much the same. But I'll find it. We've a ways to go yet. If I remember correctly, there was a rock pillar at the mouth of it, standin' all by itself like a gatepost or somethin'. I'll find it." Then he grinned at Cullen and said, "It'd most likely take me a lot longer to find it if you and Jug weren't with me."

"Huh," Cullen snorted, "that lady's out of your class."

His response caused Cody to chuckle. "I reckon she's more in your class. Right?"

"I didn't say that," Cullen replied. "I'm just sayin' she's a proper lady, and you ain't likely to have your way with her like you have with Mule Sibley's daughter."

Cody recoiled with a look of surprise. "You know about Brenda Sibley? How do you know about Brenda Sibley?"

"Hell, I'm your older brother. I ain't stupid," Cullen answered.

"Damn," Cody swore softly. "Does Jug know?"

"I don't know," Cullen replied, amused that Cody couldn't see that he had only been guessing about Sibley's daughter. "I doubt he cares." He shook his head then and laughed to himself.

The night passed without incident, and the search party got under way early the next morning. Roberta rode beside Cullen whenever the trail was wide enough for two horses abreast, a fact that Cullen could not help noticing. Cody rode out ahead, with Jug bringing up the rear. Throughout the morning and into the afternoon, they followed a creek with many waterfalls and beaver ponds that had attracted Cody's interest in the canyon before, prompting him to pause periodically to point out places where he had trapped beaver. They came to several gulches that appeared to lead into the sheer granite walls of the canyon, but Cody rejected them all. When the sun began to disappear from the narrow canyon early in the afternoon and they had not come upon the break in the canyon wall as Cody remembered it, they reluctantly decided it best to stop while there was still light enough to make camp. "You're sure we ain't missed it?" Cullen asked, his promise to Roberta foremost in his mind.

"I'm sure," Cody replied. "It's just farther up this canyon than I remembered, but we ain't missed it."

Roberta said nothing, but looked at Cullen for reassurance. "Don't worry," he told her. "We'll most likely find it early tomorrow."

As on the first night, Roberta insisted upon doing the cooking. After they had eaten and Jug decided another pot of coffee was in order, they sat around the fire to help him drink it. "It gets pretty chilly in this canyon when the sun goes down," Roberta commented. "I think I'll put on that extra coat your father insisted I take along."

"I'll get it for you," Cullen offered at once, and went to retrieve it from her saddle where his father had tied it. "This'll take the chill off," he said as he placed it around her shoulders.

She smiled gratefully and patted the blanket beside her. "Sit down beside me," she said. "I need a warm body to keep me snug."

With raised eyebrows, Cody and Jug exchanged amused glances, then looked quickly away to keep from bursting out in laughter. They were both enjoying their older brother's awkwardness around the woman, who had seemingly picked him to receive the larger portion of her attention. Cullen had always been of too serious a nature to participate in flirtations with any woman, and Cody and Jug were both encouraged to see his apparent attraction to their charming guest. *Maybe there's hope for him after all*, Cody thought. *Stranger things have happened.* He glanced at Jug again and thought, *He'll marry the first good cook he meets—doesn't matter if she's butt-ugly.* He laughed to himself then, thinking that this trip might turn up more than ol' Gabe.

Cullen's prediction proved reliable, for Cody found the stone pillar he had described to Cullen the next morning within an hour's ride of their camp. The mouth of the gulch was hidden from view by a low sandy ridge running crosswise along the deep ravine. "You sure a horse can get through that crack?" Cullen asked as he considered the narrow opening.

"Yeah," Cody replied. "It's pretty tight, but you can ride through it. We'll be ridin' single file, though." Crossing over the ridge, Cody suddenly reined his horse to a stop and signaled the others to halt while he dismounted.

"What is it Cody?" Cullen asked, and his brother pointed to hoofprints in the sand.

When Cullen dismounted to join him, Cody pointed to several more prints left by unshod hooves. "Indian ponies," Cullen said, and Cody nodded. He automatically paused to look around him. "How old, you figure? Three, four days?"

"At least," Cody replied. "No more'n that, though."

"Looks like five or six horses," Jug speculated after

he, too, moved up to study the prints. "Whaddaya think, Cody?"

"I reckon," Cody replied, "at least five." He looked to Cullen for confirmation, and his older brother nodded his agreement.

"Flathead, I reckon," Cullen said. "It's not likely they're any part of the Nez Perce moving through the valley."

All three brothers automatically became alert in case their search mission turned into something more risky than they had foreseen. Cody suggested that it might be wise for him to move out a little ahead of them to more carefully scout the rough trail leading down into the narrow gulch. All the tracks they had found led into the gulch, with none leading out, leaving the very real possibility that the Indians were still there. As Cullen pointed out, they could be hostile, or they could be friends of Gabe's. It would be best to proceed under the assumption they were hostile, maybe some of those responsible for the recent stock raids.

After leaving the others a good hundred yards behind him, Cody moved cautiously down into the deep ravine, following the tiny stream that trickled along the bottom. He paused frequently when he encountered places where the granite walls of the gulch closed in to barely allow a man on a horse to pass. As he glanced up at the ledges at the tops of the cliffs, it occurred to him how easily anyone could be ambushed by someone simply rolling a heavy stone over the edge to crush an unsuspecting intruder below. He thought back to recall the circumstances in which he had first discovered ol' Gabe's camp. He had almost been surprised by a party of Flatheads while hunting elk, and in his haste to avoid them, he had stumbled upon the entrance to the gulch behind the low ridge. It looked to be a good place to defend himself if they discovered his trail and decided to follow him, because they would have to come after him in single file. He grunted a soft chuckle when he recalled finding Gabe at the end of the gulch. It was hard to decide which of them was the more surprised, he, Gabe, or Gabe's old hound, which immediately charged with teeth bared.

Concentrating now on remembering characteristics of the narrow passage so as not to blunder around the last sharp turn before stepping out into a broad opening—as he did the first time he was there—he dismounted and led his horse. When he reached that final crook in the gulch, he recognized it at once and stopped dead still to listen for sounds that would tell him who might be waiting in the clearing beyond. There was no sound save that of the breeze rustling the boughs of the firs on the ledge above his head—no sound of Indian voices, not even a warning growl from Gabe's hound dog. And then he heard a low noise like that a coyote might make when eating. He drew his Winchester from the saddle sling and dismounted. Then moving up to the turn in the rock wall, he cautiously eased his head far enough past the corner to see the clearing. Baffled at first, he stared at the animal on the other side of the clearing for a few moments until he realized it was Gabe's hound, and the half-eaten carcass the dog was working on were the remains of a man.

Unaware of Cody until that moment, the dog turned its head and snarled a warning, but backed away a few feet in the face of the man advancing toward him. "Good Lord a'mercy," Cody uttered as he continued toward the badly desecrated body, the vile odor just then reaching his nostrils. "Git!" he yelled at the dog, but the hound, having gone without food for several days before taking nourishment from his master's body, was reluctant to yield to the intruder. Cody picked up a stone and threw it at the hound. It missed the mark by a foot, but was enough to cause the dog to retreat several yards from the body, where it again crouched and snarled its defiance.

When Cody moved up beside the carcass to take a closer look, the dog suddenly sprang up to defend his food, attacking his adversary. Cody had no choice but to shoot it. Already puzzling over the fact that there had been no tracks leading out of the gorge, he thought to himself, *I may have done it now. Anybody who didn't know we were here damn sure knows it now.* With the others not that far behind him, he hurried to take a quick look at what was left of the corpse. There was enough to determine that it had been ol' Gabe, and the next thought that came to Cody's mind was to get back down the gulch to intercept his brothers and Roberta. It wouldn't do for Roberta to see the ghastly remains of her uncle.

He caught them just as they reached the final turn before the clearing, Cullen and Jug with guns drawn. "What was that shot?" Cullen questioned immediately.

Cody held up his arm to halt them. "Just me shootin' a dog," he replied. "You'd best hold up here," he directed at Roberta, "till me and my brothers can take a look around." When she started to protest, he said, "You don't wanna see this, miss. It ain't a pretty sight."

Cullen pushed his horse forward. "What the hell do you mean, you shot a dog?" He had already assumed there were no Indians in the camp, but that didn't mean they wanted to announce their presence to whoever might be within earshot. When Cody explained, Cullen looked immediately behind him to Roberta, who, like Jug, sat puzzled and out of earshot. Turning back to his brother, he asked, "You sure it's her uncle?"

"It's Gabe," Cody replied with certainty, "or what's left of him."

Taking charge as usual, Cullen called to his other brother, "Jug, come on up here. We need to scout this campsite and see where those Indian ponies went." He pulled his horse aside to let Jug pass, then reined back to block Roberta, who had started to follow. "I expect it's best for you to stay here for a bit until we get a chance to see what's what," he told her. "Those Indians might still be hidin' around here somewhere."

With a distinct suspicion that there was something in the clearing he did not want her to see, she responded with, "If there were Indians hiding around here, they would probably already be shooting at us." She urged her horse forward.

Cullen took hold of her horse's bridle. "Roberta, please. It's your uncle, and I don't think it would be a good idea for you to see him now. Wait a few minutes till we can take care of him." He saw the immediate distress in her face, but there was also a vestige of determination.

"I'm a big girl, Cullen," she responded patiently. "I

appreciate your concern for my feelings, but I don't need to be protected from seeing my uncle's body. I had already prepared myself for the worst."

It was fairly obvious to him that he would have to physically restrain her to keep her from riding in, so he released the bridle. "Well, I reckon you know what you're doin'," he said, and backed his horse away to let her pass. "But I don't think it's the last picture of your uncle you'd want to remember him by."

"I appreciate your concern, Cullen," she replied with a sad smile, "but I'll be all right." She urged her horse forward. He wheeled the bay and followed.

Standing over the corpse, Jug and Cody turned at once when Roberta approached them. Glancing beyond her at his older brother, Cody frowned and started to protest. "Damn, Cullen . . ." Without finishing, he quickly turned to Roberta. "You'd best stay back, Roberta. You don't wanna see this." He hesitated then, not wishing to give her the horrible news that her uncle had been partially devoured by his dog. "Those Indians scalped him," he offered as a reason for her to stay away.

"Good Lord," Cullen uttered upon seeing the remains of the miner known as ol' Gabe. He immediately put his arm around Roberta's shoulders and turned her away from the macabre scene.

"Poor Uncle Gabriel," Roberta repeated over and over as she surrendered to Cullen's protective embrace, pressing close against his chest. After a moment, he led her across the clearing toward a large rock next to the remnants of a campfire. She trembled violently for a few minutes in reaction to seeing the grisly remains while Cullen held her in his arms. After a few moments more, she looked up into his face and uttered softly, "I'm all right now." She smiled at him, then stepped away from his embrace and let him seat her upon the rock.

"I'm sorry you had to see that," Cullen said. "You just sit here for a few minutes while we look the place over before we bury your uncle. All right?" She nodded and he rejoined his brothers.

"Looks like it was Indians that done him in," Cody said to him when he walked up. "What we need to do is find out where they went after takin' care of ol' Gabe. There must be a back door to this camp. I never noticed one when I was here before. 'Course, I never looked for one."

"Damn, what a mess," Cullen uttered upon his second and closer look at the half-eaten body. He glanced then at the body of the dog, its belly extended— evidence of its recent gorging on *long pig*. "There ain't much chance of us surprisin' 'em if they *are* still around."

"Well, hell, didja expect me to let the son of a bitch take my arm off?" Cody responded in defense of his action. "I didn't have a lot of time to think about it."

"I'm not sayin' you did," Cullen conceded, "I'm just statin' a fact." Then taking charge once again, he said, "Why don't you scout around the back of this clearin' to make sure we ain't expectin' company? Maybe you'll find that back door. Jug and I can start diggin' a hole to bury this poor fellow."

Jug shrugged, still staring at the body. "I wonder what people meat tastes like."

Cody looked at his brother in mock disgust. "Damn,

Jug, you do beat all." Then an impish grin appeared on his face. "I hear tell it tastes kinda sweet, like rabbit."

"Shut up, you two," Cullen scolded, taking a quick glance across the clearing to where Roberta was still seated. "What if Roberta heard you makin' fun of her uncle's body?" When it was evident that the young lady had not heard the comments, he said, "Now, let's get to work, so we can get on outta this place."

Finding a pick and shovel among the late Gabe Morris' possessions, Jug and Cullen set to work digging a grave. It was not easy finding a place with ground soft enough to dig in, but a spot was settled upon near the small stream where Gabe had excavated a sizable portion of the bank, apparently looking for pay dirt, and had dumped the dirt to form a mound large enough to hide a body. The grave digging claimed his attention for several minutes, so when Cullen looked back to check on Roberta, he was surprised to find her gone from the rock and poking around in her uncle's tent. His heart went out to her. He thought she was hoping to find some personal keepsake to take back to her aunt.

When ol' Gabe was safely in the ground, Cullen told Jug to take the dog's carcass and throw it behind some rocks near the entrance to the camp. "Just so she won't have to be reminded of it," he said, then walked over to join Roberta in the tent. "He didn't leave much behind, did he?" Cullen commented when he came up behind her. Startled, she jumped. "I didn't mean to scare you," he said. He looked around him then at the disrupted state of Gabe's possessions.

Seeing his look of astonishment, she commented, "Indians must have made this mess." She dropped a canvas war bag that had evidently held the few items of clothing lying now on the floor of the tent. "Not much to show for a man's life," she said as she looked at him and smiled sadly.

"I reckon not," he replied, then said, "Your uncle's buried. I expect you might wanna say somethin' over his grave."

"Yes, I would," she immediately responded, and turned to leave the tent. "Aunt Edna would want me to."

He glanced around the tent before following her. "They sure didn't leave anythin' right side up," he commented. The ceremony over the grave was brief with Roberta wishing her uncle a joyous journey to the reward she knew was awaiting him and finishing with a prayer for her aunt Edna's welfare without her faithful companion. Still leaning on the shovel, Jug was touched to the point that he bowed his head and closed his eyes. Cullen stood solemnly with head bowed until she was finished. Then he took her by the arm and led her over to the ashes of Gabe's campfire. "We'll build a fire and brew up a little coffee," he told her. "That always makes things better."

"I feel so bad for poor Uncle Gabriel," she said, "and I don't know how I can tell Aunt Edna that he's gone." She looked up into Cullen's eyes, her pain so evident. "Oh, Cullen, my aunt is so ill. I'm afraid the news will kill her. I don't know how she will survive." She paused and placed her hand on his arm. "It seems so improper to even think about money at a time like this, and I'm afraid you'll think ill of me, but Aunt

Edna so desperately needs the gold Uncle Gabriel told her he discovered up here in these mountains."

Cullen replied, "Any gold he found should go to your aunt, so there's no reason for you to feel bad about looking for it."

"Where would he have hidden it?" she asked.

"I don't know—any place, I guess." He glanced around him then as if looking over the campsite for the first time. "Hard to say—someplace you wouldn't think to look, I suppose."

She squeezed his arm and gazed into his eyes, beseechingly. "We've got to find that gold. Aunt Edna needs it desperately, and I'm afraid those Indians stole it, and he died for nothing."

"Well, I reckon we can search for it," he said, trying to fake enthusiasm, for he really had his doubts concerning Gabe's success in an area where no gold had been found to amount to anything. "I doubt those Indians would have carried off any gold dust. It doesn't have much value to them. I expect they were satisfied just to get his livestock."

Cody returned to find the three of them scouring the clearing. "What the hell are you doin'?" he asked Cullen. Cullen explained that they were searching for Gabe's hidden gold to give to Aunt Edna. Cody thought about that for a moment before reporting, "I found the back door. This little gulch starts climbin' after leavin' this clearin', goes about two hundred yards, then just sorta peters out up the side of the mountain. I found the tracks from those ponies and some tracks from shod stock—Gabe's mules, I reckon. They're long gone."

About ready to give up on what he considered to be

a useless search, Cullen posed a question to his youngest brother. "We've turned over every rock small enough to move and Roberta's turned the tent upside down. If you had some gold dust to hide, where would you hide it?"

Cody paused and looked all around him for a few moments, taking in the whole area of the clearing. "I expect I'd put it back where I found it in the first place."

"The stream?" Cullen responded, and turned to look at the tiny waterway making its way down the gulch. "Why not?" he decided, and he and Cody started walking slowly along the stream, paying close attention to the many turns and spills around the rocks. Almost simultaneously both men's eyes locked on a miniature falls formed where several rocks appeared to pile one upon the other. Having overheard the conversation between his two brothers, Jug joined them in the search and started to attack the waterfall with Cody. In a few moments time, they uncovered a small pouch. Untying the rawhide drawstring, Cody peered in the sack to discover a small amount of gold dust. He looked up at Cullen. "Well, here's his fortune," he said. "Ain't much to show for his trouble."

"That's too damn easy," Cullen decided, and hesitated. "I think ol' Gabe set that up as a decoy." He took a closer look up and down the stream while his brothers took the rocks forming the waterfall apart. Still, he saw nothing unusual, so he crossed over to the other side. In doing so, his foot slipped off the side of the bank, dislodging a pumpkin-sized stone under it. About to curse his clumsiness in getting his boot wet, he was stopped short by the sight of a canvas pouch barely visible behind the rock. "I got somethin' here," he sang out, and dropped to one knee to retrieve the pouch.

"Well, I'll be damned," Cody muttered as Roberta ran to join them. "So the old codger—I mean, your uncle—really did find gold."

"There's more," Cullen said as he pulled another sack out of a hole dug in the bank and handed it to Jug. In total, there were four heavy pouches of dust hidden in the bank, protected by the one rock. "Ol' Gabe found a fortune," he announced, "and from the weight of these sacks, a sizable one."

Roberta could not hide her excitement as she frantically worked at the knotted drawstring of the largest of the pouches. She opened the sack and withdrew a small handful of the precious dust, examining it closely. Then aware of the three men standing and watching her, she looked up, her face beaming. "Aunt Edna will be so pleased. There's enough gold here to take care of her for the rest of her life."

"She ain't the only one."

The words came from behind them, the voice deep and threatening. Taken completely by surprise, having been caught up in the excitement of their discovery, the three brothers were helpless to react in time. Jug and Cody recognized the three at once from the encounter in Sibley's saloon. "Reach for them sidearms and you're dead," Frank Burdette warned. Crocker and Blackie Cruz stood on either side of him with their pistols aimed at them. Caught flat-footed, the McCloud brothers had no choice but to raise their hands. There was no time to berate themselves for their carelessness. The question now was how to save their hides, for there was no doubt as to their fate. They would hardly be spared their lives. The only question was why the outlaws hesitated. There was no reason not to simply shoot them down, but Burdette hesitated, evidently enjoying the prospect of making the three brothers contemplate their execution. The air was heavy with the tension between them.

"Now, suppose you boys just back away from them sacks and unbuckle them gun belts," Burdette ordered, "nice and easy-like." A slow smile formed on his unshaven face. "Not you, young lady," he said to Roberta. "You're comin' with us." He motioned with his head for her to move toward him.

As the three brothers backed slowly away from the stream, each one feeling helpless and angry at the same time, there was a common knowledge that, no matter how desperate, they would have to make some move to save Roberta and themselves. Deliberately stalling as he unbuckled his gun belt, Jug was the first to try. Directing his words to Big John Crocker, he attempted to goad him. "You were the one doin' all the talkin' back at Sibley's. I knew you were all mouth when you said you'd kick my ass. You're lucky you were able to sneak up on me with a gun, just like the low-down coyote you are. I expect you saved yourself a good asswhuppin'."

Crocker's eyes narrowed to two dark slits. "Why, you son of a bitch, I might have to teach you a lesson before this day is over."

"But I expect you'll have to shoot me first, won't you, asshole?"

The thought of the two oversized men squaring off against each other amused Burdette. It might be entertaining at that. He'd never seen a man stand up to Crocker. "What about it, Big John?" he asked. "You wanna have a little go-round with this big mouth?"

Grinning wickedly, Crocker replied, "I'd love to."

"All right," Burdette said. "Go to it, but make it quick. We need to get outta here."

"It won't take long," Big John said, and stepped toward Jug.

"Hold on a minute till we get them pouches," Burdette said. "Blackie, help the lady on her horse. Then pick them pouches up and tie 'em on behind her." Then, addressing Cullen and Cody, he ordered, "You two back away from them guns."

"All right, Burdette," Blackie replied, "but tell Big John to wait till I'm done. I don't wanna miss the fight."

"Make it quick," Burdette ordered, then raised his pistol to aim at Cullen, preparing to finish him and Cody. Before he pulled the trigger, though, he had another thought. "I believe I'll let you two watch Big John break your brother's back before I send you to hell." He laughed at the prospect. "But don't get no funny ideas," he added, "'cause I'll just shoot you down where you stand."

Certain that Jug was doing all he could to delay their executions, Cullen felt his mind racing through his options. There were none. He glanced at Roberta, who had no choice but to do as she was ordered. She seemed to be taking the threat stoically, but he could imagine the fear and panic raging inside her as she allowed Blackie to lead her to her horse. It seemed evident that she was in a state of shock after having come so close to saving her aunt. In the short time he had known her, however, he had learned that she was not the kind of woman to weep and faint away, and he had to battle the reckless urge he felt to go to her, knowing that would destroy her chances of rescue completely. He glanced then at Cody and saw the look of quiet determination in his eye. They were of the same accord, and that was not to go down without a fight.

There was a short standoff between the outlaws and the brothers, while they waited for Blackie's return. The blatant pleasure in Burdette's eyes told of the enjoyment he anticipated in the execution of the three brothers. After a few minutes' time, Blackie hurried back after readying their horses to leave, with Roberta seated on her horse and the gold sacks secured behind her. Cullen tried to signal Roberta with his eyes to make a run for it, but Blackie had evidently considered that possibility and held on to her reins. She met Cullen's gaze and her eyes seemed to reach out to him in helpless surrender to her fate. He felt his heart about to break. "Stomp his ass," Blackie said gleefully, ready to watch the match.

Crocker grinned maliciously as the two huge men circled, watching and warily anticipating the first to make a move. Unable to wait a second longer, Crocker finally attacked, launching himself into Jug's midsection, driving him several feet backward, but failing to knock him off his feet. Surprised to find him still standing, Crocker took a step back, blinked a couple of times, then hunkered down to make another bull-like charge at his confidently grinning adversary. This time Jug was ready for him, and deftly stepped aside to avoid his charge, slamming him with a solid right hand to the side of his face. The blow sent the infuriated giant to his knees. Jug walked around him, and before he could get back on his feet, Jug launched another hay-maker that flattened Crocker's nose and sent him down on his back. Like a great cat, Jug was immediately upon him, clamping his neck in a headlock and tight-ening down. It was no contest. Jug was making quick work of it and Crocker knew it. "Shoot him!" he gasped in desperation, fearing that his neck was about to be broken. When he bellowed his frantic plea, both Cul-len and Cody dived for the pistols they had dropped on the ground. It was not in time to prevent Burdette from pulling the trigger and firing a slug into Jug's side. A half second later, Cullen recovered his revolver and shot at Burdette. With really no time to take aim, his shot went wide and only grazed Burdette's shoul-der, but it was enough to cause the outlaw to retreat.

While Cullen rolled over the edge of the stream bank, firing now at Crocker, Cody sent a bullet Blackie's way before following Cullen for cover under the lip of the bank. The shot struck Blackie in the chest, and the star-tled man sat down hard on the ground to stare down at the wound in disbelief, still holding on to Roberta's reins. The gun battle that followed was of short dura-tion, lasting no more than three or four minutes before Burdette grabbed Roberta's reins from Blackie's hand and withdrew to take cover in the narrow passage en-trance, with Crocker close behind with his and Blackie's horses. In that brief period of time, however, a lot of lead flew, most of it from the outlaws in an effort to keep Cody and Cullen pinned down in the stream.

When the firing finally ceased, Cullen tried to assess the damage to his brothers. Ignoring the burning in his side from the bullet that had creased him, he looked at Cody, who was holding his hand over a bloody shoulder. Cody yelled that he was okay. Cullen nodded, then crawled over to the edge of the stream and made his way to Jug, who had not moved since being hit in the side. The big man was alive, but only barely. His shirt was drenched with blood that continued to seep through the fingers of his hand as he pressed it tightly over the wound. "Just sit tight," Cullen told him. "Try not to move too much. You might cause it to bleed more. As soon as I make sure they've gone, I'll be back and Cody and I will help you on your horse and get you home. All right?"

Jug nodded weakly.

It was not going to be that easy. He was pretty sure the two he heard called Burdette and Big John had fled, taking Roberta and the gold with them. But his and his brothers' horses were scattered, all of them having bolted toward the back door of Gabe's camp. His concern was for his brother. Jug's wound seemed to be serious. He wasn't sure about Cody's, in spite of his younger brother's reassurance. He would take care of his brothers, but of equal concern was Roberta's fate, and this brought a feeling of helplessness on his part for not being able to pursue her captors at once. *I'll come for you as soon as I can,* he silently promised, and tried not to dwell upon her possible treatment at the hands of her abductors.

He looked back to see Cody crawling cautiously over the bank, relieved to see he appeared to still have his strength as he moved toward Jug. "Keep your gun handy till I make sure they've gone," he called. "Then I'll try to round up the horses." He hurried to the edge of the clearing just before the entrance to the gulch, and peered around the rock column. They were nowhere in sight for as far as he could see before the gulch took another turn. Wasting no time, he immediately turned then and ran toward the back of the clearing after the horses. "They're gone!" he yelled to Cody as he ran.

Having scattered initially, the horses came back together to stand in a small meadow a few hundred yards above the camp. With Cody's help, he collected all three, plus the packhorse, and led them back to the clearing. The question to be answered next was how to transport Jug. It was going to prove extremely painful to put him on a horse. A travois would be best, but the narrow walls of the gulch in many places prohibited its use. "Hell," Jug gasped, "just get me up on my horse. I'll make it somehow. I don't wanna die in this damn hole." So they managed to lift him into the saddle, a task not easily accomplished owing to the bulk of their brother. After he was safely aboard, he immediately lay forward, grasping his horse around the neck. With the feeling that time was critical, they started back down the gulch at once, leaving the clearing to be guarded by the wide-eyed corpse of Blackie Cruz, still seated upright and staring down at the hole in his chest.

In spite of their urgency, the ride back down the gulch was painfully slow with Jug threatening to fall from the saddle even at that pace. Leaving Cody to help Jug stay on his horse, Cullen rode a few dozen yards ahead to make sure they weren't riding into an ambush. But it was soon obvious that Burdette and Big John were more interested in hightailing it, probably figuring the McCloud brothers were too shot up to follow, but still too dangerous to risk exchanging more shots.

It was already getting late in the day by the time they rode out of the gulch into Blodgett Canyon again. It was getting more and more difficult to keep Jug upright on his horse, and finally Cullen decided there was no choice but to stop and let him rest. In the meantime, he told Cody they could fashion a travois to carry him the rest of the way, since they were out of the narrow gulch. "We might as well camp here all night," Cullen said, although reluctant to make the decision. It was difficult to bear the thought that the delay would only put Roberta farther and farther away, but he had to think of Jug. "If we try to take him out in the dark, we're liable to break a horse's leg or dump him in the creek," he said.

Cody agreed. He was feeling considerable pain in his shoulder by then as his arm stiffened, and he was inclined to take the time to tend to all their wounds.

The image of Roberta, looking confused and afraid, returned to Cullen's thoughts as he helped Cody look for wood for a fire, and he fought the desperate feeling of urgency to find her. When they had seen Jug settled as comfortably as possible, and had done what they could to stop the bleeding, Cullen then took a look at Cody's wound. "That doesn't look any too good, either," he said after cleaning some of the blood away. "Looks like the bullet's still in there, 'cause there ain't no hole in the back. I could dig around in there and try to get it out, but it might be best, and easier on you, to wait and let Smoke get it outta there. We oughta be able to get back home by tomorrow afternoon early."

"That suits me," Cody said, thinking that there was whiskey available at home to help with the pain of Smoke's probing. His arm was already stiffening to the point of feeling like a useless ham hanging from his shoulder. Then he nodded toward Cullen's blood-stained shirt and asked, "What about that wound in your side?"

Cullen glanced down at his side as if just then remembering it. "It ain't anythin'," he said, surprised by the size of the bloodstain on his shirt. "Just grazed me. I've been hurt worse shavin'. What was Jug talkin' about back there? Do you two know those men?"

"We had a little run-in with 'em at Mule Sibley's place. They got a little rough with Brenda and her mother. I wish to hell we'd shot 'em." Cody studied his brother's face for a few moments before asking, "You thinkin' 'bout Roberta?" Cullen nodded solemnly. "Me, too," Cody said. "You think they'll kill her?"

Cullen shook his head slowly, reluctant to admit the possibility. "I don't know," he finally answered. "If they had any notion to kill her right away, I expect we'd have already found her. Most likely they'll keep her for a while." He hesitated before finishing the statement, but finally added, "Until they're through with her." He didn't like the mental picture that suggested. He had known Roberta Morris for only a brief couple of days, but he had sensed an attraction between them. She had caused him to start thinking about things he had never felt before. Even if he was mistaken about the special connection between them, he could not bear the thought of the woman being abused by the likes of the two men who had abducted her.

Cody could read his brother well. "Go get her. The quicker you find her, the better off she'll be," he said. "I know you're worried about Jug and me, but I can get Jug home all right if you wanna get on their trail before it gets cold." He immediately saw the spark in Cullen's eye in reaction to his suggestion.

"Are you sure you can make it back all right?" Cullen replied. "Jug's wound looks pretty bad."

"Well, it ain't gonna make no difference whether you're with us or not. If you'll build that travois, I can sure as hell do the rest." He didn't need a spoken answer; he could read it in Cullen's eyes. "Let's take a look at those tracks while we've still got some light. It'd help a helluva lot if we can find somethin' unusual about 'em to help you know you're followin' the right trail."

Lady Luck favored them in this regard, for after a careful examination of the outlaws' tracks along a sandy stretch of creek bank, Cody discovered a signature for one of the horses. "Here you go!" he called out, and when Cullen hurried over to see, he pointed to one particularly clear print. "One of their horses has got a twisted shoe," he said. "See that, how that one doesn't look like it lines up on the hoof like it should? That's because whoever did the shoein' didn't do a good job. That's gonna be a loose shoe before long." He stood aside while Cullen took careful note of the print.

"I believe you're right," Cullen agreed. "It is twisted—kinda hard to tell, but it's sure as hell twisted." He felt confident then that he could follow Roberta's abductors as long as he didn't let them get too great a head start.

As darkness settled upon the narrow canyon, Cullen finished the construction of a simple travois for Jug while Cody tried to see if his wounded brother could eat anything. It proved to be a fruitless endeavor, causing Cody to remark that it was the first time ever that Jug could not eat, indicating to him and Cullen that Jug's wound was serious indeed. "I've got to get him home quick," a worried Cody opined. "Maybe I oughta try to take him to the doctor in Stevensville."

"You'd best take him home," Cullen said. "It'd take too long to take him to Stevensville. Smoke'll know what to do." Smoke had probably as much experience treating bullet wounds as the doctor in Stevensville. It was settled then and their decision made more sense when Jug seemed a bit better the following morning, although he still wanted nothing more than coffee for breakfast. They lifted him onto the travois and started out of the canyon. When they reached the valley, they paused briefly while Cody and Cullen scouted the outlaws' tracks, which turned north, leading down the valley. Torn between the welfare of his brother and the urgency to rescue Roberta, Cullen hesitated. His father's ranch was also north of this point, but in a direction northeast of the trail left by the outlaws. It was only after Cody's reassurance that he could see Jug safely home that he bade them good-bye, and started up the Bitterroot Valley in pursuit of Burdette and Crocker with a resolve to rescue Roberta while Cody veered off toward the M Bar C.

Chapter 4

There had been no consideration for sparing the horses since fleeing the steep-walled canyon. With Burdette leading and Roberta's horse between his and Crocker's, and Blackie's horse trailing, they had not stopped, even when reaching the valley a short time before dark. Turning north, Burdette continued on another four or five miles before picking a place to make camp. Guiding his horse along the bank of the Bitterroot River, he selected a small clearing on the west side lined with ponderosa pines. "I reckon this is as good a spot as any," he announced when Crocker and Roberta caught up to him. "Does it suit you, sweetheart?" he asked with an exaggerated lascivious grin. Roberta ignored the question.

"Well, it damn sure suits me," Crocker remarked. "I didn't think you was ever gonna stop. Them fellers back there ain't likely comin' after us, anyway. They're too bad shot up—and their horses was scattered up the mountain." He dismounted and paused to take Roberta's reins. "Too bad about ol' Blackie, though."

"You should have finished them off when you had the chance," Roberta stated coldly. "But you had to have that childish fight. Now we have to worry about somebody chasing us. I don't trust those brothers. If they're not hurt as bad as you think, they'll be coming after us."

Her tone was one of extreme annoyance. Burdette cringed from her scolding and sought to placate her. "Don't worry about them boys, honey. I'm bettin' they've had all the taste of lead they want, and it'll soon be too dark to cut our trail. Besides, if they do come after us, me and Crocker will take care of 'em for sure."

"Like you did back there?" Roberta replied sarcastically. "Why didn't you shoot them while they were standing there with their guns on the ground? I cut you in on this deal because you were supposed to take care of them. I didn't need you to help me find that old man's camp. That part was easy enough. Your part was to get rid of the old man and be my insurance just in case the McCloud brothers decided they should get part of the gold. But the old man was already dead, and I would have probably ridden out of there with all the gold dust." She glared at him and shook her head in disgust. "You might not have had to shoot anybody. Now they're likely to come try to rescue me. I'd feel a lot better if they were all dead." She silently berated herself for enlisting the three outlaws' help, realizing now that the McCloud brothers had no intention of forcing a share in the gold. She hadn't really needed Burdette's help. She could have pulled the whole thing off with no help, since that party of Indians had been so accommodating. But how was she to know? In fact, Cullen or Cody would probably have seen her safely back to Missoula. Now she feared one or both might be bent upon coming to rescue her. *I shouldn't have led Cullen on,* she thought. "That fight between Crocker and Jug McCloud was not a wise thing to do," she started in again. "Like two schoolboys in a schoolyard. You should have finished them all off when you had the chance," she repeated.

"I know that, Roberta," Burdette replied, getting a little bit testy from the scolding. "You done told me twice, damn it, but you ain't got nothin' to worry about from them fellers as long as me and Big John are with you." He had been led to believe that there was more promised to him than a share of ol' Gabe's dust, but the sweetness in her tone seemed to have disappeared. This sudden coolness in her attitude had never surfaced during the ride from Fort Missoula to Stevensville the week before. This was the first real glimpse of the temper that lay close beneath her sugary surface.

"Whaddaya say we divide up that gold dust?" Crocker suggested, his only response to her criticism.

Roberta glanced at Crocker, then back at Burdette, her expression softening from the frown a second before, fully aware that she had use for him yet. "Not yet," she said. "It'll be a more accurate split after we get back to Fort Missoula and have it assayed. Don't you think so, Frank?"

Relieved to see the apparent return of her gentler demeanor, Burdette replied, "You're probably right, Roberta. No sense in tryin' to divide a pile of dust when the assayer's office can tell us exactly how much we've got to split." In an attempt to further lighten the mood, he turned to Crocker then and said, "You're too anxious to get your hands on that gold, Big John. There ain't nothin' to spend it on till we get to Fort Missoula, anyway."

Crocker shrugged. What they said made sense to him. He would have preferred to divide it up right away, but he wouldn't put up a fuss over it. He didn't entirely trust the woman. She sure as hell liked to run things her way. Of course he had to admit that the whole scheme was her idea to begin with, and Burdette seemed to trust her, so he guessed he could, too. He and Burdette had pulled more than a few jobs together, along with Blackie. *Too bad about Blackie,* he paused to reflect, *but that makes it a three-way split instead of four.* He gazed at Roberta as she tucked the pouches under her saddle after Burdette had placed it on the ground for her. It occurred to him that the sensible thing to do at this point was to get rid of the woman and split the gold two ways. That was what they would have done if Burdette hadn't gotten sweet on her. *I reckon if she sashayed her little rear end around me like she does around him, I'd be the same way.*

The cooking of supper was left to Crocker, since Roberta, in an abrupt change in demeanor, insisted that she should take care of Burdette's wound. Burdette made a big show of pretending the creased shoulder was of no concern to him, and Roberta scolded him for his manly indifference to pain. The little play between the two was enough to disgust Crocker as he unwrapped a slab of bacon and sliced off enough to fill his frying pan. The woman had Burdette acting like a schoolboy sniffing around a little girl for the first time, when ten minutes before she was scolding him like a runaway slave. Before Roberta came along and charmed his partner, he and Burdette would have shared the woman. *We get back to Butte*, he told himself, *I'll have enough money to buy any woman I want*. Thoughts of the wide-open town with its many bawdy houses in the red-light district the locals called *The Line* brought a smile of anticipation to his face. *Ol' Burdette can have his true-loving with one woman. I'll have a different one every night*.

As for Burdette, he had a great deal to learn regarding the manipulative powers of a woman. He was quite flattered, overwhelmed in fact, by Roberta's apparent interest in him. When they first met in Butte, their arrangement was strictly business with the potential of a considerable payoff for all concerned. But as the venture progressed, they seemed to find a certain attraction for each other—enough so that he found himself experiencing feelings of jealousy over the short time she was to spend riding with the McCloud brothers. Therefore, he was considerably relieved to feel the soft, caring touch of her fingers upon his wounded shoulder.

When she had finished cleaning the shallow cut left by Cullen's bullet, she made a bandage from some cloth she carried in her saddlebags. "That'll do just fine," he announced. "Wasn't much to begin with."

"You need me to take care of you," she scolded playfully, causing him to grin from ear to ear.

"When you two get done playin' house," Crocker blurted impatiently, "I reckon you can help yourself to some of this bacon. I ain't gonna serve it up for you."

Roberta responded with a girlish giggle and bent

close to whisper in Burdette's ear, "I wish there was just the two of us."

"Me, too," Burdette replied, also under his breath.

"Why don't you make your bed up close to mine?" she suggested coyly.

He nodded enthusiastically. "I'll do that," he whispered, already excited over the prospect.

There was some speculation about the real possibility of their being followed by the McCloud brothers as they sat around the fire to consume the bacon and coffee Big John had prepared. Crocker seemed unconcerned about it. He was fairly certain that Jug was seriously wounded and the other two had suffered wounds to some extent. "They ain't in no shape to come after us," he said, "even if they was to try."

"Maybe we should keep a watch just in case," Roberta suggested, "at least until well after dark when it'll be too hard for them to see our trail. What do you think, Frank?"

"Maybe you're right," Burdette immediately agreed. "Wouldn't hurt to be sure." He was already thinking of the promise of time alone with Roberta. She had already expressed her reluctance to demonstrate her affection in front of Crocker. It was an attitude of modesty that Burdette had never been exposed to with the usual class of women he had known, and another quality of Roberta's that made her all the more desirable.

Not entirely taken in by the ruse he suspected, Crocker was not averse to the suggestion, however. It probably would be a smart precaution to take. "Lemme guess who you think oughta take the first watch," he said sarcastically.

"Hell," Burdette replied, "I can do it, if you don't want to. It won't be for long, anyway."

"Nah," Crocker responded, "I'll take it." He got up then, pulled his rifle from the saddle sling, and walked off in the direction of a low rise in the riverbank to pick a good spot to watch their back trail.

He was barely out of sight when Burdette got up and moved over to sit down beside Roberta. "Did any of them McCloud boys try to get too cozy with you?" he asked. "'Cause if they did, I might wanna go back and make damn sure they paid for it."

She graced him with another of her coy smiles. "That's sweet of you to care," she said demurely, "but, no, although I could tell a couple of them were thinking about it. And I didn't give them a chance. I kept thinking about you waiting for me." She leaned over then and kissed him lightly on the cheek.

Overcome with joy, Burdette was speechless for a few moments, scarcely able to believe his good fortune. He had never had a woman—one he hadn't paid—so blatantly attracted to him. And Roberta was so far above any woman he had had contact with before. Tall and trim, proper with almost a touch of elegance at times; she was a prize he never dreamed he would win. It didn't occur to him to wonder why she had become so attracted to a rough outlaw like him. "Damn," he finally uttered, "I been thinkin' a lot about you lately."

"And I've been thinking about you," she returned, meeting his hungry eyes with a frank gaze of her own that encouraged him to be bold.

Confident then that he had not misinterpreted the invitation in her eyes, he reached for her, and she made

no move to resist, coming into his arms, her face lifted
to receive his kiss. Following his natural instincts, and
having never been a party to a gentle passion, he set
upon her then, pawing and groping in his beastly fashion. She permitted his primordial exploration of her
body until he began pulling at the buttons on her blouse;
then she stopped him. "Oh, Frank," she sighed, seemingly breathless, "I want to share my body completely,
but I can't with Crocker sitting out there. I would be
devastated if he came and saw us."

Heated to a degree he had never before experienced,
Burdette was not sure he would not explode. "He won't
come back. I'll tell him to stay the hell away till we're
ready," he insisted, his voice urgent and raspy.

"I want you so," she whispered, "but I can't give
myself freely, the way you deserve, until we're away
from that man." Seeing the frustration in his eyes, she
pressed him further. "I wish he wasn't with us. If it
was just the two of us, we could live as lovers—and
we would have all the gold to ourselves."

Burdette was not an intelligent man, but he recognized a situation that appealed to him. He was quick
to come up with a solution to their problem. "Well, I
reckon I can fix it so we won't have to worry about
Crocker no more."

"Oh, Frank, do I really mean that much to you?"

"And then some," he answered. "I'll take care of
that big son of a bitch right now. I'm tired of his com-
plainin', anyway." He got up immediately, strapped
on his gun belt, and started toward the low rise where
he had last seen Crocker.

Smiling to herself, Roberta straightened her clothes,

which had become disheveled after Burdette's feverish
pawing. She felt confident that his lust for her was a
sufficient instrument to bring about the elimination of
another shareholder in the four pouches of gold dust.
A two-way split was her ultimate goal, and for the time
being, she was content to let Burdette assume that
he was the partner she planned to split it with. She
resolved to tolerate him at least until she felt she no
longer needed his protection. She could not say that
she enjoyed the rough-and-tumble style of lovemaking
practiced by Frank Burdette, or any other style, as far
as that was concerned, but she would put up with it
for as long as she thought necessary. She was not looking forward to the fulfillment of the promise she had
implied, but she knew it was necessary to maintain control of Burdette. At least it would be preferable to deal-
ing with the huge beast that was Big John Crocker. Her
total disdain for making love in general caused her to
view it as nothing more than a means to get what she
wanted. The act had never brought her pleasure, although she reluctantly admitted to herself that there
might have been a possibility with Cullen McCloud.

"You relievin' me already?" Crocker asked, surprised
to see his partner climbing the backside of the ridge by
the river's edge. He grinned then and chided, "Miss
Priss must not be in heat right now." His comment only
served to strengthen Burdette's resolve. "What's goin'
on?" Crocker asked, confused when Burdette pulled
his revolver from the holster. "What the hell are you
doin'?" he challenged nervously as Burdette raised the
pistol to point directly at him.

"There ain't no hard feelin's, Big John," Burdette responded. "I expect you'll do as a partner about as good as any man I ever rode with. But things has changed. You'd do the same if you was in my shoes."

Crocker realized at once what was about to happen. He rolled off the log he was seated upon, reaching for his rifle as he hit the ground, but Burdette shot him before he could raise the weapon and cock it. He cried out in pain and dropped his rifle when the bullet ripped through his stomach, "Oh Lord, you've kilt me!" But he wasn't dead yet. "Frank, we rode together for more'n three years. Don't do this!" His pleas ignored, he managed to get on his knees and attempted to crawl away.

Burdette stalked purposefully along with him, aiming his .44 at the back of the doomed man's skull. When he pulled the trigger, Crocker crumpled and lay still. Burdette stood over the huge man's body for a few minutes to make sure he was dead. "I didn't want you to suffer with that stomach wound," he said in explanation for the shot to the head.

His evil mission completed, he relieved Big John of his weapons and returned to the campfire and his waiting lover. He found her in the midst of mixing up some bread to be baked in a pan. Astonished to find her so employed, he blurted, "I done it. I shot him."

"I heard the shots," she replied. "We're better off without him." He was still puzzled by her mundane reaction to his harsh solution to their problem. Without looking up at him, she busied herself at the fire. "I was still hungry after that bacon and I thought you might want something more, too."

"Well, yeah," he stumbled to reply. "I reckon I could

eat somethin' else." The cold-blooded murder of his friend and partner had not been enough to effectively cool his ardor. And the fact that she apparently did not share his need for fulfillment at the moment frustrated him totally.

Finally, she looked up at him and smiled. "We're going to have to get an early start in the morning and I don't want you to go to bed hungry. We need our rest." One look at the dismay in his expression told her that she was going to have to honor their unspoken contract. She would go through with it—let him have his romp, just to keep him in the harness until she was safely in Missoula. Then she would have no further use for him.

The trail was not hard to follow. It was the only fresh set of tracks leading out of the mouth of Blodgett Canyon. After parting with Cody and Jug, Cullen headed north at a lope, seeing no need to closely scout the tracks of the four horses. He had not gone far when he noticed a circle of buzzards in the distance. Wondering if the scavengers had any connection to the tracks he followed, and troubled that it might be the scene he hoped he wouldn't find, he slowed his horse to a walk while he looked for the tracks that would tell him he was still on the right trail. Still holding the bay to a walk, he continued through a patch of high grass close by the river, his mind creating the image of Roberta resisting an assault upon her body, and the possible result that might follow. It was not a pleasant picture, and feeling the urgency to find her, he pressed the bay again for more speed.

He could now see that the buzzards were circling closer to the river than it had first appeared from a half mile back, and the tracks he followed led along the west bank of the river before abruptly turning away from the water, toward a low ridge about forty yards from the edge of the pines. Giving his horse a gentle nudge with his heels, he started directly over the top of the ridge before coming to an abrupt halt at the top. Below him, at the foot of the ridge, lay the body of Big John Crocker.

Cullen instinctively looked all around him to make sure there was no one watching him before he proceeded to the foot of the ridge to dismount. The huge man looked even larger as a corpse, sprawled facedown in the sandy soil, now stained with a pattern of blood that spread underneath it. The hole in the back of Crocker's skull was no doubt the fatal shot, but upon turning the corpse over, Cullen could see that Crocker was also gut-shot. What did it mean? he wondered. Had the two outlaws fought over the woman and this one was the loser? Maybe the big man received the stomach wound in the gunfight at Gabe's camp and made it this far. But how could the shot to the back of his head be explained? A mercy killing? Perhaps, but not likely, he decided. It made more sense to him that the two had a falling-out for whatever reason. With the amount of gold dust involved, it was not hard to imagine. He glanced up at the buzzards overhead and thought, *Thank God it's this scum and not Roberta. Maybe there's still time*.

Leaving the grisly banquet awaiting the scavengers, he followed the tracks into the trees to the clearing where they had camped the night before. There was not much to see, the ashes of their fire, the grass still matted in spots where the bed was made, little else. He could not prevent a sharp pang of despair when he determined only one large imprint, indicating that Burdette had evidently kept Roberta close to him all night. It also told him that Crocker must have been killed the night before. With a new sense of urgency, he stepped back up in the saddle and started out after Burdette once more, trying desperately not to think of the terror Roberta had to be suffering.

As he continued on their trail, he rode on through the afternoon, never stopping until his horse needed rest. As the afternoon wore on, he began to give up hope that he would overtake them before dark. And unless Burdette changed directions, he would pass within a mile or two of Mule Sibley's place. At the rate he was traveling, it would be dark before he reached that point, and since he would be forced to stop for the night, he decided that he might as well ride on in to Sibley's and pick up some more cartridges for his rifle. His estimation proved to be accurate, for darkness began to settle in by the time he reached a trail that ran from the river to Sibley's store. It occurred to him then that Burdette might have stopped at the trading post for some reason, so he followed the trail in, although he could find no tracks to verify it.

"Well, hello there, Cullen," Mule Sibley sang out when Cullen walked in the door of his establishment. "I ain't seen you in a while. Your brothers was in here a few days ago." He paused, waiting for an indication that would tell him the point of Cullen's visit. Cullen pointed toward the general store end of the room. "What brings you out this way this time of night?" Sibley asked, and followed him to the counter.

"I thought I might pick up a box of .44 cartridges," Cullen said, "if my line of credit is still good."

"Why, sure—you know it's always good," Sibley replied.

"My brothers tell me you had three strangers come by a few days ago. You haven't seen one of 'em today, have you?"

The question sparked Sibley's interest right away. "Those three? No, I ain't seen none of 'em again, and I'm just as glad I ain't. Why? You lookin' for 'em?"

"I am," Cullen replied, then went on to explain why. Sibley listened with more than a little interest, still recalling the trouble that had barely been avoided when the three outlaws were in his saloon. "I knew they was up to no good," he remarked when Cullen told him of the attack at Gabe's camp in the mountains. "I ain't surprised. I'm right sorry to hear about Jug and Cody gettin' shot, though." He shook his head slowly to show his concern. Then he asked again about the woman, Roberta Morris. "Why did you say she was lookin' for ol' Gabe?" Cullen explained that Roberta was trying to reach Gabe to tell him of his wife's serious illness, and now Cullen's concern was to find her before further harm came to her, and the gold Gabe had labored for was lost to her aunt Edna. Sibley paused to let that sink in before commenting, "Gabe didn't have no wife."

This immediately claimed Cullen's attention. He wasn't sure he had heard Sibley correctly. "What did you say? How do you know?"

Sibley went on to explain. "Hell, Gabe ain't never been married. You know, he traded with me for supplies from time to time, and he used to joke about wantin' to find enough gold to buy him a nice woman to keep him warm in his old age." He chuckled then. "I always told him at his age he was better off without one."

"Hell, maybe you think you'd be better off without one," Rena interrupted, having strolled over to listen in on the conversation.

Sibley grinned. "Now, you know I couldn't do without you, Love. Hell, who'd tend bar for me?"

"Yeah, and who'd cook for you, and wash your clothes, and clean the house, and do everythin' else around here?" Rena demanded.

Oblivious to the minor bickering between husband and wife, Cullen felt his mind going into a tailspin of confusion. Surely there was some mistake, some misunderstanding, either on his or Sibley's part. For if what Sibley said was true, then there was no Aunt Edna for whom Roberta was concerned. After the initial shock caused by this unexpected turn of events had subsided enough to permit him to think calmly again, he admitted to himself how badly he had been duped. Feeling like a prime fool, he could not prevent the anger now rising in his veins. She had played them all—Cody, Jug, his father, even Smoke—but Cullen held himself the biggest fool of all, because he had been led to believe there was something more between the woman and himself.

The picture of Roberta as she was being led away, the last glimpse of her, returned to his mind and the helpless agony he had felt when he could not get to her. Looking now at the incident from this new, painful perspective, he remembered how somberly she had reacted to her abduction, quietly allowing herself to be taken. Other thoughts came flooding back—her frantic search for Gabe's hidden treasure, turning his tent upside down—and her quick recovery after learning of her supposed uncle's demise. *God,* he thought, *it's all so clear now.* Turning again to Sibley, he asked, "You sure about Gabe not havin' a wife?"

"Sure, I'm sure," Sibley responded. "As I recollect, the only family he had was a brother named Jonah, I think." He turned to his wife then. "You recollect, Rena? You was always listenin' when Gabe was in here."

"All he had was a brother," Rena responded. "Had a farm somewhere near Coulson, back on the Yellowstone. That's what he told us."

Still somewhat stunned, Cullen barely noticed Brenda when she came from the living quarters behind the store. "Howdy, Cullen," she said, looking past him to see if he was alone. Disappointed to discover that he was, she had started to go back behind the counter when her mother told her that Jug and Cody had been wounded in a gunfight. The news stopped her immediately. She spun around to face Cullen again, her concern written clearly in her face.

"He's not bad hurt," Cullen said, knowing which brother she was worried about. "Jug's shot pretty bad, but Cody's just got a shoulder wound. Your folks will tell you about it."

Her face registered immediate relief, her concern apparently no more than skin deep. "If I know him, he probably had his nose stuck into somethin' it shouldn'ta been," she commented. "He said he was goin' to bring us some elk meat. I reckon that'll be a while if he's hurt."

Cullen couldn't help shaking his head in response. "Your folks will tell you about it," he repeated. *And I'm sure Cody will be back soon to scratch your itch*, he thought. *If I was as wild and carefree as he is, I wouldn't have been such a damn fool about the first woman I thought was interested in me.* It was difficult not to be hard on himself, when he had to admit that he had fallen for the woman he thought Roberta was. "I'll be seein' you," he said to Mule and Rena as he picked up his box of cartridges and started for the door. There were a good many more things to think about, now that he was pretty sure that Roberta was no more than a common thief in league with Burdette, out to rob a poor hard-working old man. Maybe they weren't responsible for ol' Gabe's death—he had to give the Indians credit for that—but there was little doubt they would have finished him off once they found his gold. The cold-bloodedness of their intent was enough to cause a sick feeling inside when he remembered the gentle charm with which she had enchanted them, all the while planning for their deaths. *Damn, Cullen,* he silently scolded, *could you be a bigger fool?* One thing was certain at this point: The murdering pair had to be run to ground. He was not yet certain that they had not killed Jug. As for the gold, he figured it rightfully belonged to Gabe's brother, since there was no other family. One thing he knew for sure, it would be an outright sin to let those two get away with it.

The next morning he started out again on the trail

he had followed the day before, his mind still unsettled about what he should do. He was determined to see that justice was done, but he wasn't sure that he should look to the law to take over the responsibility to bring the outlaws down. George Tyler, the sheriff in Stevensville, might be a good man, but Cullen wasn't sure of George's mettle when it came to going after someone as dangerous as Frank Burdette appeared to be. In reality, there was little George was called upon to do in the peaceful community, and as far as Cullen knew, he had never been tested in a really critical situation. *We'll see where this trail leads,* he told himself. *If it passes through Stevensville or close by, I'll talk to the sheriff.*

Chapter 5

It was close to midday when Cullen came upon the pair's campsite of the night before, about a mile south of Stevensville near a trail that led from the river to the town. There was no real reason to do so, but he felt an urge to take a closer look at the place where Roberta and Burdette had spent the night. He paused momentarily by the ashes of a sizable campfire, kneeling down to feel the lifeless coals—hours old by his estimation. The thought came to mind that if Cody was with him, his brother could probably tell him what the two outlaws had eaten for supper.

He got to his feet again and looked around the grassy bank by the river's edge. It was obvious where the horses had been hobbled. It was also obvious by the faint imprint still visible in the soft grass where the pair he followed had slept. There was but one imprint again, obvious evidence that they had shared a common bed, and he could not help scowling as he thought of the implications that suggested.

After scouting around the perimeter of the camp, he stopped to examine a single set of tracks leading to the common trail to Stevensville. They looked fresh enough to have been left the night before. And even though they were not left by the horse with the twisted shoe, he could be reasonably sure it was one of the horses he was following, so one of the two had evidently ridden into town the night before. This seemed reason enough to involve the sheriff. He decided to take the time to ride in to Stevensville to see what he could find out, since it was no more than a mile, wondering all the while if it had been Roberta or Burdette who rode into town.

The settlement of Stevensville seemed peaceful enough when Cullen rode in at dusk, which would mislead a visitor to think that the town was unconcerned with the threat of Indian trouble. In fact, however, many of the residents of the area had neglected their fields, instead working all day in a hasty effort to upgrade the long-abandoned structure that was Fort Owen in readiness to defend themselves from the Nez Perce if necessary. Word of the battle with General Oliver O. Howard's troops against the Nez Perce on the Clearwater River, west of the Bitterroots, had reached the Montana citizens, bringing a new fear that the warriors of chiefs Joseph, Looking Glass, and White Bird might still be in a warlike mood. While General Howard's soldiers had succeeded in doing damage to the Indians, destroying their lodges and much of their supplies, they had failed to prevent them from continuing into Montana.

When half-breed scout Delaware Jim, who was mar-

ried to a Nez Perce woman, first brought word that the
Nez Perce chiefs were intent upon reaching the Lolo
Trail, General Howard's failure to immediately pursue
the warriors had resulted in giving the Indians a healthy
head start. The people of Stevensville were afraid of
the heretofore peaceful tribe's intentions upon reaching the Bitterroot Valley, but were unaware that the great
exodus of the Nez Perce people was already traveling
through the valley and no more than two days from
the town. Consequently, the town was quiet enough
when Cullen rode in.

GONE TO DINNER, the sign on the sheriff's office door
declared. Cullen found it fitting, since the sheriff had a
reputation for being handy with knife and fork. The
only place in town to eat that Cullen was aware of was
the saloon at the far end of the short street, so he turned
his horse in that direction. As proof of the town's rapid
growth, he came upon a large tent erected just several
feet short of the saloon that advertised HOME COOKING.
It had not been there the last time he had been in Stevensville. Cullen reined the bay to a halt and dismounted.

Stepping inside the tent, he discovered a long table
capable of seating about fifteen men, twenty if crowded
in together. On this day, there were no more than a
dozen sitting around the table, with Sheriff Tyler at
the end. The sheriff glanced up briefly and mumbled,
"McCloud," when Cullen walked in, then returned his
gaze to the mound of potatoes he was in the process of
reducing.

"Sheriff," Cullen returned, and pulled an empty chair
over beside him.

Seeing that Cullen had evidently come specifically

to find him, Tyler paused to remove a tough piece of thoroughly chewed steak from his mouth. "This steak's got more gristle than meat," he commented. "I believe Hattie's slippin' some mule in the fryin' pan." After holding the stringy morsel up to observe it, he placed it on the edge of his plate and wiped his fingers on his trouser leg. "What brings you to town? You worried about the Injuns?"

Unconcerned about trouble with the Nez Perce at this point, Cullen related the events of the past few days. Tyler seemed genuinely alarmed, even to the extent of pausing between bites when told of the gunfight that resulted in the death of one man and the wounding of Cullen's brothers, as well as the later death of John Crocker. "A man and a woman, you say," he remarked. "Do you think they're on their way here?"

"One of 'em mighta already been here last night," Cullen replied, "and that's what I wanted to ask you. Did you see any strangers in town last night?"

"I can't say that I did," Tyler answered. It was obvious that the possible involvement with the man Cullen described was upsetting his appetite and he placed his knife and fork down on the table.

"There was a feller in the saloon last night I ain't never seen before," one of the patrons who was seated to Tyler's left volunteered. "Kind of a tall feller, wearin' a rain slicker, long black hair, and a mustache," he went on. "That sound like the feller you're lookin' for?"

"Yes, it does," Cullen replied. He knew then that Burdette had made the trip to town, leaving Roberta in camp.

"Did you talk to him?" the sheriff asked.

"Nope, he didn't talk to nobody, just bought a bottle of whiskey from Tom and went on his way. Wasn't in the place more'n two minutes."

Tyler looked relieved and picked up his fork again. He shook his head as if seriously thinking. "Well, I reckon they've passed on by us," he said. Then pausing to direct a question at Cullen, he asked, "And you say there ain't nobody at their camp by the river?" When Cullen replied that this was true, Tyler frowned and said, "Well, that's that, I reckon. No harm's come to Stevensville." He attacked the potatoes on his plate again.

"What are you gonna do about it, Sheriff?" Cullen wanted to know. "I've been followin' the two of them, but I expect the law oughta be doin' the job—maybe a posse or somethin'."

"I don't reckon I'm gonna do nothin' about it," Tyler said. "As long as they keep on goin', they ain't no problem for me or Stevensville. I ain't got no jurisdiction outside of town, anyway. Hell, I got bigger things to worry about right now. There's about a thousand Injuns that might come chargin' through town in a few days. My advice to you is to forget that pair you're chasin' and go on back home, 'cause like as not, those Injuns will run through your pa's ranch. Whatever them other two done, they're gone now. Just be glad you didn't get shot."

"You mean to tell me you're not willin' to go after murderers and thieves when they were camped right on your doorstep?" Cullen demanded.

"Like I said, I was hired to protect the town. If you want the law to help you hunt all over the territory, you can try the deputy marshal over in Butte."

Cullen was rendered speechless by the sheriff's attitude.

"You gonna eat?" came a voice behind him.

He turned to discover a short, stout woman cradling a large mixing bowl in the crook of her arm—Hattie, he presumed. "No," he answered, still astonished by the total disinterest exhibited by the sheriff and everyone else in the tent. "I lost my appetite when I came in here."

"Suit yourself," Hattie responded, her voice as apathetic as the sheriff's.

"Say hello to your daddy for me," Tyler called after Cullen when he turned and made for the door. "I always had a lot of respect for Donovan McCloud."

"Yeah, I'll do that," Cullen replied. "I'm sure he feels the same about you."

Seeing Cullen's obvious irritation, Tyler said, "Don't you go gettin' yourself shot, boy. You'd best just let it be. Sometimes that's all you can do."

"I suppose," Cullen called back, "but it ain't outside my jurisdiction." *I don't know why I expected anything different,* he thought as he climbed on his horse and wheeled the bay back toward the river. Mad as hell, he was determined more than ever to find the treacherous pair and deliver the justice they so sorely deserved. He picked up the trail again at the riverbank and followed it north. It appeared now that Burdette and Roberta intended to continue up the valley to Fort Missoula, probably planning to have Gabe's gold dust assayed.

Thoughts of concern weighed on his mind for Jug. His brother's wound had seemed to be serious, and even as strong as he was, the damage might have been too much for even a bull like Jug to recover. He had to make a choice, and the image of Jug lying helpless on the travois while one of the three murderers still rode free was the deciding factor that spurred him on to seek the vengeance he felt was demanded.

The object of Cullen's concern was not recovering as they had all hoped. Smoke did all he could for Jug, but the bullet had done more damage than he could repair and he hesitated to dig deeper for it. With Jug's decline during the next two days, Donovan McCloud decided his son had to see a doctor, and that meant a trip into Stevensville to see Dr. Brandon Elrod. So they loaded Jug up in a wagon and Donovan and Cody started out for town, leaving Smoke in charge with instructions to call on the Bailey boys for help if the trip took longer than planned.

They arrived at Dr. Elrod's office at a little before noon. The office consisted of two rooms in the front of his house—one his examining room, the other a make-shift surgery. Mrs. Elrod was just about to call her husband to the noon meal when the solemn McCloud men rolled up in the yard. She glanced out the window at the threesome and shook her head sympathetically upon seeing Jug lying in the wagon bed. It seemed that the seriously ill or injured always managed to arrive at meal-time, so she put her husband's dinner in the oven to keep warm. She could hear him talking as he stepped out on the porch to meet them.

"Donovan, Cody," Dr. Elrod said in greeting. "What have we got here?"

"It's Jug, Dr. Elrod," Cody blurted before his father could answer. "He's shot bad, and he looks like he's gettin' worse. He don't do nothin' but lie there with his eyes half closed—won't eat nothin', don't want nothin' to drink."

"Well, let's get him inside so I can take a look at him," Elrod said.

They carried him inside and put him on the bed in Dr. Elrod's surgery room. Jug seemed to be out of his head the whole time, mumbling something none of them could understand, waving his arm in the air from time to time as if signaling to someone. Once he was settled on the bed, he seemed to calm down a bit. "He's burning up with fever," Elrod said, and called for his wife to bring him a bucket of cool water and a cloth. After a cursory examination, he said, "I'm afraid you've come all this way hauling a dead man."

"Whaddaya mean?" Donovan demanded. "He ain't dead!"

"He's on his way," Elrod replied, then knowing he was being a little too frank in his preliminary diagnosis, he softened his tone. "I'm sorry, Donovan. I'm just trying not to sugarcoat it for you. I'll look into that wound more thoroughly, but I don't want you to get your hopes up. We'll see what happens after I get the bullet outta there—see how much damage has been done—then we'll see." Even before probing for the bullet, he knew there had to be extensive damage. It surprised him to know that Jug had held on for two days in his present state. "He must have the constitution of a buffalo," he remarked. "It'll take a little while, so why don't you boys go on into town, get you some dinner or something, and come back in a couple of hours?" When Donovan appeared to be undecided, Elrod added, "You'll just be in my way here."

"Maybe I oughta go find the sheriff," Cody suggested. "Cullen mighta come through here after that pair."

"Well, this time of day you'll likely find him at Hattie Moore's place eating dinner," Dr. Elrod said as he walked them to the door. When there was a question in both faces, he said, "It's a tent next to the saloon. A woman set it up a little while back."

"I'll go with you," Donovan told his son. "Might as well eat while we're at it."

Louise Elrod walked up to stand beside her husband as he stood in the doorway watching the wagon pull out of the yard. "I put your dinner in the oven to keep warm," she said. "Are you gonna be a long time?"

He shook his head, then turned to face her, closing the door as he did. "No. I might as well go ahead and eat. That man in there is already halfway dead. I don't expect there's anything I can do for him now. Maybe if I had seen him right after he got shot, I mighta saved him. I'll try to see how much damage has been done, but I expect the only thing I could accomplish right now is letting my dinner dry out in the oven. Let's go eat."

Sheriff George Tyler glanced up when Donovan and his son walked in the tent, and continued to stare at them until they in turn spotted him at his usual place at the end of the table. *Damn it,* he thought, *is my dinner gonna be interrupted every blasted day by some member of the McCloud family?* He voiced no greeting, however, and waited for them to state their business.

Both father and son took a moment to look over the food heaped upon the plates of the half dozen customers before deciding to grab an empty chair. "Howdy, Sheriff," Donovan offered as he sat down and pulled his chair back up to the table.

Tyler was pretty sure about the reason for their visit, but he asked anyway. "Mr. McCloud, Cody," he said, nodding to each one in turn. "What brings you to town?" He assumed they had come for the same reason Cullen had.

"We brought my middle boy in to Dr. Elrod's," Donovan replied. "He's been shot and Doc thinks it's pretty bad. I'm wonderin' if you've seen my son Cullen in the last day or so. If you have, you know what brings us to town."

"You gonna eat?" Hattie Moore interrupted, and Donovan nodded.

"I heard that Jug got shot." Tyler acknowledged that he had seen Cullen, and told Donovan what had been the result of Cullen's quest for help from the law. "I'll tell you the same thing I told Cullen," he said as he hacked off another generous bite of the tough steak on his plate. The beef, seemingly reluctant to be sacrificed willingly, sought to deny the sheriff's knife, causing Tyler to pause in midsentence while he applied additional elbow grease before declaring victory and shoving the hunk of meat into his mouth. "I'm sorry about your sons gettin' shot, but there ain't nothin' I can do about it. I'm too busy with other things right now to stop and worry about a couple of outlaws. Them folks never showed up here in Stevensville, so it's out of my jurisdiction." He decided it was of no value to admit that one of them had, in fact, shown up in town since Burdette left right away with his bottle of whiskey. "Accordin' to Cullen, them two he was trailin' camped overnight down by the river, maybe a mile or so below town. Then they musta kept on goin' the next mornin', and I reckon Cullen went after 'em, or turned tail and headed for home. I don't know which. It ain't in my jurisdiction."

The sheriff's comments caused a moment of concern in Cody's mind. "You said 'them two' he was trailin'. Didn't he say there was also a woman with 'em?"

"Nah. I don't know nothin' about a woman," he lied. "They didn't come in my town, so it ain't my worry."

Cody and his father reacted much the same as Cullen had to the sheriff's attitude about the fugitives. "Well, we didn't find out a helluva lot here," Donovan responded, "but at least we can get somethin' to eat. I hope we ain't put you out too much," he added sarcastically. Tyler just shrugged his shoulders in response and continued the attack on his dinner again.

"Did Cullen say where the camp was?" Cody asked, still concerned by the lack of any word about Roberta.

"I told you. 'Bout a mile below the river road."

"Which side of the river?" Cody asked.

"Hell, I don't know," Tyler replied, plainly irritated. "West, I think. It ain't my jurisdiction."

"Thank you very much, Sheriff," Cody said with more than a hint of the sarcasm his father had just expressed. "We won't bother you no more. You just go on back to fillin' that big belly of yours."

Donovan quickly shot a warning glance in his son's direction. Of the three, his youngest was the one who possessed a hair-trigger temper. Cody smiled and shrugged. The sheriff's brow knitted into an angry frown and he pointed his fork directly at Cody as he issued a warning. "Now, I'm gonna go easy on you since you've had a streak of bad luck with your brother and all, but you'd better watch your mouth or you're gonna wind up settin' in one of my jail cells for the night."

"He don't mean nothin', Sheriff," Donovan was quick to offer. "He's just concerned about his brother."

"I suppose so," Tyler reluctantly conceded. "I won't hold it against him."

The moment was defused when Hattie set two plates of food down before them. There was nothing more they could hope to gain from the indifferent sheriff, so they ate the food and returned to see how Jug was doing. The news was not good. Dr. Elrod told them he had probed around in Jug's side, but the damage was too extensive for him to do much good. It was too dangerous, he said, to try to take the bullet out. He had no choice but to sew up the incision he had made in an effort to dig the bullet out. "You'd best change that bandage in the morning and try to keep it clean. I'd guess he's got maybe a week or so before he dies. It's hard to say. He might die on the way home in that wagon. I'm right sorry, but that's all I could do for him."

This was sorrowful news to his father and brother,

almost unbelievable in fact. It was hard to think of the gentle giant of a man finished by a single bullet. Cheerful to a fault, eternally hungry, he would leave too large a void in the McCloud family. "Let's get him in the wagon," Donovan said. Cody nodded sadly and the two of them carried Jug out and laid him in the wagon bed again. When they had made him as comfortable as possible, Donovan placed his hand on his youngest son's shoulder, his sorrowful eyes slightly moist. "We'll take Jug home," he said. "Maybe Smoke can try again to get that bullet outta there."

Jug didn't seem to know where he was, or who was with him, as he lay in the bed of the wagon, softly muttering to himself, words that neither Cody nor his father could understand. Donovan had his eldest son to worry about as well. If Jug had not been so close to death, his father would have sent Cody to trail Cullen, but he knew it was important for Cody to be at his brother's side during his final moments. So they took the amiable giant home to the M Bar C to die.

Chapter 6

The trail Cullen followed north along the river was no doubt leading to Fort Missoula. He urged the bay along at a fast walk, knowing there was little chance of overtaking Burdette and Roberta before they reached that settlement. His only hope was that they would remain there for a day or two, or if they were already gone, someone could tell him where they had headed. He felt sure that their next destination would most likely be Butte. That would be the only reasonable route to take out of Missoula, but he couldn't depend on Roberta to think like a typical woman. He had already paid dearly to learn that lesson. Anxious to overtake them, he pressed his horse to pick up the pace and held him to it until the bay began to show signs of fatigue. It was while he was resting his horse that he saw the forward scouts of the Nez Perce village. Shortly after, the long column of men, women, and children came into view. Driving a large horse herd, the Indians seemed to pass by his temporary camp on the opposite side of the river for over an hour. Some walking, some riding, they paid little attention to the lone white man watching from across the river. Warriors riding as scouts on the flanks of the column came close to the river's edge, but seemed to have no interest in him. All seemed peaceful as Looking Glass had promised. In fact, there were wagons from the white farms in the valley loaded with produce, following the column and trading with the Indians as they moved through. Nothing could be more peaceful. Cullen shook his head sadly, for he was certain they felt the danger was over. They could not understand the army's obsession with stopping them. He remained by the riverbank until the last of the stragglers passed to the south. His horse rested now, he climbed back in the saddle and continued on. He arrived in Missoula at sundown.

For lack of a better idea, he decided to visit the saloons in case someone might have seen a stranger matching Burdette's description. There was no hotel, so he imagined the two he followed would make camp somewhere close to the river, just as he intended to do. Pulling his horse to a stop before the first saloon he came to, he looped the reins over the hitching post and stepped up on the board walkway. Pausing in the doorway, he scanned the room, looking for Burdette. There were several soldiers near the back of the barroom, sitting with two civilians at a table. Cullen recognized one of the civilians. Barney Quinn had served in a company of volunteers with Cullen when a hostile band of Bannocks had raided in the valley the year before. After another look around to make sure he had not missed Burdette, Cullen walked in and approached the table in the back.

Quinn glanced up from his glass of beer and did a double take when he recognized Cullen. "Well, I'll be damned," he announced. "Here comes the man we need right here." He got up to greet Cullen. Grinning broadly, he thrust out his hand. "Fellers, this here is Cullen McCloud. Ain't nobody knows them mountains better'n him."

"Hello, Barney," Cullen said. "What are you doin' back here? I thought you were goin' to work for that rancher up in Deer Lodge."

Quinn chuckled. "I was, but I never got there. I got drunk in Butte and lost all my money—ended up helpin' a feller owns a farm north of there till I heard they was lookin' for volunteers to ride with the army to make sure them Nez Perce don't start no trouble."

"Everybody up and down the whole valley is lookin' for Indians," Cullen responded. "I just came from Stevensville, and I passed Chief Joseph's people just short of there. Folks in that town are nervous as hell. They're tryin' to build old Fort Owen up to defend the town, and the Nez Perce will already be past 'em in a day or two."

"Hell yeah," Quinn replied. "There's a bunch more soldiers that got here a few days ago. The folks around here was already worried since the Flatheads have been doin' some raidin'." He shook his head and chuckled as if he was about to tell a joke. "Funny thing is, it's the Nez Perce that's got everybody shittin' their underwear now." He nodded toward the soldiers sitting at his table. "Me and some of the boys are fixin' to ride with these fellers. Captain Rawn is their commanding officer. He's the officer they sent over here to establish Fort Missoula. You oughta join up with us."

Cullen shook his head. "The Nez Perce aren't goin' to go on the warpath against the white folks in this valley. Hell, Barney, I've bought more'n a few horses from some of White Bird's people, and they've passed through this valley on their way to hunt buffalo for as long as I've lived here. Never been anything but friendly."

"It might be a different story now," Barney said, "since they've already been fightin' the soldiers over in Idaho Territory. Ol' Joseph says he ain't goin' to the reservation—soldiers say he is. He might forget he used to be friends with you and your family." When Cullen still appeared to be doubtful, Quinn changed the subject. "Well, what are you doin' here, if you didn't come to fight the Nez Perce?"

Cullen told him about the appearance of Roberta Morris at his father's ranch and the tragedy that followed, ending with his two brothers being wounded. "I followed them this far," he said. "And I'm hopin' this is where I'll find them."

"Damn, Cullen, I'm sorry to hear about your brothers. Maybe I can help you look for this feller and the woman. I can't say I've seen 'em since I've been here. Everybody here is a stranger to me."

"'Preciate the offer, but I reckon I'll just have to do the lookin' myself, since you don't know what they look like. I'll walk through town just on the chance I'll spot 'em. If I don't, I expect I'll just head on to Butte tomorrow to see if they showed up there—after I scout up and down the river a ways to see if I can find their camp." He fully realized that his was a hopeless endeavor at this point unless he was struck with blind luck. Even though he was following a horse with a twisted shoe, it was impossible to find the trail among all the many tracks in the settlement—most of them fresh—but he didn't know what else to do.

"Well, you might as well camp with us for the night," Quinn said. "We're camped close to town right in the fork of the river. You mighta passed it on your way into town."

"Yeah, I saw the camp," Cullen said. "I'm gonna take a turn around town; then maybe I'll be back later."

Roberta was a woman driven by her selfish ambitions, a woman who would not let anything stand in the way of her goals, but she was also capable of compassion in the right circumstances. Sitting by the campfire next to the riverbank, she cast an observant eye upon her traveling companion and partner in crime as he poured a cup of coffee and settled himself next to her on the blanket she had spread for the purpose. Roberta studied him as if seeing him for the first time. One could not say that Frank Burdette was not an interesting man, she decided. He might look more distinguished if his beard was trimmed properly and he was dressed in a proper suit—two things he said he planned to do when they reached Butte. He said he wanted to look like a worthy escort for her. A slight smile traced her lips at the thought. It was flattering to think she controlled the man so completely. As she continued to study him, she decided that he had served her well in her quest to become wealthy. And all he wanted was to remain with her, to protect her, to do her bidding. She decided that she owed him the one thing he longed for.

She had not resisted his animal-like attempts at making love, even though she did not participate in earnest. Perhaps, she decided, she should show her appreciation for his faithful service to her and give him the kind of response he longed for. She placed her coffee cup carefully down and lay back on the blanket. Curious, he paused to watch her as she arranged herself comfortably on her side. She smiled at him then and beckoned him to come closer. Confused and unsure at first, he hesitated, thinking he must have misunderstood—she had never been aggressive in that regard before—and for the last couple of days she had seemed especially distant. She parted her lips slightly and gazing at him longingly, bade him to come to her.

Still not sure he had not misinterpreted her gesture, he moved over closer to her—cautiously at first—until she smiled and motioned for him to lie next to her. Then resembling a trembling puppy more than the rough outlaw he was, he scrambled to her, his excited heart pounding in his chest. He at once began his usual pawing and groping, but she stopped him and whispered, "Lie back. Let me do it." She made love to him then in a fashion not known to him before, accustomed as he was to the rough-and-tumble style of prostitutes and rapists in his lawless life. For the first time in his thirty-four years he was permitted entry into a tender, loving paradise that he never knew existed. When it was finished, he lay contented and helpless in her arms, a defenseless and grateful puppy. He paid no attention to her movements as she casually reached behind her for the long stiletto she always kept under the edge of her blanket. With her other hand, she grasped a handful of his long dingy hair and gently pulled his head back. Still in a blissful stupor, he smiled at her, only to recoil in shock as the long blade was suddenly and forcefully thrust up under his chin, buried to the handle.

Like a chicken whose head had just been chopped off, he convulsed violently, clawing at the knife desperately. Choking with blood, he was unable to scream as he writhed in excruciating pain, his eyes bulging as if about to explode from their sockets. She moved away a few feet to stand and watch him die. It did not happen as quickly as she had imagined, so she casually went to her saddlebag and withdrew her Colt .44. Returning to stand over him again, she patiently waited for him to remain still long enough to make sure her aim was accurate. The fatal shot was no doubt as welcome to the suffering victim as it was to his callous executioner.

Silently complimenting herself for her sacrifice in giving her body to the trusting outlaw as a reward before his termination, she rolled his body off the edge of the blanket. He had already managed to soak a corner of it with blood, a fact that irritated her somewhat, and she frowned to think it would be ruined. *I'll try to soak it in the river to see if the cold water will remove the stain,* she thought, but she didn't hold out much hope for salvaging it. Then she smiled when she reminded herself that she was a very wealthy woman. She could simply discard the blanket just as she had the man. Frank Burdette had outlived his usefulness as soon as

Roberta had realized she was reasonably safe upon reaching the town. And with all the soldiers now posted at Fort Missoula, she no longer feared for her safety. Still, she admitted, Frank Burdette and his partners had proved to be useful. All things considered, it had turned out well, the only downside being the necessity to sacrifice her body to the vile and disgusting outlaw. *It would have been nicer,* she thought with a mischievous smile, *and a lot more interesting had it been Cullen McCloud instead of Burdette. I might have even enjoyed it.* With that thought in mind, she went to the water's edge to thoroughly clean herself, with the intent to wash away all traces of Frank Burdette.

Now that she was free of the last of her temporary partners in her venture, she prepared to move into town. There was no hotel, but she did remember seeing a rooming house at the end of the street. The thought of sleeping on clean sheets in a real bed was enough to cause her to make up her mind, but first, there was a great deal of preparation before she could risk a trip into town. There was the question of four heavy sacks of gold dust to be dealt with. She would have preferred to convert the dust to cash, but there was no assay office in Missoula. It would have to be converted in Helena. Thinking to sell the horses in Missoula, she decided to keep one to carry her fortune, so she spent most of the next morning packing the gold in four different saddle packs to be carried on only one of the horses. Once the gold dust was situated evenly, she disguised the packs as best she could with pots and pans, blankets and clothing until she was satisfied that the horse appeared to be loaded with household posses-

sions. Everything else of trade value, like her late partners' weapons, she loaded on the other horses, and
leading the extra horses, she rode into Fort Missoula.

"Why, you poor dear," Martha Gooding uttered upon
hearing Roberta's accounting of the tragedy that brought
the slender young woman with the long dark hair to
her doorstep. "Of course we can rent you a room for
the night. Come inside out of the chilly wind." She
looked, somewhat curiously, beyond her visitor at the
horses tied at the corner of the porch.

Quick to satisfy Martha's curiosity, Roberta explained, "That's all that I have left of my family," she
said sadly. "When the Indians attacked our camp in
the mountains, my dear husband fought them bravely,
but after he was killed, I managed to escape with the
horses and the few things I could quickly save. It's not
much to show for five years of marriage."

"Bless your heart," Martha responded. "You have suffered enough, but we're glad to make you comfortable if
we can. How long do you intend to stay with us?"

"Not long. I'm going back to my family home in
Butte on the first stage that goes that way. That is, if I
can find someplace to sell my horses and some firearms that Frank had accumulated."

Just then, entering the living room and overhearing
the conversation, John Gooding remarked, "Bob Strother down at the livery stable will most likely take 'em
off your hands, and there's a stagecoach leaving out in
the mornin' for Butte."

"This is my husband, John," Martha interjected. "John,
this is Mrs. Lawrence. She has just lost her husband."

John nodded politely. "I'm pleased to meet you, ma'am, and I'm sorry 'bout your husband." She extended her hand and he shook it. "Like I said, Bob Strother oughta be willin' to take them horses off your hands. If you want, I'll go with you to see that he gives you a fair price."

Roberta fashioned a timid smile for his benefit and replied, "You are too kind. I do appreciate it very much. I know my late husband would appreciate it as well. He always tried to take care of me as best he could."

"Well, let's get your things inside and make you comfortable," Martha said. "I'm gonna put you in the front room. You'll be our first customer. John's still finishing the rooms on the back of the house. Our sign hasn't been up but a month."

"Will my things be safe in your barn?" Roberta asked demurely. "They're everything I own to start a new life."

"Oh yes, ma'am, your things are safe here," John assured her. "If it'll make you feel any better, I've got a big padlock I can put on that barn door tonight."

"That would be so thoughtful of you," she cooed. When he started to lead the horses away, she insisted that she should help him. "Some of those packs are very heavy, with big pots, my skillets, my irons, and so forth. I couldn't bear to leave anything behind."

"I understand," he said, even though he was still amazed at the weight of the packs on one of the horses.

Early the next morning Cullen crossed over the river after finding no evidence of a camp on the east side. He had ridden no more than a few hundred yards when he came upon the body. Backing his horse a few feet from the edge of the riverbank, he looked around him cautiously, taking in the thick stands of evergreen trees that almost reached the water's edge. Though right on the bank, the camp was well concealed. It was no wonder that he had almost ridden over the body before seeing it.

After satisfying himself that there was no one waiting in ambush, he dismounted. With the toe of his boot, he rolled the corpse over to reveal the horrified look of fear frozen on Frank Burdette's face. In addition to the bullet wound, there appeared to be a deep knife wound up under his chin. *She made damn sure he was good and dead,* he thought. *Looks like the lady is on her own again.* He paused to consider the fact that Burdette was wearing no britches, a rather undignified way to enter the great beyond, and cause for speculation on Cullen's part. He chose not to dwell on it for long, still uncomfortable with thoughts it created of a conscienceless black widow. Looking into the face of the corpse, he could almost hear the agonizing cries of the deceased as he realized his fate. Bringing his mind back to the reality of the matter, he tried to estimate how long Burdette had been dead. As stiff as the corpse was, he guessed it had to have happened sometime the night before. The question now was where did Roberta escape to? Surely she must have gone on into Fort Missoula. Without further speculation, he climbed back into the saddle and turned the bay toward town, with no thoughts toward burying the outlaw's body. *I hope to hell the buzzards don't get the bellyache from that sorry meal,* he thought.

"Where would she go?" Cullen asked himself as he

returned to the settlement at a lope. He decided that wherever she lit, she would most likely have put her horses in the stable, so that was his first stop.

"Yes, sir," Bob Strother replied. "I just bought them horses you're lookin' at there, yesterday evenin'."

"You bought 'em?" Cullen replied. "All of 'em?"

"Them three," Strother answered. "The lady that sold 'em to me said she didn't need to keep but one to tote all her household possessions."

"When did you buy them?" Cullen asked. When Strother repeated that it had been the night before, Cullen realized that he had managed to catch up with her. "You remember her name?"

"Mrs. Lawrence is what she told me," Strother replied. "Now, listen, if there's somethin' wrong here, if these horses is stolen, it ain't none of my worry. I paid good money for 'em, so ain't nobody got any claim on 'em but me."

Lawrence, Cullen thought, *so that's what she's calling herself now.* Looking back to an increasingly agitated stable owner, he quickly shook his head. "Nope, they're not stolen—'preciate the information." He turned to leave, but turned back after a few steps to say, "One of 'em's got a twisted shoe. You might wanna take a look at that before it works loose."

It didn't take long to determine that Roberta was no longer in Missoula. There was no hotel in the town, although one was in the early stages of construction. When asking about possible places where a woman alone might find lodging, he was directed to the Goodings' home.

He was met at the front door by Martha Gooding.

"Mrs. Lawrence?" Martha responded. "Why, yes, she stayed with us last night. Are you a relative of hers?"

"Ah, no, ma'am," Cullen replied. "It's just important that I catch up with her." He hesitated, then added, "Important news about her family."

"Oh, I hope it's not bad news," Martha said. "She was such a sweet girl."

"Yes, ma'am, she sure is. Will she be back here tonight?"

Martha looked dismayed. "Oh no, young man. I'm afraid you've just missed her. She took the stage to Butte this morning."

"The stage? I didn't know there was a stage runnin' between here and Butte," Cullen replied. "How long has that been goin' on?"

"Only about a month," John Gooding answered for his wife as he came out on the porch to join them. "Fellow name of Ruthers got a contract to deliver the mail between here and Butte. I think he's just runnin' it for somebody else that's got a bigger line east of here." When the young stranger seemed slightly perplexed, John went on. "I figure it's a hundred and twenty or thirty miles to Butte. They claim they can make the run in thirteen or fourteen hours with swing stations every fifteen or twenty miles to change the horses. 'Course I don't know how much that'll change when winter sets in."

Cullen took a moment to consider what he had just been told before speculating, "Pretty much follow the Clark Fork, I reckon."

"Yep," Gooding replied, "right up the river."

"Where's the stage office?"

"A little board shack next to the stable," Gooding answered.

"Thanks," Cullen said, and turned to leave, thinking that Bob Strother might have saved him considerable time had he mentioned that the stage office was right next door to his stable.

He was already tracing the trail along the Clark Fork River in his mind while he walked his horse to the stage office. It had been some time since he had last ridden that valley, but he remembered the terrain quite well. Finding the stage office door unlocked, he opened it and walked in to find a bald man eating his supper. Pulled up to a squat table, using a nail keg with a short piece of board across the top for a seat, the man looked up without pausing in his consumption of a plate of beans. "Help ya?" he asked without enthusiasm.

"That stage that left here this mornin'," Cullen asked, "what time you figure it'll get to Butte?"

The station attendant paused to wipe his mouth with the back of his cuff while he thought. "Well, they pulled outta here right at seven this mornin', so if they don't run into no bad luck, they oughta be in Butte before ten o'clock tonight."

"That quick, huh?" Cullen replied, thinking how long it would take him to ride that far on the bay.

"Yessir," the man replied. "We ain't got no Concord coaches on this line. We're using the Celerity coach— mud wagons, as we call 'em. They ain't as fancy and comfortable as a Concord, but they're lighter and faster. They'll getcha there quicker, especially with a six-horse team and six swing stations between here and Butte.

Yessir, they'll make Butte, maybe by nine o'clock, and that's with a one-hour stop to eat."

"Where's that?" Cullen asked.

"Little ranch settlement called Garrison," the attendant answered, " 'bout ten miles short of Deer Lodge."

The prospects for catching up with Roberta were getting smaller and smaller in Cullen's mind. It would take him maybe two days of hard riding to get to Butte, maybe a little more than that—with the risk of killing his horse in the process. There was nothing to do, however, but to start out. "Much obliged," he said as he turned to leave. Then he paused and asked, "Was there a young woman on the stage—traveling alone?"

"Yes, there sure was." He reached behind him and took a pad from the shelf. "A Miss Lawrence. She took the stage and wanted to tie a packhorse on the back. I told her the stage would run that packhorse to death, so she packed her stuff on the stage and sold me the horse for ten dollars. I couldn't pass that up."

"Much obliged," Cullen said.

Outside the stage office, he saw the familiar figure of Barney Quinn ambling his way, leading his horse. Beside him, Captain Charles C. Rawn was in pace with him. Barney threw up his hand when he spotted Cullen. "Hey, Cullen," he hailed, "I been lookin' for you." Cullen stopped and waited for them. "I been tellin' Captain Rawn here that you was in town, and ain't nobody knows the mountains better'n you."

"I don't know about that," Cullen said as he nodded to the captain. "I expect there's a lot of men that know those mountains better'n me."

"I'll get right to the point, McCloud," Rawn said.

"I'm leading a detachment of cavalry and some civilian volunteers to keep an eye on those Nez Perce passing through the valley. I'd like to have you ride along with us."

"Why?" Cullen asked.

Surprised that he would ask the question, Rawn replied, "Because Quinn here says you live in the valley and know every foot of it."

"Captain," Cullen said, "Nez Perce, Flatheads, and Gros Ventres have been ridin' back and forth across the Bitterroot Valley for longer than I've been born. I appreciate Barney's recommendation, but anybody can follow their trail. Hell, there're about eight hundred of 'em and God knows how many horses. You can't miss 'em, and I've got other business I need to attend to right now."

Captain Rawn was obviously disappointed with Cullen's response. "I'd like you to consider the needs of your fellow citizens here in the valley," he said. "I'm asking you to consider how important this business of yours is in comparison to the safety of hundreds of people that are your friends and neighbors."

There was no hesitation in Cullen's response. He was quite frankly weary of talk about the dangerous threat descending upon the people of the Bitterroot Valley. "Captain, I know these people. If you just leave them alone, they'll pass through the valley peacefully. There wouldn't have been any fightin' in Idaho if the government had just left the Nez Perce the hell alone, or at least let Joseph and the others go peacefully with their families and horses."

Rawn was clearly perturbed. He glanced at Barney

and then back at Cullen. "So you're telling me you refuse to go?"

"Like I said, you don't need me to follow them."

"Quinn didn't tell me you were an Injun lover," Rawn said. "I'm sorry I've wasted your time, as well as my own." He turned abruptly and walked away, leaving a bewildered Barney Quinn to stand alone with Cullen.

After watching silently for a few moments as the captain stalked away, Barney shrugged. "I'm sorry, Cullen. I thought you mighta changed your mind about goin' with us."

"Any other time, Barney," he replied, "but I've got family business to take care of now." Barney nodded without commenting further. Cullen went on. "And if you leave White Bird and Looking Glass alone, they'll leave you alone. You oughta see if you can get that into that captain's head."

"I hope to hell you're right," Barney said. "Hope you get your business took care of." He turned to stare at the officer's back. "Now I've got to go catch that captain you pissed off."

He figured the afternoon was already wasting away, but he needed new supplies before setting out in pursuit once more. Looking up into a cloudless sky, he turned to the west. Before long the sun would be settling down behind the Bitterroots, but there would be a three-quarter moon that night, a good night to travel. He paused to stroke the bay's neck. "You've been workin' pretty hard, boy, but we've got a lot of ground to cover." Untying the reins, he led the horse back to the stable to buy a sack of oats, figuring the bay was going to need some extra nourishment.

Chapter 7

Jack Sykes sat in a side chair in his sister's hotel room in Helena, his feet propped on the corner of the bed. He took a deep drag on his cigar. Smiling in response to Roberta's frown when he flicked ashes on the carpet, he was feeling very satisfied with himself. It had gone pretty close to plan, just as Roberta had predicted. And Burdette and his two stooges had all been eliminated, also as his sister had promised. *God, she's a cold-blooded snake*, he thought, smiling to himself. *I'm glad we're on the same side*. If he had the capacity to be honest with himself, he would have admitted that he practically worshipped his sister. He had spent time in the territorial prison in Deer Lodge, but his was not the devious, conniving mind of his sister's.

There were some details of the past days that were not entirely clear to him, things that didn't matter nearly as much since he and his sister were in possession of his uncle's gold. He might have wondered what became of the horses that had belonged to Burdette and his partners, as well as some weapons that could have been acquired. Roberta had told him when he met her at the stage station in Garrison that the horses had all been lost except the one she sold. She had three pouches of gold dust to split between them. Jack couldn't help chuckling when he thought of the gold and the irony he enjoyed now that he and Roberta had gotten their hands on it. If his uncle Gabriel had lived to have his way, it would have all gone to his brother Jonah's family, and none to the Sykes side of the family. *Well, me and Roberta were always the black sheep of the family, but I guess they can all go to hell now.*

"There's still some business that has to be taken care of," Roberta said as she tidied up her hair in front of the mirror on the dresser. "McClouds." She turned to face her brother then. "I didn't figure them to be as big a problem as they may turn out to be—Cullen, especially. He was eating out of my hand by the time we got to that camp." She paused when Jack laughed and made a comment regarding her ability to charm a fence post if there was something it could do for her. "I'm sure he thinks I was sweet on him, and I know he'll try to come rescue me. If he finds out the truth, he'll probably come even harder. And he wasn't wounded. I'm pretty sure of that. I think Cody got shot, but I don't know how bad."

"Hell," her brother said, "them folks back there has got plenty to worry about with all them Nez Perce comin' outta the hills. They ain't got time to be chasin' you. We couldn't have timed it better."

She pointed her finger at Jack as if to threaten. "They'll come after me. I know they'll try to find me.

Cullen especially. He's one of those 'do the right thing' kind of men. I guess I only have myself to blame. I should have stopped short of causing him to fall in love with me."

Jack chuckled. "You sure are somethin'," he crowed. "Them McCloud boys ain't no problem, though. I can have that taken care of for a couple hundred dollars— same way I got Burdette and the other two. I ran into Bob Yeager the other night in the Red Dog Saloon. He was at Deer Lodge the same time I was—just got out about a month ago—and he's bound to be lookin' for some fast money. So first, we've gotta go to the bank and change the rest of that dust into cash. After we divide it up, we'll split the cost of taking care of the McCloud boys, right? Equal shares."

"Equal shares," she repeated, "just like everything else." As she said the words, she couldn't help wishing she had told him there had been only two pouches of dust, instead of three. It had been hard enough, however, to hide the fourth pouch in her saddlebag from him. It was a good thing he didn't have a courteous bone in his body. Otherwise, he might have offered to carry the saddlebag for her. If he had, he might have wondered why it was so heavy. *Like most men*, she thought, *dumb as a stump*. "Jack," she emphasized, "it's got to be taken care of right away. How do we know this Yeager can handle it?"

"Oh, there ain't no worry about Bob Yeager," Jack assured her. "Takin' care of troublesome people is his business. Him and three fellers he rode with gunned down a deputy sheriff in Virginia City six years ago and they got away with it slick as you please. He was in prison for robbin' a stagecoach outta Bozeman. They never did find out he was the one killed the deputy— shot him in the mouth with his .44."

"How do we know he won't come back around later on, looking for more money?"

"'Cause he knows I'll shoot him if he does," Jack boasted with a smirk. "Besides, he don't have to know about the gold and he don't have to know why we want the McClouds dead. All the same to him, as long as he gets paid for the job."

"Just be sure this deal is between you and him," she said. "I don't want him to know I'm involved in any way." She had big plans for the money that gold would buy and she wanted no chance of some saddle tramp killer showing up at her front door looking for hush money.

Jack snorted impatiently. "Don't worry, Your Highness. I ain't gonna tell him about you." Knowing his sister's fetish for neatness, he couldn't resist making a point of deliberately tapping his cigar over the rug and smiling when the ashes hit the floor. "You know, it'd help a helluva lot if I knew what these jaspers look like. I don't reckon they'll ride into town wearin' a sign around their necks that says 'We're the McCloud boys.'" He chuckled in appreciation for his joke.

She could not be sure both brothers would be trailing her. It would depend on how serious Cody's wound had been. "I'll describe them as best I can," she said. "They're both taller than average. Cullen's the oldest. He's clean shaven and has dark hair. Cody's hair is much lighter and he has a mustache."

"That don't tell me a helluva lot," Jack responded.

"Helena's a fair-sized town. There's a lot of jaspers walking around that fit that description."

"If they're both following me, you can tell them by the horses they ride. Cullen rides a light bay with white stockings, and Cody rides an Appaloosa, one of those Indian-bred horses." She paused to watch his reaction, then thought of another suggestion. "Why don't you have this Yeager person ride back toward Garrison, and maybe he'll meet the McClouds before they get to Helena?"

"How do we know they ain't already here?" Jack asked.

"We don't," she replied calmly. "And they may not show up here at all. I never mentioned Helena to them, so they should suspect that I'm going to Butte." She held up a finger then as if making an important point. "But they're both like a couple of Indians when it comes to tracking, so there's a small chance they might be on their way here. And I want all the little possibilities taken care of, so go find this Yeager person and send him on the trail to Garrison Station. If Cullen and Cody haven't showed up there, tell him to wait until they do."

Just as he had figured, Jack Sykes found Bob Yeager at the Red Dog Saloon, a seedy, run-down saloon on the northern fringe of Helena. It was run by a man known simply by the name Stumpy, in obvious reference to the peg-leg strapped to the stump of his right thigh. The Red Dog was seldom frequented by the peaceful citizens of Helena, because of its reputation as a hang-out and meeting place for those who walked the dark line between the law-abiding and those who had drifted

over that line. It was a natural attraction to men like
Jack Sykes and Bob Yeager. Yeager, a dark, brooding hulk
of a man, was easily recognized by a long white scar
that ran through his beard from his left earlobe, across
his cheek to almost touch the corner of his mouth. He
sat at a table in the rear of the saloon, hovering over a
glass of beer, much like a dog guarding a bone. Stumpy
sat across from him. Both men looked up when they
heard the door open and Jack walked in.

"Jack Sykes," Stumpy announced in bored greeting.
"What can I do for you? Whiskey?"

"Nah," Jack returned, "just give me a glass of that
beer." He nodded at Yeager then, who had not changed
his sullen expression and offered no response to his
nod. "I thought I'd find you here," Jack said.

Stumpy got up to draw a beer for him, but paused
long enough to ask, "I reckon you've got some cash
money on you, 'cause I'm flat done with sellin' beer on
the cuff." He gave Yeager a hard glance that Jack could
easily interpret as meaning that the sullen man was
drinking on credit. Jack was pretty confident then that
his bargaining position was strengthened considerably.

"Yeah," Jack replied, "I can pay for my beer, and I'll
buy one for Bob, too." He reached in his pocket and
laid the money down, enough for a couple more to boot.
It was enough to cause the somber Yeager to raise his
head and look directly at him. While Stumpy went to
the bar to fetch the beer, Jack pulled a chair over closer to
Yeager. "Don't look to me like things has been goin'
too good for you since you got outta prison."

"Things *has* been better," Yeager replied.

"Well, maybe I've got a little job for you that's right

up your alley, that is, if you're interested in makin' a little money."

This ignited an immediate change in Yeager's disposition, bringing a spark of interest to his otherwise dull gaze. "Maybe," he replied. "Who you want kilt?"

"Hold on a minute," Jack cautioned, and looked over his shoulder to see if Stumpy had heard Yeager's response. "This job has to be kept quiet."

"Hell, Stumpy ain't gonna tell nobody," Yeager said. "He knows I'll kill him if he does."

"All the same," Jack insisted, "I'd rather keep this between me and you. I'll talk to you outside. Besides, who said anythin' about killin' somebody?" He glanced at Stumpy again, who was still at the bar.

"Hell, what else would it be?" Yeager grunted. "I ain't much of an expert in any other trade." His curiosity caused him to raise an eyebrow then and almost brought a twinkle to his eye. "How much does this little job pay?"

Speaking in a whisper now, as Stumpy approached the table carrying three glasses of beer, Sykes replied, "Two hundred dollars, gold," he said, and sat back to let Yeager absorb that while Stumpy placed the glasses on the table and sat down with them. The sum mentioned was enough to cause Yeager to raise the other eyebrow, just as Jack figured.

"It feels so damn good to finally have a payin' customer this mornin' that I decided to have a drink with you," Stumpy announced. "Seems like ever'body is feelin' hard times these days."

Confident now to rebuff Stumpy's criticism, Yeager favored him with a smirk. "You crabby ol' skinflint, maybe I won't have to drink no more on credit in this dump you call a saloon."

"Is that so?" Stumpy replied, and cast an inquiring look in Jack's direction. Sykes simply shrugged in response, feigning any knowledge of the basis for Yeager's remark. "Did somebody die and leave you a fortune?" Stumpy asked. Then exercising his sense of humor, he continued. "Or is somebody just *fixin'* to die?" He chuckled then in appreciation of his wit.

Jack shot Yeager a warning glance, which Yeager answered with a lazy grin. To Stumpy, he said, "None of your business, old man. Get up and fill them glasses again." He tipped his glass back and drained it, then set it down hard on the table for emphasis.

When Stumpy raked the remaining money off the table and went to the bar, Jack told Yeager to meet him outside. Yeager nodded, and Sykes got to his feet then and headed for the door with a casual wave to Stumpy as he walked past the bar. "Don't hurry off," Stumpy called out to him, reluctant to see a paying customer leave with money still in his pocket.

Jack waited by the hitching rail for Yeager to follow him. He was about to lose his temper as well as his patience when the gruff ex-con finally appeared on the short porch of the saloon. "What the hell took you so long?" Sykes demanded irritably. When Yeager replied that there had been beer bought and paid for that he couldn't let go to waste, Jack snorted in response, "I'm talkin' 'bout a job that's worth two hundred dollars, and you're worrying 'bout fifty cents' worth of beer?"

"You ain't told me what the job is," Yeager said, "and I ain't seen no two hundred dollars, neither."

"You'll see it when we've got a deal," Jack promised. He then explained what he would be paid to do. "Two hundred dollars," he emphasized when he had finished. "One hundred for each man—and damn it, I want proof of each kill."

"You said there might not be but one of 'em showin' up," Yeager said. "I get the two hundred whether both of 'em show up or not, or I ain't interested."

Jack had to think about it for a few moments before agreeing. "All right, two hundred if it's one or if it's twenty that shows up, but you don't get a cent until the job's done."

"I'll be damned," Yeager complained. "How do I know you'll pay? Hell, how do I know you've even got that much money?" He had never known Jack Sykes to be any more than a down-and-out outlaw like himself, and he was asking for a helluva lot to be done on trust alone. "Hell, I've got expenses—supplies and cartridges—if I'm gonna have to track somebody between here and Garrison Station."

Sykes thought it over for a few seconds before giving in to his demands. "All right, I'll tell you what I'll do. I'll give you fifty dollars up front and the rest of it when the job is done, but I want those two brothers dead."

"We got a deal," Yeager said, "just as soon as you give me the fifty dollars." He was more than happy with the arrangement. It was more than he had expected. He would have killed two men for fifty dollars, had that been the total offer. He had one more question, however, that had puzzled him. "Where the hell did you get that kinda money?"

"Never you mind about that. I've got it. That's all you need to know." The thought occurred that Yeager might be thinking about cutting himself in for a bigger portion of the gold once he got his foot in the door. It was not a matter that caused Jack any concern. *If he wants a share, all he'll get is a deposit of lead—enough to mold one .44 bullet,* he thought.

So the deal was struck to eliminate one—or two—of the McCloud brothers with Jack agreeing to meet Yeager the following morning with the cash advance of fifty dollars. He could have given the outlaw the fifty then and there, but he preferred not to hand it over while the night was still young, and Stumpy's was still open. So it was that the following morning Bob Yeager set out on the trail west toward Garrison with fifty dollars in hand and a very sketchy description of the men he was to kill. Sykes had never seen either of the two men he hired Yeager to kill, and could only offer Roberta's description of them. "One hundred and fifty dollars, waitin' for you when you're done," Jack reminded him as he rode away, in case the temptation to simply disappear with the fifty was working on his mind.

Bob Yeager kicked dirt over the remains of his campfire, pulled his rifle from the saddle sling, and checked it before returning it and stepping up into the saddle. He figured he was halfway between Helena and the stagecoach stop over on the Clark Fork. Had he been in a hurry, he could have made the ride in one day, but he was in no hurry. If Jack Sykes' hunch was right, he ought to meet the man, or men, he was looking for. There was still some question as to whether there was one or two of the McCloud brothers stalking Jack. Sykes had been a bit hazy about why they might be looking for him. And there was still the possibility these brothers might be heading for Butte instead of Helena. *Well,* he thought, *If I don't meet up with them before I get to the Clark Fork, I'll head for Butte.* He guided his horse the short distance back to the trail and continued west.

Not a solitary soul did he meet before striking the Butte road and the stagecoach swing station on the river. Pulling his horse to a stop, he sat undecided whether to head south toward Butte or follow the road in the opposite direction toward Missoula. "This is crazy as hell," he exclaimed. "How the hell do I know whether the son of a bitch has done come and gone, or ain't even got this far yet?" Then he thought about the fifty dollars he had in his pocket, and the prospect of turning it into two hundred. *Jack must want this bastard dead pretty bad,* he thought, *so I'll look for him. Sykes wants proof he's dead, so I'll cover the trail as best I can. Then if I don't find him, I'll shoot somebody and tell Jack it's McCloud. Hell, he ain't ever seen them fellers himself.* He decided then to ride on up to the stage station and buy himself something to eat, now that he could afford it. He could ask if they had seen anyone of McCloud's description in the last day or two. There was a good chance that McCloud had stopped there.

It was close to sundown when Cullen came to the modest settlement called Garrison. He guided the bay toward a low frame building, sprawled close beside the riverbank with a couple dozen horses in the corral, indication that this was the stagecoach station. Cullen was ready to stop for the night in any case, for his horse was in need of rest and maybe a ration of oats. Approaching the door, he stopped to knock instead of walking right in, since the building didn't have any appearance of a commercial establishment. In a few minutes' time, the door was opened by a cheerful-looking woman wearing a long apron. Stepping back in frank appraisal of the tall stranger, she said nothing for an awkward moment before inquiring, "Can I help you, sir?"

Looking past her, Cullen could see that he had guessed right in hesitating to walk in uninvited. It was a home with a proper parlor behind the woman, and he at once started to apologize for bothering her at suppertime. "Beg your pardon, ma'am," he said. "I was lookin' for the stage station, and I thought this might be it. I saw the horses in the corral back there." He touched his hat and turned to leave, but she stopped him.

"You're in the right place," she said. "The stage line changes horses here. What can we do for you? Do you need to speak to my husband about the horses?"

"Ah, no, ma'am," Cullen replied. "To tell you the truth, I was thinkin' that this might be a dinin' room or somethin' where the stage stopped to feed the passengers. I was lookin' to buy some supper."

She laughed then and took a step back. "Like I said, you're in the right place. Come on in. You're just in time. Supper's still on the table." She paused as he stepped inside. "If you don't mind, sir, you can leave your gun belt and pistols here on this table. We prefer not to have guns in the dining room."

"Yes, ma'am," he replied, and unbuckled his belt

and placed his weapons on the small table with a belt
and pistol already there. Although not of great interest
to him, he did note that the holster for the Colt .44 was
backward so that the pistol sat handle forward, the
style that a lot of men preferred in order to draw the
weapon faster.

The lady led him through the modest parlor to
pause in the doorway to a large dining room where all
the furniture had been removed except a sideboard and
a long table. "My name's Myra Sullivan," she said. "Me
and my husband, Fred, have an arrangement with the
stage line to cook a meal for the passengers on days
they're running from Missoula to Butte. We charge the
passengers fifty cents apiece for supper, and I reckon
we can do the same for you." She paused. "If that's all
right with you."

"Yes, ma'am, that'd be fine with me."

He looked beyond her at the diners already seated
at the table. Only one end of the table was being used,
since there were only five places set. Those already
well along in their supper turned to look at the new
arrival. The gray-haired man at the head of the table
nodded to Cullen. Myra introduced him as her husband, Fred. To Fred's left, a young boy of perhaps thirteen or fourteen stared at the stranger while still working
on a biscuit, his curiosity insufficient to interrupt his
supper. Cullen was told that this was their son, Jimmy.
That left one to be introduced, a brooding, broad-
shouldered man with a full beard and heavy eyebrows
like dark thickets over eyes set deep in his skull. The
feature that set the man apart was a long white scar
that cut a line through his dark beard that resembled a

trail through a thick forest. "This is Mr. Smith," Myra said. "He's like you, just traveling through and decided to stay the night."

Cullen nodded to the somber Mr. Smith, who seemed to be looking him over with some curiosity; then he turned back to Myra. "It's mighty neighborly of you folks to let me take supper with you."

"Well, to tell you the truth of it," Fred Sullivan responded, "we plan to turn the place into a regular dinin' room if this business with the stage line catches on, so we're glad to see folks like you and Mr. Smith stop in. If we get enough calls for it, I'm gonna build a section of rooms onto the back of the house, so if a body wants to stay over for a day or however many, he can rent a room." He smiled at Smith then and said, "And he won't have to sleep in the barn like Mr. Smith, here." Turning back to Cullen, he said, "I didn't catch your name."

"McCloud," he answered, "Cullen McCloud."

"Well, Mr. McCloud, set yourself down at that empty plate there," Myra said, and watched for a moment while Cullen hung his hat on the back of the chair and sat down. Then she went to the kitchen door and called to her daughter, "Marcy, bring one more plate and some silverware. We have another guest."

Cullen had wondered who the extra plate was for, since everybody but Myra was already well into their supper. Satisfied that the menfolk were all taken care of, Myra sat down across from Cullen. In a minute or two, a young woman of perhaps eighteen or nineteen came from the kitchen with another place setting and sat down with it next to her mother. She nodded politely to Cullen before getting up again to fetch the coffeepot. In a few seconds she was back, and Cullen watched her as she went around the table, filling the empty cups. He could not help admiring her obvious grace as she cheerfully poured the hot coffee from a large gray metal pot. Cullen found himself studying her auburn hair and the one stray lock that fell across her forehead to be constantly brushed aside. Her eyes, bright and laughing, locked on his and captured his gaze. He quickly looked away, embarrassed to be practically gaping at her. The cups filled, she returned the pot to its place on the edge of the stove, then came back to her chair.

Although there had been no reaction in the somber gaze of the man introduced as Mr. Smith when Cullen identified himself, there was a sudden tightening of the muscles in his forearms. It was a natural reflex upon having the man he waited for suddenly walk right in and present himself before him. Without conscious thought, Bob Yeager dropped his hand down to his side where his .44 normally rode. His first inclination was to pull the derringer he kept hidden in his boot and earn his two hundred dollars right then and there. He was dissuaded from doing so, however. The Remington derringer held only two shots, and if anything went wrong, he might have to race the two men and the boy to the table beside the front door for his gun belt and pistol. His heavy eyebrows lowered to a deep frown as he pretended to concentrate on the slab of ham on his plate and he considered the wisdom of killing McCloud in front of so many witnesses. Telling himself that it would be much wiser to wait and bushwhack Cullen on the trail, he forced his attention back on his supper.

After everyone had finished the meal and Marcy filled the coffee cups one final time, Cullen sat back to listen to Fred Sullivan's plans to expand his little business venture. Everything hinged upon the success of the spur stage line; otherwise, he said, he would have to continue to depend upon farming to feed his family. "How often does the stage run?" Cullen asked, not really caring, but aware of Fred's enthusiasm for talking about it.

"Right now," Fred answered, "once a week—once from Butte to Missoula, and once back to Butte."

"So there was only one stage from Missoula this week," Cullen said. "How many passengers were on it?"

"Six. Isn't that right, Myra?" He looked at his wife for confirmation.

"That's right," she said, "six, but we fed seven. There was that one man who met one of the passengers here. So there weren't but five that went on to Butte."

Her comment sparked an immediate interest for Cullen. "Someone got off the stage here, instead of goin' on to Butte?" When both Sullivan and his wife nodded, Cullen asked, "Was the passenger who got off by any chance a woman?"

"Why, yes," Myra replied, "a rather pleasant young woman. Her brother met her here with a couple of horses. They stayed to eat, and then went on the road to Helena, I think."

I'm damn glad I stopped here for supper, he thought, for he had assumed Roberta was heading back to Butte. Then it occurred to him that he had never asked, neither here nor in Missoula, if there was more than one woman on the stage. "How many women were on the stage?" Myra replied that there were two. He had to be sure, so he asked one more question. "Do you remember the name of the woman who got off here? It might be somebody I know."

She paused to recall. "No, I don't remember what her name was."

"Roberta," Marcy supplied. "Her name was Roberta, but I don't remember her last name." She hesitated to watch Cullen's reaction, then asked, "Is she a friend of yours?"

He didn't answer right away. His mind was already thinking about the trail to Helena, estimating the time it would take to reach the town and who the brother might really be. Finally, he smiled at Marcy and replied, "No, she's no friend of mine. I was just curious."

His comment stirred a spark of curiosity in the sullen Mr. Smith as well. Always on the lookout for an extra payday, Yeager wondered why McCloud was asking about a woman who left the stagecoach and went to Helena instead of Butte. To Yeager, he seemed to be a little more than just curious. Jack Sykes was pretty tight-lipped about why he wanted McCloud killed. *And where the hell did Jack Sykes get his hands on enough money to pay me two hundred dollars to get rid of this son of a bitch?* he wondered. He downed the last swallow of coffee from his cup, thinking about Cullen's interest in the woman and wondering if she had anything to do with Sykes. Maybe Sykes was the brother who met her here. *There might be a bigger payday than two hundred here*, he thought. *Jack might be onto something he don't wanna share with nobody.* It was enough to ignite a genuine interest in what Sykes was up to. The decision was made to wait to see if McCloud changed his mind about going to Butte, and set out on the road to Helena instead. Yeager wasn't particular about which trail he did the job on, but if Cullen did head for Helena, it might be a pretty strong indication that the woman had something to do with whatever gold mine Sykes had struck. *And that little son of a bitch might as well cut ol' Bob in on the deal.*

"Will you be wanting breakfast in the morning, Mr. Smith?" Myra asked when Yeager pushed his chair back and prepared to take his leave.

"No, I reckon not," Yeager answered. "I changed my mind. I reckon I'll be headin' on out tonight. I'd best be gettin' along."

"Well, remember us next time you're traveling this way," Myra replied, not really sure she meant it. The man seemed to have a shroud of doom around him that made her uncomfortable. She turned to face Cullen then. "How about you, Mr. McCloud? Are you leaving now, too?"

Cullen thought about it for only a second. "No, ma'am," he replied. "I think I'll spend the night in your barn, and get started after breakfast in the mornin' if that's all right with you."

"Glad to have you stay over," Myra answered with a smile, always happy to earn another fifty cents for breakfast and an extra fifty for a bed in the hay.

No one noticed the crooked little smile that appeared on Yeager's unshaven face after the exchange between Myra and Cullen. He waited until Cullen pushed his chair back under the table, then walked with him to the little table beside the front door, taking the measure of the man he planned to kill tomorrow. Cullen found the man odd, his expression one of amusement as he strapped on the gun belt and adjusted the revolver to settle on his hip with the handle turned out, all the while gazing at him as if expecting some comment. With no desire to make conversation with him, Cullen strapped his belt on and walked out the door. "Be seein' you, McCloud," Yeager called after him.

Cullen looked back at the grinning man and replied, "Yeah, maybe so," and headed for the barn to take care of his horse. Once inside the barn, he spied a bucket hanging on a nail driven in a post and remembered that he wanted to feed the bay some grain. He decided to help himself and add it onto his bill in the morning. He was still feeding his horse when Yeager came in from the corral, leading a blue roan that was almost all black—two white socks and a blaze on its face the only white showing. The heavyset brute grinned at Cullen as he threw his saddle on the horse, although he did not speak again. Cullen was glad to see him finally climb in the saddle and ride out of the barn. He felt a sense of distrust for the scar-faced stranger and was relieved that he would not have to share the stable with him for the night. He might have given Mr. Smith more thought, but Jimmy Sullivan walked into the barn at that moment. "Pa sent me to see if you needed any help with your horse or anything," the boy announced.

"Nope, we're all set," Cullen replied, "but thanks just the same." Then he remembered. "Tell your pa I owe him for a half pail of grain."

Bob Yeager rode away from Fred Sullivan's house at a leisurely lope, up from the river, and north on the road to Missoula. His ride was not very far, however, for after about a half mile, he reined the blue roan toward the river again. Then, walking the horse back toward the stage station, he continued until he found a spot to camp where he could watch the lane from the Sullivan house to the road. "We'll just set here and wait," he told himself. "If he rides outta there in the mornin', and heads for Butte, then I reckon I'll just earn me two hundred dollars. But if he takes out after that woman to Helena, then there's somethin' bigger goin' on, and two and two might add up to a helluva lot more than four." He would kill the man, as he had contracted to do, but he was determined to find out what Jack Sykes and the woman were up to.

"Mr. McCloud . . ." Cullen heard the voice outside the barn. He had just saddled the bay, so he led him out the door. From the sound of the voice, he assumed that it was Jimmy, but was surprised to find that it was the girl, Marcy, waiting outside. "Good morning," she said. "I just came to tell you breakfast is ready."

"Good morning," he returned, understanding why she had called him from outside the barn instead of walking right in. "I'm all ready to ride." He led the bay up to the hitching rail in front of the house and she walked along beside him.

"Do you ride this valley very often," Marcy asked, "or are you just passing through this once?"

He looked down at her and smiled. "Well, I'm just passin' through this time, I guess." She nodded and said nothing more as they stepped up on the porch. *A pleasant-looking young lady*, he thought. Now as the early rays of the sun peeked over the eastern slopes behind him to scamper playfully across her young face, he couldn't help noticing the shy freshness of her smile. "Marcy, was it?" he asked, embarrassed that he had to.

"That's right," she answered.

He felt that he should like to say more, but couldn't think of anything appropriate. He wasn't comfortable trying to make casual conversation with young ladies. He lacked the glibness of his brother Cody—or even the bluntness of Smoke. A thought struck his mind that he was more at a loss than he had been with Roberta, and he realized how much she had dominated any conversation. He smiled to himself when he thought of the ornery cook, and guessed that Smoke would just tell Marcy that she was pretty. That sort of comment was all right for Smoke, but from Cullen, it was not in his manner to make a blunt statement like that. *Hell*, he thought, *it's just a girl telling me that breakfast is ready.* He shook his head then, wondering why he was even bothered by it. *I'm getting as bad as Cody*, he thought, *thinking I need to cozy up to every female I meet.* He was saved from having to make further conversation when Jimmy stepped out on the porch.

"Breakfast is gettin' cold on the table," Jimmy said. "What's takin' so long?"

Myra Sullivan set a fine table. It was well worth the

fifty cents she charged stagecoach passengers. Cullen was surprised when she told him that she was only going to charge him a quarter for his breakfast since he was paying to sleep in the barn and grain for his horse. "Well, I'm much obliged, ma'am," he said, and glanced in Fred's direction to see if there were any signs of disapproval on his part. His glance was met with a broad smile.

"That's right," Fred said. "Last night you were just a customer. This mornin' you're company." He looked at his wife and chuckled. "That bein' the case, we ought not charge him a quarter, Ma." Myra laughed and promptly agreed. The Sullivans had decided they liked the tall, gentle stranger. Possibly it was because of the sharp contrast to the brooding hulk with the scarred face who had occupied a chair at their table for two meals before Cullen arrived. In fact, Fred was aware of a light and jovial mood at the breakfast table without the baleful glances from the dark figure as he hovered guardedly over his plate.

"Well, I expect I'd better get goin'," Cullen announced, after finishing another cup of coffee. He found it difficult to bring his concentration back to the task he had undertaken. It was tempting to forget about the villainous woman he had been tracking, but then he thought about Jug, lying helpless on the travois as Cody had ridden away, and his resolve quickly returned. Roberta already had an almost insurmountable lead on him, and she was more and more likely to disappear the longer he delayed. Getting up from the table, he said, "I'll be sayin' good-bye, then. Thank you for the breakfast."

"Come back to see us," Myra said.

"I will," Cullen replied. "I'll be back on my way home." Noticing the smile on Marcy's face as she stood in the kitchen door, he had a feeling that he definitely would.

It did not take long for him to return his focus to the job he had set out to do, to find the black widow who had left a trail of bodies as she made her way out of the Bitterroot Valley. He could not help wondering how a woman could be so free of conscience that she could use men up and destroy them when she was finished with them. He was driven to find her, even though he was still not sure what he was going to do if he found her. Kill her, as she would do in the reverse situation? Even under the circumstances, it was difficult for him to think of shooting a woman. She had stolen a considerable fortune that rightfully belonged to Gabe Morris' family, but how could he recover gold dust that had no doubt been converted to cash and dispersed who knew where? It was a lot to think about, and enough to trouble his mind. If killing a woman was out of the question, he was at least determined to make sure she spent the rest of her life behind bars.

There were other thoughts to command his attention as well as he started on the road to Helena. He berated himself for his foolish infatuation for the mysteriously charming woman who had shown up at his father's ranch searching for her *beloved uncle*. "Damn, what a fool I was," he complained to his horse. Looking back at that regrettable time, he was drawn to compare Roberta with the young and shy Marcy Sullivan. This was the thought in his mind when he was suddenly slammed in the back by a .44 rifle slug that knocked him out of the saddle. Landing hard on the ground, stunned and confused, the wind knocked out of his lungs, he was not sure what had happened, having not heard the shot that caught him between the shoulder blades. After a few moments, while he struggled to get to his hands and knees, he tried to reach for his Colt revolver. But he didn't seem to be able to control the movement of his hands and arms, and he felt as if there was a heavy weight buried deep in his chest. He heard horse's hooves approaching. The sound seemed unusually loud, and he knew he must pull his pistol, but he seemed unable to do it. Halfway up on his hands and knees, he crumpled helplessly flat on the ground again.

Silently complimenting himself on the rifle shot, Bob Yeager reined his horse to a stop before the wounded man. "That was a pretty damn good shot," he boasted as he stepped down from the saddle. "Most of a hundred yards, I expect, and I hit you square between the shoulder blades. You look pretty much a goner to me," he commented unemotionally, "but it wouldn't hurt to make sure." He drew his revolver and pumped two shots into the body for good measure. "That was an easy two hundred dollars," he said as he dismounted. Rolling Cullen over, he unbuckled his gun belt and pulled it from him. Checking his pockets for cash then, he came up with a few more dollars. Then his attention was drawn to Cullen's bay gelding, and he moved to secure the horse before it took a notion to depart. "That's a fine-lookin' horse," he said, admiring the light bay, all the while becoming more and more pleased with his profits from this one job. Ready to ride, he climbed aboard his horse, giving the bleeding body one last glance. "Well, it was a pleasure meetin' you, Mr. McCloud. Say hello to the devil for me. Tell him Bob Yeager sent you." Then with a gruff laugh, he kicked his heels into the blue roan's sides and was off to claim the rest of his payment from Jack Sykes, and maybe find out a little more about the mystery woman.

Chapter 8

Cody McCloud suddenly sat up, startled awake by something—he could not explain what. He had been sound asleep in the chair beside his brother's bed. He looked at once toward the patient, wondering if Jug had made some outcry, but Jug was lying quietly, although his eyes were open. Confused by the feeling that something was wrong, Cody wondered if it was caused by a dream. If so, he couldn't remember it. Then the thought of Cullen came to his mind, and he wondered if his brother was all right. His father walked in the room then.

"I see you woke up," Donovan McCloud said softly. "I brought you some coffee. Smoke made some breakfast, and he's already grumblin' about it gettin' cold."

"Thanks," Cody said, reaching for the cup. "I didn't even know you'd left the room. I went to sleep."

"Yeah, I figured you could use some coffee after last night," Donovan said. It had been a rough night for the father and son keeping a vigil beside Jug's bed. All indications had pointed toward Dr. Elrod's prediction being accurate—that Donovan's middle son wouldn't make it, and it seemed to be coming to a climax that night. Feverish and apparently out of his mind for much of the night, Jug had finally lapsed into sleep in the wee hours of the morning. And now his father stood over his bed gazing sadly at the still figure lying there, his eyes open, but apparently seeing nothing. A moment later, Donovan was startled when the eyes shifted to look toward him.

"I could use a little of that coffee myself."

Coffee splashed on the floor and the bed as Cody and Donovan both jumped uncontrollably when the words came from the patient. "I didn't mean I wanted to wear it," Jug said. His voice was weak, but lucid for the first time since he had taken a turn for the worse two days before.

"Here, take this!" Cody exclaimed, offering his cup.

"Help me sit up," Jug replied. His father and brother immediately set their cups down and hurried to lift him to a sitting position in the bed. "Take it easy," Jug complained. "I still got a damn hole in me."

After he was situated comfortably, and taking a few tentative sips from the coffee cup, Cody gazed down at him, still marveling at the transformation from a few hours before. "Hell, I thought you were dead," he commented. "Doc Elrod said you were gonna die."

"Well, I reckon he didn't ask me about it," Jug said. "Might be Smoke's a better doctor than Elrod, anyway."

"I wouldn't be surprised," Smoke agreed as he came through the door at that moment. He had heard exclamations coming from the room and had come to investigate the cause. He walked over to stand close to the bed and took a hard look at the man returning from the dead. Satisfied that Jug had an unmistakable spark of life in his eyes, he snorted and asked, "You ain't havin' one of them clear spells just before you die, are you?"

His insensitive question brought a weak smile to Jug's harried face. "Hell no. I ain't never had no notion to die."

"Well, I reckon I better make sure we've got plenty of meat in the smokehouse," Smoke said.

Suddenly feeling exhausted, Donovan McCloud sank heavily into his chair on the other side of Jug's bed, finally confident in his son's ability to defy the doctor's diagnosis. The last few days, when Jug was fighting for his life, had been hard on the head of the McCloud family. The odds of Jug's recovery were dead set against him, and they were all resigned to the prospect that the likable, easygoing giant of a man would soon pass out of their lives. Donovan had spent many long moments in the tiny graveyard on the ridge close to the river, talking to Charlotte, asking his late wife to be on the lookout for her second son, Ryan. Jug would need her help, Donovan pleaded, being on his own after so many years looking to Cullen for guidance. Now, unable to keep a tired grin off his face, he watched what some might think a miracle, and he had a feeling that it was just some of Charlotte's work. Even Smoke had a smile on his face, which was a miracle in itself, for Donovan could not recall having ever seen one on the craggy face before. Glancing from Smoke, to Jug, and then to Cody, everyone was grinning except Cody. His youngest son was standing at the head of Jug's bed, obviously thankful for his brother's unexpected rally, but he wore a troubled look on his face.

"I expect we'd all best get outta here and let him get some rest, now that his fever's broke and he don't look like he's gonna check out any time soon," Smoke advised.

"I expect so," Donovan agreed, and got up to leave.

"I'm gonna need somethin' to eat," Jug protested weakly.

This brought an immediate laugh from his three visitors. "Yeah, I reckon he's back all right," Cody said.

"I'll fix you somethin'," Smoke said, and led them out of the room.

"What's workin' on your mind?" Donovan asked Cody when they had walked out into the hall.

"I don't know," Cody answered. "I'm thinkin' about Cullen. I guess I just got a feelin' that he might need help. And now that I'm sure Jug is gonna make it, I'm thinkin' about headin' out toward Missoula to see if I can find him." He didn't need to express other concerns that they both knew. Cullen had been taken with Roberta Morris. Cody feared what it might do to his brother if he was too late to save her.

Donovan nodded thoughtfully. There was a strong bond between all three brothers, and he had long ago stopped questioning their tendency for one to know when the other needed help. "All right," he said, "I think that's a good idea. Me and Smoke will be okay here. We'll take care of Jug. Go find your brother, and, Cody, you be damn careful."

"I will, Pa. I'll find him."

Early the next morning, Cody once again threw his saddle on the six-year-old Appaloosa gelding named Buttermilk. Of his string of horses, he would have to say that he favored Buttermilk when the job called for endurance and speed. Smoke put a fresh bandage on the wound in his shoulder, which looked to be close to the point where he could go without one. The stiffness was gone, and that was all that mattered to Cody. After promising his father again that he would be careful, he turned the Appaloosa's head toward the north and started out to find his brother.

"Not again!" Jimmy Sullivan exclaimed. It was the second time this month the spirited young stallion had managed to squeeze through a small gap between a corral post and the barn. And just like the first time, it took off up the road toward Helena. It was Jimmy's job to find him and bring him back. His father planned to geld the young horse in the early fall when the flies weren't so bad and the cooler temperatures would tend to keep the swelling down after the procedure. Gelding was usually done in early spring or late fall. Jimmy's father could have done it in the spring just passed, but he wanted to give the horse time to develop a little muscle definition and aggressiveness first. The leggy stallion was not quite a year old. Its withers hadn't grown to be level with its croup yet. In Jimmy's opinion, the horse had already developed enough aggressiveness to be a nuisance. *You'll settle down to more respectable ways after you've had your balls lopped off*, he thought.

The first place Jimmy had looked for the rebellious young horse was the meadow just above a band of pine that ringed the lower slope of a low mountain. This was where he had found him the last time, and sure enough, that was where he found him again. It took a little cussing, and a fair amount of time, but Jimmy finally got a rope on the renegade. With the ornery stallion in tow, he guided his horse down through the pines with the intent to come out on the road to Helena. The stallion followed reluctantly, jerking and tossing his head in protest to Jimmy's rope. Emerging from the trees that lined the road, Jimmy's horse shied away from an object lying beside the trail, some thirty feet away. It took a second look before Jimmy realized it was a body. "God A'mighty!" he exclaimed involuntarily, and hauled back on the reins. Hesitant to move closer at once, in case someone might be watching him, he sat there and looked up the road in each direction, then back to the still form lying beside the track. When he felt sure there was no one else around, he nudged his horse closer until it was plain to see the cause for the body to be there. It was covered with blood, the obvious work of an Indian or a road agent.

Still in the saddle, Jimmy walked his horse slowly around the body to take a better look before riding for home to tell his father. The face seemed familiar and it occurred to him then that it was the man who had spent the night in the barn. McCloud was the name he recalled. Shocked, he didn't wait any longer, but gave his horse a kick and galloped off for home, the leggy young stallion in tow.

As soon as Fred Sullivan heard his son's excited report, he sent him to the house to fetch his rifle, while he hitched up the wagon. There had been no Indian trouble in this valley all summer, but with recent reports of the Nez Perce fighting in Idaho, and the prospect of their arrival in the neighboring valley west of the mountains, he had reason enough to be cautious. Jimmy said the dead man was Cullen McCloud. It was hard to believe he had been killed practically on their doorstep. It had been only hours since he had shared breakfast at their table. His womenfolk had commented on what a nice fellow he seemed to be. The least he could do was to give the man a decent burial. The team hitched, he waited for a few moments until Jimmy came running from the house with the rifle. His mother and sister followed the boy out the door, their faces etched with concern. "You women stay in the house," Fred ordered, "till we get back."

As the wagon rumbled along the rough tracks of the Helena trail, Fred kept a sharp lookout for any signs of treachery awaiting, but all seemed peaceful enough. They had gone no more than three miles when they rounded a sharp turn in the road and Jimmy sang out, "There he is!" He stood up and pointed to the body lying beside the road. Fred pulled the team to a halt beside Cullen, and as his son had done earlier, paused to look all around him for any signs of danger before getting down. There was no sign of anything wrong, and no sound except a gentle whisper of the wind in the tall pines with the occasional call of a crow. Whoever had done this evil piece of work had obviously long since departed.

"Let's get him in the wagon," Fred told his son, and

climbed down to take a closer look. It was McCloud, all right. It was hard to tell how many times he had been shot because of the blood-saturated shirt. "Who woulda done such a thing?" Fred murmured, noticing his gun belt was missing and his pockets turned inside out. "Bushwhacked by a murderin' thief." He turned to Jimmy. "Take hold of his feet, son, and we'll see if we can get him loaded. He's a pretty good-sized feller, so mind your back." Fred slid his hands under Cullen's shoulders. "All right, you ready? Let's pick him up."

Man and son strained and started to lift the body, but raised it no higher than a few inches before releasing him and jumping back startled when a slight groan came from the supposedly dead man. "Jesus!" Fred exclaimed. He looked at his son, astonished, wondering if he had heard the sound. The wide-eyed look on Jimmy's face told him that he had. Fred knelt down beside Cullen to get a closer look, and recoiled slightly when Cullen's eyes flickered open for an instant before closing again. "Good Lord in heaven," Fred uttered. "He's alive." He had to sit back and think for a few moments. He had known what to do before, when he had a dead man to deal with. Now with a man clinging to life, he wasn't sure there was anything he *could* do for him. Considering all the blood soaked in Cullen's shirt and trousers, Fred wondered if there could possibly be much left in his body. "Come on, son," he finally said. "We'll put him in the wagon and get him back to the house. It ain't fittin' for anybody to die lyin' out here by the side of the road."

Both Myra and Marcy came out of the house to meet them when they rolled back into the yard. Sev-

eral steps in front of her mother, Marcy was the first to
reach the wagon. Before she could ask, Jimmy blurted,
"He ain't dead yet!"

Marcy looked to her father for confirmation and
Fred nodded in response. "That's a fact," he said.

Moving up to stand beside her daughter as they both
stared at the wounded man lying in the wagon bed,
Myra uttered in disbelief, "My Lord, Fred, how could
he *not* be?"

"Don't ask me," her husband replied, "but he ain't."
He scratched his head while he thought the problem
over. "We could haul him over to the doctor at Deer
Lodge, but the ride would most likely finish him off. I
don't think he'd make it."

"Well, we can't leave the poor man out here in the
wagon," Myra said, a worried look on her face. She
was clearly troubling over what to do with the dying
man. As if concerned that Cullen might hear, she whispered to her husband, "Maybe it would be best to put
him in the barn. It'll be easier to clean him up in there."
She paused, then said, "For however long it takes for
him to die."

Hearing her mother's comment, Marcy protested.
"We can't put the poor man in the barn with the horses
and the cow, Mama. We have to help him if we can. He
may not be as badly wounded as it looks."

Fred shook his head, all the while studying the grim
scene in his wagon bed. "I don't know, Marcy. He looks
pretty much finished to me. Your mother may be right.
He's gonna need a lot of cleanin' up, and it'd be a
whole lot easier in the barn, a lot easier to clean up the

barn, too. We can make him a bed in that stall where he slept last night—put some fresh hay in there. It'd be clean as in the house." He ignored the pointed glance Myra aimed his way for the remark.

Although it still seemed insensitive to her, Marcy realized that her parents might be right as far as making it less trouble to care for the man. She confessed to having more compassion for the wounded man than had her mother and father, and it tore at her heart to see him in such a desperate state. "I guess you're right," she conceded reluctantly. "Mama and I will clean him up and make him as comfortable as we can."

"Oh, I don't know if that's the thing to do, or not," Fred replied hesitantly. "I reckon me and Jimmy could do it."

"Don't be silly, Fred," Myra responded. "It isn't like we've never seen a man in his underwear before. Besides, you two clumsy bodies would probably kill him in the process."

"I guess you're right," Fred replied sheepishly. Still undecided what else he should do about the wounded man, he suggested, "Maybe I ought to send Jimmy over to Deer Lodge to tell the deputy about this." Then reconsidering, said, "He'd most likely tell me there wasn't anythin' he could do about it."

The matter settled, Fred drove the wagon on over to the barn and the four of them carried Cullen inside and settled him as comfortably as they could in a corner of the stall. Their patient had not spoken a word during the entire process until he was lowered onto the fresh hay prepared for him. He opened his eyes briefly as Marcy bent over him to brush a stray wisp of hay from his face. Looking up to meet her gaze, he formed one silent word, *Thanks*.

"Don't worry," she whispered. "I'll take care of you."

With their problem temporarily resolved, Myra sent Jimmy to build up the fire in the kitchen stove and put a bucket of water on to heat. She went to the house to fetch her scissors and an extra quilt to cover Cullen after she had cut his shirt away and cleaned his wounds as best they could. She sent Marcy to pull down the bolt of cotton material from the rafters over the washroom. She had bought it in Helena to make curtains for the dining room, but had never gotten around to it. She could use some of the material now for bandaging. Hesitant at first, she had caught some of her daughter's empathy for the unfortunate man lying in the barn, and resolved to make his final hours as comfortable as possible.

"You're sure he's dead?" Jack Sykes asked.

"I don't reckon I'd be wearin' this gun belt with his initials scratched on the inside if he wasn't, now, would I?" Yeager replied sarcastically. He unbuckled the belt and placed it on the table, then pointed to the initials as proof that the job had been completed. "Now let's talk about a little matter of a hundred and fifty dollars."

"Hell, how do I know you ain't just stole that gun belt?" Sykes shot back. "Besides, it mighta belonged to somebody else with the same initials. Hell, you mighta scratched them initials in there yourself. I told you I wanted proof that he was dead."

"This son of a bitch was ridin' a light bay with white stockin's, like you told me, and he said his name was Cullen McCloud," Yeager said, his tone taking on a hint of temper. "If you wanna see the damn horse, I can show it to you. There ain't nothin' more to argue about. He's dead. I pumped three slugs into him and left him lyin' in a wagon rut beside the road. I did the job. Now I want my money."

"All right, all right," Sykes replied. He was convinced that the job had been taken care of, and to question Yeager further might prove to be risky for his own health. He pulled a roll of bills out of his pocket and began counting out one hundred and fifty dollars.

"Wait a minute," Yeager said. "I thought you said a hundred and fifty, gold."

"Damn it, Bob," Sykes protested. "I ain't got it in gold. The paper's good. Hell, a dollar's a dollar, paper or gold, in any saloon in the territory."

"All right," Yeager grumbled. Then in light of his curiosity about the source of Jack Sykes' apparent wealth, he changed his attitude. "Sure thing, Jack, I know the money's good. Tell you what. Let's have a drink on it— I'm buyin'." He yelled for Stumpy to bring a bottle.

"Hell," Sykes replied, "let me buy you one." He would have preferred to part company with the man now that their business was completed, but he realized the possibility that he might need him later on for a similar type contract. According to what Roberta had told him, there was one more McCloud to worry about, depending upon how seriously Cody had been wounded. Aside from that, he wanted as little to do with Bob Yeager as possible. Yeager, on the other hand, was intent upon staying close enough to Sykes to keep an eye on him. He had something going for him that was evidently worth a lot of money, and Yeager was determined to cut himself in on the deal, whatever it was. He was especially curious about the woman who had gotten off the stage at Garrison, and he had a strong suspicion that Jack might have been the man who met her. So both men affected a cordial smile when Stumpy ambled over with a fresh bottle.

"You know, Jack," Yeager said after they had downed a couple of shots from the bottle Sykes bought, "I don't know what you've got goin' on, but judgin' by the size of that roll in your pocket, I'd say it was somethin' that pays pretty good." When his comment was met with a silent pause from Sykes, Yeager continued. "I ain't tryin' to horn in on nothin'. Hell, I say more power to you. I'm just tryin' to point out that a lot of folks think I'm a handy man to have around for them jobs that other folks don't wanna get their hands dirty on. And you know me, Jack. I can keep my mouth shut. Me and you go way back to Deer Lodge."

Sykes filled the glasses again while Yeager studied him intently, waiting for his reply. "What makes you think I've got some deal workin'?" he finally responded. "I just needed to have you take care of somebody who was givin' me trouble. There ain't no deal. I'm just tryin' to get by, same as you."

"Damn, Jack, I ain't the smartest son of a bitch around, but I've got enough sense to know that roll of bills you're carryin' didn't come from no rich uncle. And I ain't heard of no bank gettin' robbed lately. I ain't askin' for an equal share of whatever you've got goin'. I'm just askin' you to throw a little business my way."

"Damn it, Bob," Jack replied, getting a bit hot under the collar, "I already threw a little business your way and paid you good for it. If I need somebody else took care of, I'll throw you a little more, but there ain't nothin' else goin' on right now."

Yeager leaned back and thought about it for a minute, still studying Sykes intently. "Who's the woman?" he asked bluntly.

"What woman?" Jack responded, taken aback, but trying hard to keep the look of surprise from showing.

He was unsuccessful in the attempt. Yeager read the startled expression and knew he had struck a chord. "That woman that got off the stagecoach at that little swing station over on the Clark Fork. McCloud was mighty interested in that woman, and he took the same trail to Helena she took with a feller they say looked a helluva lot like you." Yeager had no description of the man who met Roberta at the stage, but he decided to throw a bluff at Sykes. Judging from Jack's expression, he was sure he had guessed right. "Them folks over there said she was your sister, or so she said." Feeling smug now with the confidence that he had struck a sensitive area in Jack's mind, he sat back and watched Sykes' reaction.

Damn! Sykes swore to himself, thinking that he'd better put a lid on that. Roberta would be fit to be tied if she knew Yeager had found out she had any connection to him or McCloud. "You've been drinkin' too much cheap whiskey," he said. "There ain't no damn woman, and I sure as hell ain't rode down to meet no stage."

"All right, then," Yeager replied after a long pause. "I reckon it was somebody else." He could see that Sykes had no intention of sharing whatever he had working, so he pretended to be done with the matter. *I'll just keep a sharp eye on you, you lying little son of a bitch.*

After a few minutes more, Sykes announced that he had to be getting along—he had other business to attend to. "You can keep the rest of that bottle," he said. "I'll look you up if I need you again."

"You do that," Yeager called after him as he headed for the door. He sat there for only a moment until Sykes had gone out the door. Then, grabbing the half-empty bottle, he quickly followed. Standing in the doorway, he paused to watch Jack make his way across the muddy street, then turn toward the hotel at the end. "Stayin' in a hotel," Yeager murmured to himself when Sykes stopped in front of the building and looked back toward the way he had come before going inside. "Yep, ol' Sykes is come a long way since sleepin' in the cell next to mine at Deer Lodge. Well, he might as well make up his mind he's got a new partner."

Chapter 9

Cody could only guess where the two outlaws might have gone after leaving Blodgett Canyon. Sheriff Tyler in Stevensville had certainly been no help, but Cody figured he couldn't really blame him. If Roberta's two abductors had not shown up in town, there was little Tyler could do. The thing that worried Cody now was the likelihood that the lady might have already met with a tragic fate. The two men would certainly avoid Fort Missoula if Roberta was still alive, but where else would they be heading? The more he thought about it as he rode into Missoula, the more he suspected he should have gone back to try to pick up Cullen's trail, for now he was simply trusting to luck. Regardless, there was little choice left to him except to ask around. Missoula was not that big a settlement, even with the additional folks seeking protection from the Nez Perce. Someone surely must have seen two men fitting Burdette's and Crocker's description, or maybe Cullen's. Thinking that his brother might have gone to the fort's commanding officer for help, he decided to try there first.

Captain Charles C. Rawn looked up when his company clerk came to his door to announce that there was a civilian wishing to speak to him. He was not inclined to spend much time listening to the problems of another civilian. Things were still uneasy in this part of the valley even after the threat of Indian attacks had passed. His decision to accept the Nez Perce chiefs' word that they would pass through the valley peacefully had proven to be a wise one. With his troops in reserve, he had backed away from the Lolo Trail and taken no action when the Indians descended the trail and started their peaceful trek to the south. Had he tried to stop the tribe's advance, it would have more than likely resulted in the loss of his entire command, especially since most of the civilian volunteers had left to return to their homes. Now with the Nez Perce already past Missoula and moving up the Bitterroot Valley, he was still concerned that there might be some minor incident that would spark an attack. They were not out of the woods quite yet.

"Another McCloud brother," Rawn remarked when told the visitor's name. "Well, send him in." He rose from his chair to receive Cody. "What can I do for you, Mr. McCloud?" When told that Cody was looking for his brother, Rawn said, "I tried to talk your brother into scouting for me, but he said he was trailing a woman, and I think she took the stage to Butte."

This only served to confuse Cody, since there was no mention of the two men who had abducted Roberta. Had she somehow managed to escape? This would be welcome news, indeed, if that were the case. Maybe the absence of the two outlaws was Cullen's doing. It would not have surprised Cody. Then a thought occurred that caused him to grin. Maybe Cullen was now following Roberta for another reason. There was no doubt that his older brother had been unsuccessful in hiding his infatuation for the handsome woman. As Cullen had been before him, Cody was surprised to hear of the stage line between there and Butte. He thought it a good idea to see if he could make sure the lady who had taken the stage was in fact Roberta.

"Next to the stables," Rawn replied when Cody asked directions to the stage office. "Say, you aren't looking for a job as a scout, are you?"

"Reckon not," Cody answered. "Might later on, though."

Bill Sawyer turned through the pages of his passenger log, pausing to run his finger down each page, searching for the name. "You're the second feller wantin' to know about that woman," he said as he continued his search. "She must be a special lady."

"You could say that," Cody replied. "This other fellow, was he a tall man, clean-shaven, ridin' a light bay?"

"That sounds like the feller. Friend of yours?"

"He's my brother."

Sawyer looked up to scrutinize Cody a little closer. "You don't favor him that much." Then he halted his finger on a name. "Here it is—last Thursday—Mrs. Roberta Lawrence," he said.

"Lawrence?" Cody responded, confused. "You mean Morris, don't you?"

"Lawrence is what she gave me," Sawyer said, and shrugged indifferently. "Your brother didn't say anything about it. He just took off after her."

Cody nodded solemnly, trying to make sense of the many confusing thoughts in his head. Something wasn't right, and he felt an urgency to find his brother and straighten the jumble of facts that he had encountered. *Morris, Lawrence; Mrs., Miss*, he wondered, hoping Cullen could explain. "Much obliged," he said, and started out along Clark Fork, heading for Butte.

Fred Sullivan was almost disappointed to find their patient still breathing the next morning. It would have made things a good deal less complicated for him if his only obligation was to dig a hole and bury the man. When he walked into the dark barn, he was surprised to see the glow from a lantern in the back stall, and Marcy already there. "You're here mighty early," Fred greeted his daughter. "How's he lookin' this mornin'?"

She saw no point in telling her father that she had remained by Cullen's side for most of the night. "I don't know, Papa," she replied. "He doesn't look much different from when we carried him in here last night." She glanced again at her patient. "He is still alive, though. Right now he's sleeping. Even when he's awake, he just lies there real quiet. He doesn't moan or say anything, just lies there with his eyes kinda half open."

Fred stroked his chin whiskers as he stared at the unconscious man, hoping he would see some sign of change, either for the better or worse. "Well, I think he still looks too near gone to haul him ten miles over to the doctor." He studied the problem for another few seconds before deciding. "We'll let him be for another day, and see if there's any improvement in the mornin'. If he shows some signs of knowin' where he is and looks like he might be gettin' better, me and Jimmy will haul him over to see Dr. Hicks."

"What if he's not any better?" Marcy replied.

"Well . . ." Fred hesitated. "I don't know. I guess we'll have to wait and see tomorrow." He cocked an eye at his daughter. "Don't you be gettin' all softhearted over this feller. He ain't one of your stray animals you're always tryin' to rescue."

She frowned indignantly. "I'm not getting softhearted or anything else. The man deserves the best care we can give him. At least his wounds aren't bleeding anymore, so that's got to be an improvement."

"I reckon so," Fred replied, still unsure. "We'll see how he makes it through the day, then decide tomorrow."

Reluctant to drag herself away from her patient, Marcy nevertheless had chores to do, so she attended to her duties, but managed to check on Cullen's progress throughout the day. Without intentionally doing so, Myra gradually deferred most of the patient care to her daughter, so that after only that one day, Cullen became Marcy's patient. She eagerly accepted the role.

Unaware of the discussion regarding his health, Cullen seemed suspended somewhere between life and death. There was no conscious concern for the direction fate might take him—recovery or death—it seemed so unimportant to him that he didn't care which was the final destination. He wasn't sure where he was, but it was a soft bed, much like a nest. When he was conscious, he lay as still as he could because even the slightest movement of his body brought on sharp spasms of pain. He was aware that it was always dark, not realizing that he was in a barn and his eyes were only half open. The voices he heard were soft—maybe the voices of angels, he could not be sure—especially one. He had no idea of the passing of time, but it was the morning of the second day that he became fully aware of the pain caused by his wounds, and the image of the scarred face of his assailant returned to bring his mind back to recall, *Tell him Bob Yeager sent you.* The words came back to jar his memory. His reaction automatic, he immediately tried to sit up, but dropped back in an overwhelming grip of pain.

"Easy, easy now. You have to lie back." It was the soft angelic voice he had heard before, and he could feel her hands on his shoulders, gently restraining him. Realizing then that he was in no immediate danger, he relaxed, his eyes blinking open wide for the first time since he'd been shot. As if he were awaking from a dream, things gradually began to come into focus, and he found himself gazing into the smiling face of Marcy Sullivan and he felt her hand on his forehead. "You lie real still," she said, "and I'll be right back with some water and a cool cloth." She left him then and he heard her calling out as she ran from the barn, "Papa! He's awake! He's gonna be all right."

A short time later, Marcy and her mother and father were standing over him, all three studying him intently. He wanted to speak, to thank them, but it seemed difficult for him to form the words, so he tried to smile instead. Fred was the first to speak, and he was not as encouraged as Marcy had been. "It's still too hard to tell if he's gonna be all right or not," he said. "Those wounds still look pretty bad and I don't think it'd be safe to try to move him. What do you think, Myra?"

His wife shook her head slowly while gazing at the unfortunate man. "He's a long way from getting out of the woods. He needs to see a doctor and get those bullets out of his body, but I don't see how he could make it that far in the wagon."

"I'll go fetch the doctor," Jimmy volunteered, having just entered the barn to find them all standing over the patient.

"All right, son," Fred replied almost reluctantly. "That's his best chance of livin', I guess. I'll help you saddle up. If you get started right away, you oughta get there and back before dark." Relieved to have the decision made for him, he followed Jimmy out of the stall.

"Thank you."

The voice was weak and a bit shaky, but the unexpected suddenness was enough to startle her. Marcy paused to smile at her patient as she applied a fresh bandage to one of the wounds in his shoulder that had started to bleed again. "So you're finally back, Mr. McCloud," she said. "I'm happy to see you can talk again."

"Cullen," he said, correcting her. "How did I get here?" His words came with great effort.

"My brother found you beside the road to Helena," she said. "He and my father brought you here." Her expression changed to one of concern. "How do you feel?"

"I don't know," he replied honestly. "I thought I was dead."

She laughed. "You looked like you were dead, but I'm going to take care of you and you'll be all right. Jimmy went to Deer Lodge to fetch the doctor. He should be back before long." A thought popped into her mind then. "Do you know where you are?"

"I think so," he said. "I know I remember you."

His answer pleased her. "Good," she said. "Now you lie back and rest a while."

He did as she instructed and was able to fall asleep again. A little after dusk, Jimmy returned from Deer Lodge. He was alone, which surprised no one, because Fred didn't expect Dr. Hicks to come until morning, so he would have enough time to see the patient and return home before dark. This was not the case, however, for Jimmy told them that Dr. Hicks was not coming. "He said he couldn't ride all the way down here," Jimmy related. "He said he was too busy to leave for the whole day, and we'd have to bring Mr. McCloud to Deer Lodge. That was the only way he could take care of him."

This was not good news to Myra or Fred, and Marcy was appalled. "Did you tell him how serious his wounds were?" she asked. Jimmy replied that he had. "Did you tell him he had been shot three times?" she implored. Jimmy nodded in response. "How could he be so indifferent?" she demanded.

"Take it easy, Marcy," Fred advised. "It don't surprise me none. We'll just have to take care of him the best we can. Maybe he's strong enough to pull himself through on his own."

"He needs a doctor," Marcy commented to no one

in particular. Then turning back to her patient, she said, "Maybe we can at least move him into the house."

Her suggestion brought an immediate, although weak, response from Cullen. "If you don't mind, I'd just as soon stay right where I am." His reaction was not entirely due to a desire to cause as little trouble as possible. Every move he made caused excruciating pain, and he didn't relish the idea of being hauled into the house by the four of them. There was also the matter of answering nature's calls. Cullen was a very private man and he speculated that this could be accomplished much easier where he was. All he needed was a bucket and the cooperation of Jimmy to empty it for him.

Marcy was the first to object and insisted that it would be unthinkable to keep him in the barn like a sick animal. She was met, however, with Cullen's feeble protests that the barn was where he wanted to be. "It don't seem fittin'," her father said, "but he may be right. It might be best not to move him till he's a little stronger. Then we can take him in the house."

Reluctantly, Marcy gave in, but promised Cullen that she would continue to check on him frequently. "Now," she said, "I'm wondering if you're strong enough to take a little something to eat." He had had nothing but a few sips of water since they had brought him in, and there had been no signs that any internal organs had been struck by the bullets. So she thought some form of nourishment might speed up his recovery. "Maybe you could handle some broth with a little meat in it," she suggested.

Cullen attempted a smile for her benefit. "I could handle a little coffee," he said.

Pleased to notice a bit of fortitude, she replied cheerfully, "Coming right up. Then we'll see if you can eat something."

He was to find that, miserable as he felt, he was not to suffer from lack of company. Thankfully, he slept much of the day, and it seemed that almost every time he awoke, it was to find Marcy smiling down at him. It was after one of these catnaps in the afternoon that she appeared carrying a bucket of hot water, a washcloth, and towels, causing his immediate concern. "Just leave 'em beside me," he said. "I can manage."

"Fiddle-de-dee," she replied. "You men don't know how to wash yourselves even when you're not shot up, and I intend to see that's it done properly. Now sit up a little, so I can get you out of that shirt. I'll help you. Just hold on to my shoulders. We'll get that shirt off and you can wear this one of Papa's."

"Really," he protested, "I can take care of it myself. I've already ruined one of your pa's shirts."

"I don't want any sass out of you," she insisted cheerfully. "And I don't see how you can change those bandages. So if you just do as I tell you, and don't give me any trouble, we'll have you all cleaned up and feeling better in no time."

Realizing that it was useless to protest for the sake of his modesty, he surrendered to the care of his attending angel. She tenderly applied the washcloths after removing his bandages, cleaning around the wounds as best she could without causing him too much pain. It was obvious to her, however, that his wounds were showing signs of festering, and it worried her to admit that he needed a doctor's care.

After tying fresh bandages on, she completed the bath of his torso, down to his belt buckle where she was stopped by his hand on hers. "I reckon I'd best do the rest, myself," he said. "Just leave me the bucket of water."

"Oh, fiddle," she scoffed. "You don't have anything too precious to see." She started to pull her hand out of his grasp, but was surprised by the strength in his grip.

"I'd best do it," he repeated softly.

"I expect he's right," Fred Sullivan said, entering the stall at that moment. "I can help him with that part."

"Much obliged," Cullen said, "but I reckon I'll manage it myself." Fred was visibly relieved.

"Silly men," Marcy remarked. "Here, let me unbuckle your belt and unbutton your pants. Then we'll spread the quilt over you and Papa can grab your pants legs and pull them off. All right?"

With all parties in agreement then, they left Cullen alone with the task of cleaning himself. "I'll have Jimmy get rid of all the wet hay and put in some fresh," Fred said in parting. Outside the barn, he spoke to his daughter. "Those wounds need some attention. They ain't gonna heal on their own." It was an unnecessary comment, for she was already of the same opinion. "And, Marcy," he continued, "it's best if you don't go gettin' yourself too wound up in takin' care of that man. He seems a nice enough fellow, but we don't know anythin' about him. There must be some reason somebody shot him."

"Oh, Papa," Marcy responded impatiently, "I'm not wound up in anything. We'd take care of anybody in his condition." Even as she said it, she knew inside that she would probably not give as much attention to the average person.

"I'm just concerned about you, darlin'. Like I said, we don't really know anythin' about him."

Jimmy dumped the wheelbarrow full of wet hay out back of the barn and spread it around with his pitchfork so the sun could dry it out. Laying the pitchfork in the empty wheelbarrow, he had started back toward the front of the barn when a man on a horse out by the road caught his eye. The rider had stopped where the lane to the house turned off the road, and he was sitting there as if deciding whether or not to follow it. Always with a keen interest in horses, Jimmy paused to admire the gray spotted Appaloosa. The rider, seeing him then, turned the horse toward the lane, and Jimmy stood watching as the Appaloosa traveled the two hundred yards at a gentle lope. Jimmy could not help taking notice of the easy way the rider moved in rhythm with the horse's motion as if he were part of the horse.

Pulling up before the boy, Cody said, "Howdy."

"Howdy," Jimmy returned.

Cody looked around him, glancing at the barn, the house beyond, and the corral, now holding two dozen horses that Jimmy and his father had recently brought in from the pasture. Cody nudged the Appaloosa and slowly walked him by the corral, looking the horses over just in case he saw Cullen's bay. Then turning back to the boy, he asked, "Is this the swing station for the stagecoach line?" When Jimmy confirmed that it was,

Cody considered stopping for the night, since it was already close to dusk. "Can I buy some supper here? Or is that just for the stage passengers?"

"Yessir, my mama will fix you some supper for fifty cents, and I'll take care of that Appaloosa for you." He stepped back and watched the stranger dismount, sizing him up, just as he had with the horse. He was not unusually tall, Jimmy speculated, maybe a shade taller than his father, but he looked a good deal more powerful through the shoulders, and he stood balanced, as though he was poised to spring. Jimmy was reminded of a mountain lion. "You headed for Butte?" he asked.

Cody smiled. "Maybe—I'm lookin' for someone. Mighta rode this way a while back. Maybe you've seen him—tall fellow, ridin' a light bay horse with white stockings."

Jimmy knew at once he was describing Cullen, but in light of recent circumstances, he was careful about answering questions from strangers. He might be looking for Cullen for the same reason the man who shot him was. "Is he a friend of yours?"

"He's my brother," Cody answered.

Jimmy studied the stranger's face for a moment before deciding. There was no hint of meanness in the intense blue eyes. In fact, it was a face that hinted at lightheartedness. Jimmy decided to risk the gamble. "He's in the barn, bad wounded." He saw the sudden change in the pleasant features, now frozen in puzzlement. "Come on, I'll show you," he said. Leaving the wheelbarrow where it was, he spun around and led Cody into the barn.

"Damn!" Cody exclaimed when he saw Cullen lying in the stall. Instantly concerned, then just as quickly angered, he rushed to kneel at his brother's side. He was about to ask if he was dead, but Cullen opened his eyes at that moment. Cody glanced back at the boy and demanded, "What the hell's he doin' in the barn?"

Before Jimmy could answer, Cullen formed a weak smile. "Hello, Cody. I was wonderin' when you'd show up."

Having just left one of his brothers who ignored the doctor's pronounced death prediction, Cody was not prepared to find Cullen in like condition. "What—" he stammered. "How bad is it? . . . What happened?" And before Cullen could answer, he fixed his accusing eye on the boy and demanded again, "What the hell is he doin' out here in the barn?" Jimmy was left to absorb all of Cody's anger.

"Don't go blamin' Jimmy or his folks," Cullen said. "They wanted to take me in the house, but I didn't wanna be moved." He paused to take a deep breath as if the talking was tedious, then continued. "I'm hurt pretty bad, shot three times, but I reckon I'll make it if my luck holds out. What about Jug? Is he gonna make it?"

"Hell yeah. He laid around for a couple of days. Then we knew he was all right when he started yellin' at Smoke for some grub. I'll tell you all about it later. What I wanna know now is who shot you and what happened to Roberta." While he talked, he lifted the edge of one of the bandages and peered at the wound. "Damn!" he snorted, wrinkling his nose in protest as the odor of infection assaulted his nostrils. "That looks bad. Has a doctor seen these wounds yet?"

Jimmy answered, "I went to fetch the doctor at Deer Lodge, but he wouldn't come. He said we'd have to bring your brother to his office."

Cody's reaction was evident on his face. He looked back at Cullen and asked, "Can you make it? How far is Deer Lodge?"

"I swear, I hate to admit it," Cullen said, "but I don't think so. Every time I move I start bleedin' again."

"Well, we'll just bring the doctor here, then," Cody said. "I just pulled one brother through. I ain't plannin' on losin' you."

"I thought I saw a strange horse at the barn door."

Cody turned at the remark to see Fred enter the stall with Marcy at his elbow. "You a friend of Cullen's?"

"I'm his brother," Cody replied.

Noticing the agitated expression on Cody's face, Fred was quick to explain. "We were gonna bring him in the house, but he didn't wanna be moved."

"Yeah, he told me," Cody said. "He needs a doctor. I'll go fetch him. What's his name?"

"Hicks," Fred answered, "Dr. Hicks. He won't come, though. We already sent Jimmy to get him."

Cody took a long look at Fred, then let his gaze settle on Marcy for a moment before he smiled and remarked, "He'll come. Jimmy probably wasn't askin' him real politelike. How far is Deer Lodge from here?"

"Ten miles," Fred answered, "but he'll be gone to bed by the time you get there."

"Ten miles, huh?" Cody replied, ignoring the rest of Fred's comment. "I need to borrow a horse—mine needs a rest. Any of those horses in the corral saddle-broke, or is haulin' a stagecoach all they know?"

"You can take my horse," Jimmy piped up, already impressed with Cody's aggressive manner. "He's fast and he's strong." Then remembering his place, he asked, "Is that all right, Pa?" Fred nodded his consent and told Jimmy to switch Cody's saddle over.

"Much obliged," Cody said, smiling at the boy. Then he turned his attention back to Cullen to hear all the details that resulted in his brother lying wounded in a barn. After hearing the complete story, he only became more and more angry, especially with the part that Roberta had played in the evil deceit. "I swear, she had us all fooled," he commented, shaking his head in astonishment for the gullibility they had all shared, even Smoke, who was cynical about everything. "This fellow that shot you—Bob Yeager you said his name was— you never saw him before?" Cullen shook his head. "Would you recognize him if you saw him again?"

"That shouldn't be hard to do," Marcy spoke up. "He looks like Satan himself, and he has a long scar from his ear all the way down to the corner of his mouth." She had been standing, silently observing the reunion between the two brothers and watching her patient's reaction to Cody's sudden appearance. She decided that there was a great deal of affection between the two. "You'll be wanting something to eat before you go," she said.

"Why, thank you, miss, but I expect I'd best not wait around for that. I think the sooner I get back here with the doctor, the better, so I'll get goin'."

"I won't be but a minute," she said, and hurried out of the stall. By the time Jimmy led his horse to the barn door, Marcy was back from the kitchen with a ham biscuit wrapped in a cloth. Handing it up to Cody, she said, "Here, this will hold you for a little while." She stepped back then and added, "Good luck."

"Thank you, miss," Cody replied, and touched a finger to his hat politely. Turning to Jimmy, he said, "Take care of my horse. He could use a portion of grain. His name's Buttermilk." With that, he turned the roan toward the Butte road, disappearing from their sight in the growing dusk.

"Who was that?" Myra Sullivan asked, just joining them as Cody rode up the lane to the road.

"Cullen's brother," her husband answered. "He's gone to fetch Doc Hicks."

"I thought you said—" Myra started.

"We told him," Fred replied before she had a chance to finish her remark, "but he thinks he'll come with him."

"He'll bring him," Cullen spoke up then. "Cody's used to accomplishin' whatever he sets his mind to do."

Marcy moved over closer and placed her hand on Cullen's brow. "You're starting to feel a little feverish again. You'd better rest now. There's been too much talking going on." She gave them a stern look then and ordered, "Everybody go on out of here now and let him rest."

"Now, who can that be at this hour?" Nora Hicks complained, dressed in her nightgown and preparing to join her husband, who was already in bed. "Somebody's probably having a baby, or some young'un's got a bellyache." She was well accustomed to late visitors knocking on her door, although the townsfolk knew that her husband went to bed with the chickens.

"Tell 'em to come to the office in the morning," Dr. Hicks called from the bedroom, knowing that these late-night callers were seldom emergency cases. It was usually something that bothered them all day. Then when it didn't improve by bedtime, they thought they had to see the doctor.

Nora opened the front door and held the oil lamp up to see who was knocking. The face she saw in the flickering lamplight was not one she recognized. "Yes?" she asked.

"I need the doctor, ma'am," Cody said. "My brother's bad wounded and he needs Dr. Hicks right away."

"The doctor's already gone to bed," Nora said. "He'll be in the office in the morning. Come to see him then."

"Ah, no, ma'am," Cody said as politely as he could manage. "It won't wait that long. He's lying in a barn with three bullet holes in him, and they don't look too good."

Listening to the conversation from the bedroom, Elbert Hicks was already pulling on his trousers. In a few minutes' time, he came to the door to talk to the man. "Gunshot, huh?" he asked, and looked beyond Cody, expecting to see a wagon with a body. "Where is he?"

"He's at that stagecoach station back down the road a piece," Cody answered.

"Well, good God, man," Hicks responded impatiently, "I can't treat him if you don't bring him here. I already told that boy to bring the man to my office."

"The thing is," Cody explained very patiently, "he's too bad off to move. It might kill him."

"That place is ten miles from here, maybe more," Hicks protested, growing more and more irritated by the stone-faced expression on the stranger's face. "From what the boy told me, the man's been lying in that barn for a couple of days. One more day ain't likely to make the difference, so let me know in the morning if he's still the same, and I'll take a ride down there to see him. That's about the best I can do for you." As far as he was concerned, the discussion was over, and he placed his hand on the door, preparing to close it.

"I don't think you understand," Cody said calmly, and blocked the door with his foot. "This is my brother we're wastin' time jawin' about. He needs a doctor now. I wasn't askin' you if you wanted to come with me. I apologize for not makin' that clear right from the start, but we won't waste any more time. You'd best pull a coat on. It's a bit chilly in the evenin' air. I'll just come in while you're gettin' ready to go, and then we'll go out to the barn and saddle your horse."

Hardly able to believe the audacity of the stranger, Dr. Hicks retorted, "What are you gonna do, shoot me if I don't go?"

"I'd just as soon," Cody replied, still calm, "but I need you to take care of my brother, so I'd probably shoot her first." He nodded toward the doctor's wife, who had now backed against the doorframe, her mouth as well as her eyes gaping wide.

"You're insane to think you can kidnap me," Hicks continued to protest. "We have laws in this town. My

God, man, you're only a stone's throw from the territorial prison."

"You ain't the first to call me crazy and I was hopin' I wasn't gonna have to show you how crazy I can get when folks insist on wastin' my time." He dropped his hand to rest on the handle of his .44. "Now let's get goin'. Get your bag or whatever you need to treat a gunshot wound. We've got a fair piece to ride." He glanced at the doctor's wife, who was still paralyzed in a state of shock. She seemed incapable of moving, but he was not willing to chance her sudden awakening and call to action, so he said, "You'd best come along with us to the barn while we saddle up."

He was forced to draw his pistol when the doctor attempted one final effort to resist, causing Cody to dispense with all pretense of politeness. "Let's get one thing straight," he warned. "You're gonna make a house call tonight, and it's gonna be up to you how you do it. Tied up and lyin' across the back of your horse, or sittin' up in the saddle—it doesn't make any difference to me. But if it was me, I'd rather ride in the saddle instead of bouncin' on my belly for ten miles."

"All right, damn you," Hicks gave in. The look in the young man's eyes conveyed a clear message that it was no idle threat. "But don't think you're going to get away with this outrage," he threatened.

"You just saved yourself a lot of bother," Cody said. He gave no thought to the consequences that might occur from abducting the doctor. His only concern was that his brother needed medical attention. He herded the doctor and his wife out to the small stable where Hicks kept his horse and waited while the doctor saddled the horse and climbed aboard. Then, taking the reins, he led him outside to Jimmy's horse. Worried to the point of collapse, his terrified wife dutifully handed her husband his coat and medicine case when instructed to, then stepped quickly back. Cody nodded toward the path to the road and Hicks headed out. Cody held back a few seconds, then leaned down close to Nora's ear and whispered, "I ain't really gonna hurt him. Don't worry about him. He'll be back in the mornin' safe and sound." Then he loped off after the doctor.

Not a word passed between them as they rode through the night, their way lit by a three-quarter moon riding in a clear starry sky, but thoughts ran rampant through the doctor's mind. When the last of the farmhouses was behind them, and there was nothing but the night surrounding them, his anger began to give way to concern for his safety. The relentless man behind him was undoubtedly insane, and what would stop him from murdering the doctor when he had served his needs— especially if he was not successful in the treatment? Speculation upon the question was fuel enough to make for a long, worrisome ride to the Garrison station.

It was well past midnight when they reached the lane leading to the Sullivan house, but Cody could see a lantern glow coming from the back stall in the barn. He directed Dr. Hicks toward it. "In the barn?" Hicks questioned, his first words since leaving Deer Lodge. "Did you kidnap me to treat a horse?"

Cody didn't bother to remind him that it was his brother he had come to see. "Just ride right on into the barn," he directed. As they were dismounting, Jimmy came from the back stall to meet them. "How's he doin'?" Cody asked.

"About like he was when you left," Jimmy answered. "Marcy's with him. She stayed with him the whole time. Mama and Papa finally went to bed about an hour ago." He took the reins of both horses. "I see you got the doctor."

Dr. Hicks offered no more than a low grunt in response as he pushed by the boy, his recent fears giving way once again to anger. He was met at the door of the stall by Marcy.

"You came!" Marcy greeted him. "Bless you, Doctor. It was so good of you to come. I didn't know what else to do for him."

Finding it difficult to be gruff in the face of such an honest show of appreciation, Hicks muttered his reply. "Your friend here is very persuasive." He glanced at Cody, who answered with the hint of a smile. "All right," Hicks said then. "Let's take a look at the patient." He figured that as long as he was there he might as well do what he could. Glancing at Marcy, he said, "Maybe you can help me here. Are you his wife?" He made the assumption based on her apparent concern for the patient.

"We ain't got around to that yet," Cullen answered weakly while Marcy flushed red with embarrassment.

Mildly surprised when Cullen spoke, Hicks said, "Oh, so you're alive." He turned back to the blushing young lady then and instructed, "Go ahead and remove those bandages and we'll see how bad those wounds are." He looked at Cody and said, "I'm gonna need some hot water."

"I can get that," Jimmy volunteered, and was immediately off to the kitchen.

After Marcy removed Cullen's bandages, Dr. Hicks knelt beside him. "Good Lord," he exclaimed in a whisper. "No wonder you're sick as hell. It's a miracle you aren't dead." He motioned to Marcy. "Bring that lantern over closer, so I can see. What was your name?" When Marcy told him, he continued. "Well, Marcy, I'm gonna have to do some cutting here and I'm gonna need you to help me." He opened his bag and took out several instruments. "I need to have these in a pan of boiling water, so we don't introduce any more infection than he's already gotten in those wounds." He paused and looked around him at his improvised surgery, then shook his head in disbelief. "I'm gonna need some coffee, too," he called after Marcy as she left with the instruments to be sterilized.

In the absence of whiskey, which Cody considered the anesthetic of choice, Dr. Hicks spoon-fed the patient laudanum. The bitter mixture of alcohol and opium was intended to help with the pain as well as make Cullen sleepy. "He'll most likely need it more after I work on him than he does now. This will help a little, but he'll probably pass out from the pain when I get into those wounds."

When Marcy returned with the boiled instruments, she was accompanied by her father. Hicks had finished cleaning around the wounds with the water Jimmy had brought and was waiting for her. "Mighty considerate of you to come down here to help this man," Fred Sullivan said. "My wife is makin' you some coffee. She'll bring it down directly." Hicks nodded a half-hearted acknowledgment, then turned his full attention to his patient.

The first rays of the morning sun peeked through the small windows in the side of the barn, casting shadows across the hay-covered floor of the stall as Hicks stood back and gazed at the still form on the bed of hay. Taking his cup from a shelf by the window, he drained the last of the now cold coffee and announced, "That's about all I can do for him."

Jimmy tiptoed into the stall and asked, "Is he dead?"

Hicks shook his head and sighed. "No, but he oughta be."

"Mama said to tell you she's got breakfast ready any time you want it," Jimmy said.

Hicks answered with a weary nod of his head. He turned then to confront Cody, who stood waiting in the doorway. "You did a helluva fine job, Doc," Cody said. "I appreciate it and I'll pay you your fee for coming down here."

Hicks shook his head in tired amazement, finding it hard to remain angry at the persistent young man. "Don't thank me too soon," he replied. "He ain't out of the woods just yet. It's up to him now, but I'd say he's got a fifty-fifty chance. I got the bullet out of his back and one out of his chest. I couldn't get to that other one near his lung. I'da killed him sure enough if I had probed any deeper. They'll leave some pretty bad scars, but I can't help that." He turned to face Marcy then. "I'll leave this bottle of laudanum with you. He's gonna be in a lot of pain, but go easy on this stuff, one or two teaspoons. No more than that or you're liable to kill him. You can give him a dose when he wakes up."

"Come on, Doc," Cody said, "let's go on up to the house and get some breakfast."

"I need to wash up first," Dr. Hicks replied, and looked down at some spots of blood on his chest, just then remembering that he was still wearing his night-shirt tucked in his trousers. "I reckon I'm lucky I pulled my boots on," he mumbled. Then casting an eye at Cody, he quipped, "I suppose you would have shot me if I had tried to put on my shirt."

Cody laughed. "Ah, Doc, you know I wasn't ever gonna shoot you."

Hicks studied Cody's face for a long moment before admitting, "Well, you may well have saved your brother's life. If those wounds had gone untreated, infection would have probably killed him. At least now he's got a chance."

Eager to show her appreciation for the doctor's work, and in view of the conditions under which he had been enlisted, Myra Sullivan went all out in preparing a break-fast of bacon, eggs, potatoes, biscuits, hot coffee, and fresh milk. Never before had a hostage been treated so royally. Before the breakfast was over, Dr. Hicks found himself chatting neighborly with Fred and Myra, and telling them the news from Deer Lodge.

When it was finally finished, the doctor announced that he had better be getting back before his wife had a posse out looking for him. Cody offered to ride back with him, but Hicks insisted that he didn't need an escort. "Besides, Nora's probably got hold of the sher-iff by now, and there might be a welcoming party wait-ing for you."

"All right," Cody said, "if you say so. How much do I owe you for the call?"

Hicks had to chuckle, astonished by his new attitude. "Nothing," he said. "I'll take a dollar for that bottle of laudanum. Myra's breakfast was payment enough for the surgery."

"That's mighty kind of you, Doc," Cody said. "Put it down in your ledger that I owe you a favor." He walked to the corner of the corral with him where Jimmy was waiting with his horse. When Hicks was seated in the saddle, Cody grinned and said, "If you change your mind by the time you get home and decide to tell the deputy marshal 'bout being kidnapped, I'll be gone by the time they can get here."

"I'll keep it in mind," Hicks replied. "Tell your brother I'll come back in a couple of days if I can, just to see if he's still alive."

"'Preciate it," Cody said. He was only halfway joking when he had said he'd be gone before the sheriff could get there. He would stay long enough to make sure Cullen was going to make a recovery, but then he would be on his way as soon as he got a little more information from his brother about the man who shot him.

Chapter 10

It was her belief that the world owed Roberta Sykes a hell of a lot for the injustice she had suffered when God, fate, or whatever decreed that she should be born the daughter of a penny-ante drunken gambler named Wilfred Sykes. Sykes was an abusive husband and father, and Roberta was glad when he was knifed to death in a barroom brawl. She was only twelve at the time, but she remembered the feeling of grim satisfaction when seeing her father's body, his shirtfront starched with dried blood from his wounds. Although her mother sobbed at the funeral, Roberta was convinced the tears were shed because of the poor woman's despair for being widowed with two young children, and none wasted for the demise of the worthless husband.

It was pick and scratch for Bonnie Sykes and her two young'uns for the next three years, but for Roberta, it was the only happy time of her young life. Sadly, that ended when her mother met widower Jonah Morris. It was soon evident that Morris was looking for a wife to replace his dearly departed one, but he was not in the market for children. This was soon blatantly demonstrated when Roberta and her younger brother, Jack, were instructed to address their new stepfather as *Uncle Jonah,* instead of father. This was in an effort to appease the Morris side of the family. Naturally this helped ensure that the Sykeses and the Morrises never got along, and in fact, enjoyed open hostility between the offspring of the two sides of the union.

Jack was the first to break away from the arrangement. Being more like his father, he naturally gravitated toward the lawless side of society, establishing himself as a certified member of the outlaw world when he killed a man in a bar fight. Unlike his late father, he came out of the confrontation the winner, but found himself wanted by the law. Roberta remained in the unpleasant home environment until her mother died from pneumonia. While Jonah Morris was never abusive, he was instrumental in furthering Roberta's disgust for men in general when he suggested that she might consider taking her mother's place and become the third Mrs. Morris. A concept that was certainly repugnant to anyone with a modicum of decency, for Roberta it aided in an outright hatred for the male species. Just turned seventeen, she left the home of Jonah Morris, determined to make her way in the world on her own, promising herself that she would never be subservient to any man. She soon discovered that her main attribute was the beauty she inherited from her mother, unlike Jack, who seemed to be a replica of his father. It naturally followed that she learned that this asset gave her power over men, and she never hesitated to use it to her advantage.

Now, as she strolled out of the hotel on her way to the haberdashery to look at some material for a new gown, she enjoyed a smug sense of accomplishment for her aggressive acquisition of Gabriel Morris' fortune. The cost in human lives had been dear, but not to her, for there were none lost that she deemed worth saving. While ol' Gabe's gold was substantial, she was shrewd enough to know it would not last forever, and would best be used to invest for her future. The investment she had decided upon came to her quite by accident when a gentleman she met in the hotel dining room told her that he was traveling through this part of the country mapping out future lines for the railroad. In the intimate privacy of his bedroom, he confided to her that the next year would see the tracks reach as far as Coulson. Contrary to common belief by the people of Coulson, however, the railroad planned to go beyond that town about six miles to a new settlement called Billings. Roberta was smart enough to know that land for the new railroad would be worth a great deal, so she decided to use her fortune to buy up as much of that land as she could before the news reached the locals of that small town on the Yellowstone. She frowned when reminded of that portion of the gold dust that was wasted on Jack. *Like so many men*, she thought, *Jack hasn't got enough sense to handle that amount of money. It's too bad I had to cut him in for part of the deal.* It had been necessary, however, for she had required his outlaw connections to take care of the messy parts of her plan. She registered an involuntary shudder, accompanied by an expression of disgust when she thought about the sacrifices she had made of her body.

Calling her mind back to more pleasant thoughts, she smiled at the prospect of an even greater increase in her wealth as a landowner, but was suddenly stopped cold by the sight of a man on a horse near the end of the street. "Damn!" she uttered softly, not sure at once, and stepped inside the doorway of the hardware store until she was certain. "Damn," she hissed again, for after a hard look, she recognized Cody McCloud. *That worthless son of a bitch,* she thought, thinking of Bob Yeager, who had been paid to take care of the McCloud brothers. She watched for a moment more until certain that he was going to continue down the street past her. Then she stepped inside the store to watch him through the window. How did he even know to look for her in Helena? And there was no doubt in her mind that he was looking for her.

"Can I help you, ma'am?"

She turned to give the proprietor a cursory glance and replied, "No, thanks. I was just looking at these tools you have in the window." She pretended to look at them until Cody rode on past the store toward the stables at the end of the street. Forgetting the haberdashery then, she left the hardware store and made her way quickly back to the hotel.

"Howdy," Malcolm Barnes greeted Cody when he reined up before the stable door and stepped down. "You lookin' to board your horse?"

"Yeah," Cody replied. "I don't know for how long, though, so I'll just pay you a day at a time."

"All right," Barnes said. "You can stow your saddle in the tack room." He turned and pointed. "You want grain?"

"Yep," Cody replied as he loosened the girth strap and pulled the saddle off. Barnes walked over and held the gate open while Cody led Buttermilk into the corral, pulled his bridle off, and gave him a slap on the rump. He closed the gate again, then stood with a foot propped on the bottom rail and looked over the other horses in the corral. "See any strangers in town the last few days?"

Barnes shrugged. "Some," he said.

"Who belongs to that bay over there against the fence—the light one with the white stockin's?"

"I don't know his name," Barnes answered. "Feller brought him in here with another horse."

"Have a long scar across the side of his face?"

"Matter of fact he did," Barnes replied. "Friend of yours?"

"Yeah," Cody said softly. "Know where I can find him?"

"Nope. I ain't got no idea."

"Know when he's comin' back?"

"He didn't say. Didn't seem to be in any hurry, though."

Cody turned his attention away from the horses to gaze at Barnes. "Much obliged for the information. How much you charge to sleep in the barn?"

"Quarter."

"Fair enough," Cody replied, and paid Barnes what

he owed for one night plus a portion of oats for Buttermilk. When Barnes asked if he needed anything else before he went back to the house, Cody said, "Have you got a file I can borrow for a minute? I think my horse has a burr on one shoe that needs filin' off." Barnes went to get the file while Cody carried his saddle into the tack room and pulled his rifle out of the sling.

"Here you go," Barnes said when he returned. "Just leave it in the tack room when you're done. I've got some dinner gettin' cold in the house."

"Much obliged," Cody said. He waited until Barnes walked away before opening the gate to the corral. He had no difficulty then cornering Cullen's horse. The bay knew him well and stood patiently while Cody filed two deep marks in his right front shoe. *That'll make it a little easier if I have to find you later on*, he thought. That done, he picked up his rifle and headed back up the street to check in the saloons for the man with a scar.

"Feller down at the desk said you were lookin' for me," Jack Sykes said when Roberta opened the door. "What's goin' on?" He walked into her room when she held the door wide for him. She didn't look pleased.

"There's a little matter of some business that wasn't taken care of," she said. "I just saw Cody McCloud riding down the middle of the street. He didn't look very dead to me."

Jack grimaced. "You sure it was McCloud?"

"Of course I'm sure," Roberta responded. "So you need to find that damn Bob Yeager and tell him to finish the job he was paid to do. And I mean right now. This town isn't big enough to avoid McCloud."

"All right, all right," Jack replied. "I'll get him. I know where he's probably at. Don't get all riled up about it. I'll take care of it."

He started to leave, but she stopped him. "After you see Yeager, get our horses from the stable. We're checking out of here today."

"And goin' where?" Jack asked.

"Coulson," Roberta replied.

"Coulson?" her brother replied incredulously. "What in the hell would we want to go back there for?" He couldn't believe she would want to return to the place where Jonah Morris and his clan lived. They had both escaped the little settlement to get away from them.

"Because I found out that the railroad is going to run their tracks that far within a year. Not many people know it, but they are going to bypass Coulson and go about five or six miles west of there to a new settlement called Billings. I plan to buy up as much of that land around there as I can with Gabe Morris' money. If you're smart, you'll let me use your share, too." Seeing the instant frown on his face, she said, "It'd be a lot smarter than spending it on whiskey and whores." When he still seemed hesitant, she continued. "Picture the look on old Jonah Morris' face when he finds out we own the whole damn valley. And the joke of it is we'll buy it with his brother Gabe's gold."

That brought a smile to Jack's face. "Maybe you're right. That'ud be somethin', wouldn't it?"

"Good," she concluded. "First thing, though, is to take care of Mr. Cody McCloud."

"I'll go find Yeager." He left her then, his head filled with thoughts of returning home a wealthy landowner.

He chuckled when he thought about his shrewd sister and realized how fortunate he was to be able to benefit from her gall. *I wonder if I'm still wanted by the law over there.*

As Jack suspected, Yeager wasn't hard to find. With his recent accumulation of cash, he had practically made the Red Dog Saloon his center of operations. Having earned a new status of respect from Stumpy as soon as he flashed a sizable roll of greenbacks, he seemed content to languish in the rough saloon on the edge of town, even renting one of Stumpy's spare rooms to sleep in. Jack found him seated at a corner table in the rear with his back to the wall. When Sykes walked in the front door, Yeager favored him with a scornful sneer as he approached his table. He was still irritated by Jack's rejection of his attempt to become a partner in what he suspected was a moneymaking caper. "Well, well," he slurred sarcastically, "if it ain't my old pal, Jack Sykes. You got another little job you want done?"

Jack glanced at Stumpy long enough to order a glass of beer, then pulled out a chair and sat down. Fixing a stern eye on Yeager, he replied, "No, I'm wantin' you to finish up a little job you already got paid for."

Not sure what he meant, Yeager tilted his head back to glare at Sykes for a long moment before responding verbally, "What the hell are you talkin' about?"

Jack waited for a few seconds while Stumpy placed a glass of beer before him on the table and waited for payment. When the peg-legged bartender went back to the bar, Jack continued. "I'm talkin' about Cody McCloud walkin' around town big as life," he said, making an effort to keep his voice down.

"Who?" Yeager responded.

"McCloud, damn it," Jack said, "the other McCloud brother. There were two of 'em. You only got one of 'em, and you were paid to take care of both of 'em."

"Now, wait a damn minute." Yeager rose, indifferent to whether Stumpy heard him or not. "The deal was to take care of 'em, one or two, however many showed up. Didn't but one of 'em show up and I by God took care of him." He paused to toss back the rest of the shot glass of whiskey, then looking calm again, said, "Our business was finished." He sat back to watch Jack's reaction.

"How the hell can it be finished when there's still one of 'em walkin' around lookin' for trouble?" He refrained from saying *looking for Roberta*. "You don't understand," he continued when an idea struck him. "I'm just tellin' you as a favor. I expect Cody McCloud is in town lookin' for the man who killed his brother. He ain't lookin' for me. He ain't ever laid eyes on me. I'm just tryin' to warn you that you'd better get him first." He could tell by Yeager's reaction that his comment had struck home.

A sudden change of expression from insolence to one of concern revealed that Yeager had not given thought to that possibility. He was giving it his attention now. To begin with, he had no way of recognizing Cody McCloud other than the fact that he rode an Appaloosa. If they met him walking on the street, neither he nor Jack would know him from the man in the moon.

"Hell, I can't just shoot him down in the street, even if I did know what he looks like," Yeager complained. "They got law in this town."

"I expect you'd best figure out what he looks like before he finds out what you look like," Jack suggested, his enjoyment of the situation growing with Yeager's obvious concern. "And you'd best do it quick." He had expected to have to pay Yeager more money to take care of the second brother. He was complimenting himself for placing the onus upon the assassin. "I just wanted to warn you so you could get the jump on him before he finds you."

"Don't you worry none about that," Yeager said, trying to regain a portion of his previous arrogance. "He'll cuss the day he ever found Bob Yeager." In spite of his bluster, he was strongly considering the wisdom of hanging around waiting for Cody to come after him. It might be better to simply leave town. If he knew what McCloud looked like, he'd risk bushwhacking him if the situation was such that he could avoid witnesses. The more he thought about it, though, the more a move to Butte or somewhere else seemed attractive.

The same thoughts were going through the minds of both men, and the realization that Yeager just might elect to head for parts unknown occurred then to Jack. To prevent Yeager from running before McCloud was taken care of, he decided it was a good idea to sweeten the pot a little. "We'd all be better off if that McCloud feller ran into a bullet," he said. "It'd be worth another fifty dollars to me if you'd go ahead and finish the job."

It was enough to cause second thoughts for Yeager. "Maybe I'll take you up on that," he said, still undecided. After Sykes left him, he decided to stay one more night in Helena on the chance he found some way of identifying Cody McCloud, and was able to get a shot at him.

While the man he searched for had withdrawn from the saloon for the night in one of Stumpy's back rooms, Cody left the first saloon he had visited, heading for the second one, which was on the opposite side of the street. It proclaimed itself to be the Last Chance Saloon, in obvious reference to the gulch that was the source of the gold that gave birth to the mining town when four prospectors from Georgia made their strike. The Georgians had called the gulch Last Chance Gulch and when the town was built, the name remained to distinguish the main street, which ran alongside the gulch.

As he had found in the first saloon, there was no one inside who sported a scar quite as distinctive as the one Cullen had described. When asked if he knew a man named Bob Yeager, the bartender could not recall anyone answering to that name. "There's two more saloons no more'n a stone's throw up the street," the bartender offered. "Maybe one of them has seen him."

"Much obliged," Cody said, and headed for the door. Stepping outside on the board sidewalk, he paused to look up the street in the direction the bartender had mentioned. It was past sundown by then, and a dull haze was settling in over the dusty street. Had he thought to look back toward the stables, he might have noticed a man and woman preparing to step up in the saddle, before guiding their horses toward the end of the street, a heavily laden packhorse being led by the man. His mind set more toward the scar-faced man he sought, Cody's concentration was on the next saloon in line.

His luck was no better in either of the two, so he decided to have a drink in the last one, a new establishment called Jake's. It occurred to him as he tossed his whiskey back that there was a good possibility that Yeager might have made the same sleeping arrangements that he had. When asking Malcolm Barnes at the stable about Cullen's bay gelding, he had not asked, nor had Barnes volunteered, where Yeager might be spending the night. *That might have been the bright thing to ask,* he berated himself silently. Saying good evening to Jake, he started to leave, but Jake mentioned that there was another saloon he might try out on the edge of town. "It's the Red Dog Saloon," he said. "Feller named Stumpy owns it. Don't many respectable folks go there, but maybe your friend did."

"How far is it?" Cody asked. When told that it was a little over a mile, he decided to go back to the stables for his horse, but was intercepted before he passed the Last Chance Saloon.

"Hold on there a minute, young feller." Cody turned to see a man wearing a sheriff's badge coming out the door of the saloon. Sheriff Wendall Price, a lean, raw-boned man with a long handlebar mustache, stepped down to face Cody on the walk. Cody stopped and waited while Price strolled casually up to him. "Ain't ever seen you in my town before," the sheriff said.

"Ain't ever been here before," Cody replied.

"I'm always interested in meetin' strangers in town, you know, find out why they're visitin' Helena." As the sheriff talked, Cody noticed that he was looking him over thoroughly, paying special attention to the

Winchester rifle Cody was carrying. "What brings you to town?"

"I'm just passin' through," Cody answered, "and as long as I was here, I thought I'd look for a friend of mine." So far, the interview was polite and friendly enough, but he was convinced there was a deeper reason than mere curiosity. With all the strangers who surely passed through the bustling town of Helena, Cody had no illusions that the sheriff greeted each one in this manner. It only took a few moments more to confirm his suspicions.

"What's your name?" Price asked. When Cody answered, the sheriff asked, "Who's this friend you're lookin' for? What's his name?"

Not happy with the way the conversation was going at this point, Cody answered cautiously, "His name's Bob Yeager. Maybe you've seen him."

"No, can't say that I have. What do you want with him?"

Cody hesitated for a moment before answering. Finally, he gave the sheriff a little smile and replied, "Well, now, I reckon there's a little business between us that doesn't concern anybody else. Like I said, he's a friend."

"Everybody's business in this town concerns me," Price said, "especially when a stranger comes to town with a rifle in his hand, lookin' all over for somebody."

Cody smiled again. "This is a strange little town you got here, Sheriff. You got laws against carryin' a rifle and laws against lookin' for a friend. I expect your jail ain't big enough to hold everybody that's breaking those laws."

"Well, there's another little matter that we need to talk about," Price said. "There's a young lady over at the hotel that says a feller by the name of Cody McCloud has been followin' her all the way from Fort Missoula, and she fears for her life."

Cody could only gape dumbfounded for a second, amazed by Roberta's unabashed gall in going to the law for protection. Until that moment, he had not suspected that the conscienceless vixen was even in Helena. Unprepared as he was to answer, he stumbled for an explanation, not at all certain that the sheriff would accept his version of the story Roberta had already told. "Sheriff, you ain't the first man that's swallowed that woman's lies."

"That a fact?" Price replied, showing little emotion. "Well, you can understand my position. A right respectable lady comes to me, sayin' she just got to town and there's a man chasin' her. Then I get reports that that same man is lookin' all over town for somebody with a scar on his face. You say he's a friend, but somehow I don't believe that's the case. But it sure makes for an interestin' story, so I think we'll just let you rest up in our fine jail tonight, and we'll see if we can sort some truth outta all this in the mornin'." His tone was not unlike that of a patient father, disciplining a troublesome child. "Now, you'd best hand me that Winchester and ease that pistol outta the holster."

Cody looked at the sheriff for a long moment, amazed by the sharp turn of events. The man who shot Cullen and the woman Cullen had been chasing were both here, right now, in Helena—and this fatherly, almost apologetic, lawman wanted to put him in jail. There was no time for this nonsense. He gazed at Price, with his hand extended to take his rifle, for a few moments more before shaking his head slowly and speaking. "Sheriff, I know you're just doin' your job, but I'm afraid I can't hand over my rifle right now. I don't have time to go to jail, and I'm gonna need my rifle."

Price didn't seem overly disturbed by Cody's statement. He remained standing there with his hand outstretched for the weapon, a benevolent expression upon his face, while Cody took one cautious step back. He took a second step before feeling the impersonal touch of a rifle barrel in the small of his back. "Like to introduce you to my deputy," Price said. "Lonnie, say howdy to Mr. McCloud."

"Pleased to meetcha," Lonnie said, reaching around Cody to relieve him of the Winchester. Cody had no choice but to release it.

He glanced behind him to get a glimpse of the deputy. "You move pretty quiet for a fellow your size," he commented as he felt his .44 Colt being lifted out of his holster.

"Don't he, though?" the sheriff replied. "I make him wear a cowbell when he's hangin' around the office."

"I don't suppose you're interested in hearin' my side of the story," Cody said.

"'Course I am, son," Price replied at once. "I bet it's a helluva story. I look forward to it. Let's get on along to the jail now, and you can tell it there." He motioned to Lonnie, and the deputy prodded Cody with his rifle. As they walked toward the sheriff's office, Price said, "We've got a peaceful town here. The folks who pay my salary like it that way, so you might as well set back and enjoy your stay with us, and we'll get to the bottom of who's tellin' the truth." He cocked an eye then and shook his head. "But I tell you, boy, that young lady don't look to me like somebody who'd go around makin' up wild stories."

Yeah, that's the trouble, all right, Cody thought as he was herded down to the sheriff's office, where he was locked away in a cell for the night. He made an honest attempt to convince Price that he was innocent of any crime, but the sheriff was not inclined to believe the deeds Cody credited to Roberta Morris, who had registered in the hotel under the name of Lawrence. Shortly after his prisoner's incarceration, the sheriff went home to supper and Cody found that Lonnie had no interest in his protests at all. The stoic deputy closed the cell room door, propped his feet up on Price's desk, and proceeded to catch a nap. Gripped in a vise of frustration he could not recall the likes of, he could see no solution to his predicament. *Both my brothers are lying in bed, shot full of holes, and I'm stuck in jail,* he thought. *And the people responsible for our trouble are right outside this damn building.* His vexation would have been complete had he known that while he paced back and forth in his eight-by-ten cell, the woman who had wrought such evil upon his family was on her way to Three Forks—on horseback, accompanied by her brother.

"Well, looks like I did a pretty good job on you," Dr. Hicks commented in praise of his stitching on Cullen's chest and back. "You must have a pretty good nurse, too," he went on, "as clean as those wounds look." He looked up from his patient and smiled at Marcy, who responded with a shy smile of her own. Returning his attention to Cullen, he told him, "To tell you the truth, you're one of the luckiest people I've seen in a while. If two of those bullets had been an inch left or right, you wouldn't have made it. You'da been dead before your brother shanghaied me here."

"Like you said, Doc," Cullen replied, "I'm a lucky son of a gun." He glanced at Marcy then. "And I've got a mighty good nurse." Out of the barn and resting now in a bed set up for him in the house, he was subject to almost constant care from the young lady. And he had been getting stronger every day. Dr. Hicks' visit on this day had surprised all of them. No one had expected him to return to see how Cullen was recovering, even though he had told Cody he would.

"Don't go pushing yourself to get on your feet too soon," Hicks warned. "You lost a lot of blood and you've got a great deal of healing to do yet." He glanced toward Fred and his wife then and smiled. "The real reason I came back down here was to see if I could get another shot at Myra's cooking."

Delighted, Myra chuckled and replied, "I think your chances couldn't be better. You got here on a pretty good day. The stage from Butte is due any time now, so I've fixed enough food to feed a gang of passengers." She paused then to send a smile Cullen's way. "Your patient has started to recover his appetite, too."

"That's a good sign," Hicks said. "Means he's healing up just fine." Then in order not to give Cullen too much encouragement, he warned again, "That doesn't mean you can't give those wounds time to heal properly."

"You heard what the doctor said," Marcy scolded. "You can't be impatient to get back on your feet." She had scolded him before when he had made attempts to get out of bed, only to fall back exhausted.

"Yes, ma'am," Cullen replied. "You're the boss." Although his response was cheerful, the urgency he felt to get on his feet again was difficult to resist. Burdened with concern for Cody, he found it hard to simply lie back and enjoy Marcy's attention. As much as he hated to admit it, he had given up hope of ever tracking Roberta down. Too much time had passed.

Hearing the exchange between patient and nurse, Myra and Fred exchanged glances, both fearing that their daughter was showing more than a casual interest in the serious young man. Their concern was not for the quality of the man, as he seemed to be honest and levelheaded, but they feared that he did not return the fascination for Marcy that she exhibited toward him. They had realized for some time now that their daughter was certainly of marriage age. But she was also of an age to suffer a broken heart over a one-sided infatuation.

The gathering in Cullen's room was interrupted then by the appearance of Jimmy Sullivan in the doorway. "They're comin', Pa. The stage is comin'." His announcement served to cause an immediate response from his family. Jimmy and his father hurried out to the corral to prepare to switch the team of horses already in harness with the tired horses pulling the coach. Myra and Marcy hustled to the kitchen with Dr. Hicks in tow. With everyone gone from his room, Cullen threw his legs over the side of the bed and helped himself up, holding on to the bedpost to test for himself how much strength he had regained. Still far too unsteady, he settled back in bed, knowing that Marcy would soon be in with his dinner.

Along with the half dozen passengers who arrived on the stage to Missoula, there appeared another man on horseback. Seeing the stagecoach, and the teams in the process of being changed, as he passed by, he decided that he might find some food there for himself. He pulled his horse up by the hitching rail in front of the house and, seeing a young boy by the coach, asked, "Can anybody get some dinner here?"

"Sure can," Jimmy answered, "if you've got fifty cents."

The stranger smiled and said, "Much obliged," and entered the front door. He was not easily unnoticed, and Myra glanced up in surprise when the imposing figure filled the dining room doorway. "The boy outside said I could get some dinner," he said in explanation for his sudden appearance, "even if I wasn't on the stage." The noisy banter of passengers, stiff from a long bumpy ride, fell silent while all eyes were fixed on the oversized stranger.

"Why, yes," Myra replied. "We charge fifty cents for dinner or supper for as much as you want." Taking in the size of the man, she added, "For as long as the food lasts." Then concerned that he was holding his rifle, she said, "If you wouldn't mind, we'd like you to leave your firearms by the table back at the door." She hesitated before continuing. "It's a request we have for everyone," she said in case the fearsome-looking man took it as personal to him.

"Yes, ma'am. I'm sorry, ma'am. I didn't think about it." He turned to do her bidding, and the banter around the dinner table promptly returned.

Relieved that he seemed not at all as his physical appearance implied, Myra smiled and directed him to a chair at the end of the table. "You sit down here. You look like you need a lot of room."

He had barely settled in the chair when the gathering of dinner guests was startled by shouts from one of the back bedrooms. At once alarmed, Marcy and her mother exchanged startled glances. Marcy quickly handed Myra the serving bowl she had been holding and ran to determine the cause for Cullen's raving. Fearing he had suffered a relapse to the semiconscious condition he had been in when first brought to the barn, she was not sure she heard his shouting correctly. It sounded like he was yelling, *"Jug, Jug."* Maybe, she thought, he wanted whiskey, and she was certain that he was not going to get it—not in his condition. When she finally arrived in his room, it was to find him on his feet, holding on to the bedpost. "What are you do- ing out of that bed?" she scolded. "Sit down before you fall!"

Cullen sat down, but he did not calm down. "Jug!" he repeated. "I'd know that voice anywhere!" Still she looked at him astonished, puzzled by his excitement. "It's my brother Jug," he explained.

Then she remembered his having referred to a brother named Jug. "Are you that sure?" she asked. "Maybe it just sounds like your brother."

"It's Jug," he replied with absolute assurance. "Big fellow, with shoulders wider than the door?" he asked.

The description surely fit. "You stay there," she ordered. "I'll go see if he's your brother. If he is, I'll bring him in."

She returned to the dining room and promptly asked the huge man already well into a plate filled with food, "Is your name Jug?"

Surprised, he looked up and responded, "How'd you know that?"

"Are you looking for your brother?"

Astonished to the point where he suspended a fully loaded fork halfway between the plate and his mouth, he repeated, "How'd you know *that*?"

She laughed and shook her head as if perplexed. "I know your brothers. Come on, Cullen's in the other room."

Still mystified by the happenstance reunion, he pushed his chair back and got to his feet. Looking at Myra, who was equally astonished, he nodded toward his plate and said, "I'll be back to finish that."

"I'll put it in the oven to keep it warm for you," she said, looking back and forth between her daughter and the huge young man.

"Thank you, ma'am," he said, then reached down and picked up a biscuit before following Marcy out of the room.

Marcy watched the joyful reunion between the two brothers in silent fascination and caught herself wondering how it would be to have the huge man as her brother-in-law. She quickly reproached herself for allowing such far-fetched daydreams and left to fix a plate of food for Cullen. While she was gone, Cullen expressed his surprise that Jug was recovered enough to be in the saddle again. He had not expected a recovery of such short duration. "I don't know why I'm surprised," he commented, joking. "You've got the constitution of a mule—and the good looks, too," he added.

As for Jug's part, he was far more shocked than merely surprised to find his eldest brother in such a state. "So Cody found you," he said when Cullen told him that his younger brother was on his way to Helena, following Yeager and maybe Roberta. Like Cody, Jug was amazed to hear of Roberta's part in all that had happened. He paused when Marcy returned with food for Cullen as well as Jug's plate from the oven.

"You looked as if you were reluctant to leave your plate," she teased, "even when you found out we had your brother in here."

"Well, now, that is a fact," Jug replied with a wide grin, happy to be reunited with his plate. They ate while they talked, and Jug decided that he should head for Helena right away to see if he could pick up any trace of Cody's whereabouts. "Since I don't have to worry about you anymore," he concluded. "Looks to me like you're in pretty good hands," he added with the hint of a twinkle in his eye. "That gal looks at you like she'd like to pour syrup on you and eat you up."

"Huh . . ." Cullen grunted. "You're still dizzy from that hole in your side." The idea pleased him, however.

Chapter 11

Having already decided that he was going to take a cautious look around town for Cody McCloud, Bob Yeager searched the face of every man he met on the street as he walked from one saloon to another. After all, fifty dollars was nothing to pass up if the odds were in his favor. He paused in front of Jake's Saloon to look up and down the street once more before entering to have a drink of whiskey. Standing in the doorway, he surveyed the room, looking for anyone who might be the man he was hunting, but the only customers in the place were a few men sitting at the tables playing cards. Weighing heavily on his mind was the fact that he had no description of Cody McCloud. He could be any one of the men seated at the table. To make matters worse, McCloud probably knew he was tracking a man with a hell of a scar on the side of his face. Uncomfortable with that thought, he walked up to the far end of the bar where he could watch the door.

"Yes, sir?" Jake asked, then seemed to stare openly at him.

"Whiskey," Yeager ordered, "and none of that watered-down stuff."

"I don't serve watered-down whiskey here," Jake informed him while still gazing at him intently, taking special note of the scar on the side of his face. "Did that feller ever find you?" he asked.

The comment served to bring Yeager up short, but he managed to remain calm. "What feller would that be?"

"Young feller's been lookin' all over town for somebody with a scar on his face," Jake replied. "No offense, but I couldn't help noticing. I thought you mighta been the man he was lookin' for. Don't make much difference, though, 'cause he's in jail."

"In jail?" Yeager responded, totally surprised. "For what?"

"Sheriff Price said he was stalkin' some woman in town."

"Is that a fact?" Yeager replied. A slow grin began to form beneath the heavy beard, for he had a pretty good idea who the woman might be—the one Jack Sykes denied knowing. "In jail, huh? Well, ain't we lucky we got a sheriff that knows his business?" He tossed his drink back and slammed the empty glass on the bar while he endured the burn of the whiskey in his throat. "Damn, that's terrible stuff. Wish I had a barrel of it." He put his money on the counter and promptly left the saloon, feeling that Lady Luck was smiling his way. Outside, he headed on a diagonal line across the street toward the jail.

He took a casual stroll by the sheriff's office, look-

ing the building over carefully, paying special attention to the barred windows in the rear where the cells
were. *I ain't ever shot a man in jail before*, he thought.
The notion was sufficient to prod his sense of humor.
*That would be something. He sure wouldn't have no place to
hide.* He took another look at the cell windows. *Might
have to be on my horse to reach them windows.* The idea
intrigued him. "Hell, why not?" he asked aloud. "I'll
just wait till after dark and collect another easy fifty
dollars."

Pacing back and forth like a caged animal, Cody was
helpless to do anything about his situation. Lonnie had
brought him a plate of food for his supper, but had
offered no information regarding the sheriff's plans for
the accused. All he could tell Cody was that the sheriff
had gone in search of the woman who complained,
but so far he had not been able to find her. She had
checked out of the hotel, leaving no word of her immediate plans. This alone was enough to drive Cody
to despair. When the sheriff returned to his office after
dusk, Cody learned that he had no plans to release
him.

"If the woman who made the charges has left town,"
Cody argued, "then why in hell are you still holdin'
me?"

"What's your hurry, son?" Sheriff Price responded.
"Ain't we feedin' you proper? Ain't Lonnie takin' care
of you?"

"You've got no reason to keep me locked up," Cody
complained, thoroughly frustrated by Price's paternal
attitude. Roberta was getting farther and farther away

while he lingered there bickering with the sheriff. "I haven't broken any of your damn laws. You can't hold me for somethin' you think I *might* do."

Price hesitated for a moment to consider the matter before giving his final decision. "You might be right, considerin' the lady ain't showed up yet to press charges." Seeing a glint of hope in Cody's eyes, he hastened to add, "But I've got to make sure she's left town before I can turn you loose, so you just make yourself comfortable and enjoy another night of Helena's hospitality."

Disgusted, Cody could not stop himself from exclaiming, "Why, you old hardheaded son of a bitch! You're lettin' a murderer get away. Let me the hell outta here, so I can do your job for you!"

"You just got yourself another night in jail," Price said, with still no show of emotion. Fighting to restrain his anger, Cody turned away from the bars and retreated to his cot to avoid any additional jail time.

Finally resigning himself to another night in jail, Cody lay down on his cot to try to get some sleep. He lay awake for a while, long after the town had quieted down for the night and only the sound of Lonnie's snoring in the next room registered on his mind. It was well after midnight when he was stirred from sleep by a sound like scratching on the wall outside the window over his cot. Fully awake then, he got up to investigate, realizing there was someone at the window.

"McCloud?" a loud whisper called in the dark. "Is that you?"

"Yeah," Cody answered. "Who is that?"

"A friend," the voice came back. "Step up where I can see you."

At once suspicious, Cody immediately pressed flat against the wall. He knew he didn't have any friends in Helena. "All right," he said, and slid along the wall until he was right beside the window. Standing with his feet on the frame of his cot, he could see the shadow of a pistol played across the iron bars. "Here I am," he said, and in the next instant, the pistol was thrust through the bars. Cody grabbed hold of it and tried to pull it away from his would-be assassin. A ferocious tug between him and Bob Yeager took place then, with each man strong enough to hold on, but not powerful enough to wrest it from the other's hand. Finally in desperation, Yeager pulled the trigger in hopes of hitting Cody somewhere. The crack of the .44 sounded like an explosion in the confines of the cell, waking Lonnie in the office. "Is that you, Yeager?" Cody taunted, calling his assailant by the name Cullen had remembered. Startled, Yeager cocked the single-action revolver and pulled the trigger again just as Lonnie burst through the door with a shotgun. Seeing the muzzle flash from the pistol, he cut loose with the shotgun, aiming at the window. Already seeing it coming, Cody had to release his hold on the pistol and drop to the floor to keep from being hit by Lonnie's shotgun blast. Yeager didn't waste any time withdrawing from his perch on a rain barrel outside the window. He ran down the alley behind the jail where his horses waited, and in no time at all, galloped away into the darkness, cursing the lost opportunity.

"What the hell's goin' on?" Lonnie demanded, and

rushed to the window, only to find Yeager long gone. Too flustered to make heads or tails out of the attack on his prisoner, he went back in the office and returned a few moments later with a lantern. "What the hell's goin' on?" he repeated to Cody, who was getting up from the floor. "Who was that done the shootin'?"

"The son of a bitch that shot my brother," Cody exclaimed, "the man you and that grandpappy of a sheriff oughta be chasin' instead of lockin' innocent people up."

Lonnie continued to stand there confused for a long moment before it occurred to him to bolt out the front door of the jail and run around to the back, where he discovered the overturned rain barrel. He stood there for a few moments peering into the empty darkness before returning to confront Cody again. "Why was he tryin' to shoot you?" he asked.

Impatient to the point of frustration with the bull-headed deputy, Cody replied, "Because he's a hired killer, damn it. Somebody hired him to kill my brother and me, and I've got a pretty good notion it was that woman you and the sheriff think is such a fine lady." He could see that it was too much for Lonnie's simple mind. "So unlock this damn door and let me outta here."

"What's goin' on, Lonnie?" Sheriff Price strode purposefully through the door, his revolver in hand. "I heard shots up at the house. Who's doin' the shootin'?" Lonnie related the events that had just taken place, and reported that the perpetrator had managed to escape before he could get around behind the building. Appalled to think someone could attempt murder on a prisoner in custody, Price turned his attention to Cody then. "Who was it, son? And don't tell me you don't know. You're mixed up in somethin' and I intend to find out what it is."

Cody sighed in frustration. "Like I've been tryin' to tell you all along, it's some hired killer named Bob Yeager. He shot my brother and he's out to get me."

"Why?"

"Because that woman who got me locked up doesn't want me to catch up with her."

"And why is that?" Price responded, then frowned as Cody painfully reiterated the explanation he had related several times since his arrest. As before, Price turned it over in his mind, but remained reluctant to release Cody. "Somethin' don't sound right about the whole thing," he decided. "You're up to somethin' that just don't have a good smell about it, so you ain't goin' nowhere till I get to the bottom of this."

"Jesus!" Cody exclaimed, his frustration becoming overwhelming.

"It ain't gonna do you no good to take the Lord's name in vain," Price admonished. "I don't allow that around here. You just go on back to bed." To Lonnie, he said, "You'd best lock the front door in case his friend tries it again, and I'll see you in the mornin'."

Lonnie passed a plate of biscuits and gravy to Cody the next morning, then went into the office to enjoy his breakfast. Ordinarily he had his breakfast at the café across the street before going home for the day, but the sheriff had a meeting with the mayor this morning, so he asked Lonnie to stay past his normal hours. He didn't like to leave the office empty when there was a prisoner in the cells. Lonnie was in the process of sopping up the last bit of gravy with the one biscuit left when he was interrupted by a visitor.

He swung his chair around, dropping his feet to the floor when the door opened and the stranger walked in. Lonnie was larger than the average fellow, so he immediately took note of the man's size. And when he rose from the chair, he was aware that the stranger was half a head taller than he. "Can I help you?" Lonnie asked.

"Yep, I wanna file a complaint," was the answer.

"Well, the sheriff'll be back in about an hour," Lonnie responded. "He's the man you file complaints with."

"This is kinda urgent," the visitor insisted. "I need to have it taken care of right now."

Lonnie had little patience for taking care of anything this early in the morning, especially when he was supposed to be relieved of duty after spending the night there, but he tried to remain civil. "What kind of complaint have you got?" he asked.

"My brother's locked up in jail and he didn't do nothin' wrong."

Lonnie didn't know how to respond at once, but he soon realized his choices were limited when the imposing stranger drew a Colt .44 from his holster and leveled it at him. "Whoa!" he blurted involuntarily. "You can't do that!"

"I reckon I'm doin' it," Jug replied, and cocked the hammer back.

"Take it easy!" Lonnie exclaimed as Jug motioned him toward the cell room door. "I'm goin'."

"Cody!" Jug yelled. "You in there?"

"Jug?" came the surprised reply from the cell room. "Yeah, I'm in here."

"Be there in a minute," Jug called, then directed his next remark to the shaken deputy. "I expect one of those rifles in the rack yonder belongs to my brother. You'd best unlock it." He moved to a position from which he could see the contents of the drawer when Lonnie got the key in case there was a handgun kept there. After the deputy unlocked the gun rack, Jug said, "All right, let's get that cell door open."

"Well, damn, Jug," Cody remarked, "looks like your wound musta healed up pretty good. I can't say I ain't happy to see you. I see you met Lonnie." He stood aside when Lonnie opened the cell door and Jug nudged him into the cell. "That cot has a lumpy mattress," Cody told the now sullen deputy. "But I expect the sheriff will be back before too long, so you oughta be comfortable till then." As an afterthought, he added, "Watch out for that window, though. You never can tell what might come through it."

"You gonna eat the rest of that biscuit?" Jug asked when Cody came out of the cell. Cody shook his head, not really surprised. "Well, ain't no sense in lettin' it go to waste," Jug said, and stepped inside far enough to reach it.

Cody chuckled. "I would say we could go to the café for some breakfast, but under the circumstances, I don't think it's a good idea."

"That's all right," Jug said while stuffing the last of the biscuit in his mouth. "I ate at the café before I came over to get you. That's how I found out where you were."

Outside the sheriff's office, they attempted to appear casual, even though they weren't sure how much time they had. "We've got to get my horse from the stable," Cody said. "But I want to take a minute to look behind the jail." Hurrying around to the rear of the building, he told Jug of the attempted murder by the same man who had shot Cullen. Finding the overturned barrel, he searched the ground for tracks, but there were none left by horses. The few footprints he found led down the alley. "Come on," he said. "He musta left his horses down there somewhere. We've gotta go that way anyway to get to the stables." He looked up at the window above his head then. "You all right in there, Lonnie?" There was no answer from the cell. He glanced at Jug and remarked, "I think Lonnie's mad at us." They hustled off, following the alley—Cody ahead and searching the ground for tracks, Jug behind him, leading his horse.

A couple dozen yards down the alley, behind the hardware store, they came to a spot where two horses had apparently been tied, and Cody stopped to study the tracks more closely. In a few seconds, he announced, "This is what I'm lookin' for." He pointed to a hoof-print in the hard dirt for Jug to see. "See that? I took a file and cut a couple of marks in that shoe. That's Cullen's bay." He paused to take a quick glance behind them. "I know we ain't got much time, but we need to see which way he headed. He's the bastard that shot Cullen."

"What about the woman?" Jug asked. "Have you seen her?"

"No, for a fact, I ain't," Cody replied. "But she's

seen me. That's how I ended up in jail. The bitch musta spotted me as soon as I came to town, then went and told the sheriff that I was stalkin' her. Accordin' to the sheriff, she's checked out of the hotel. No doubt she's left town and I don't have a notion which way she went, her and some feller she calls her brother. I'm more interested in findin' this Yeager feller first. He's the one that left Cullen for dead beside the trail, and I can track him if I have half a chance." Luck was with them, for the hoofprints told them that Yeager had headed straight out of town after leaving the alley. "Let's get my horse. Then we can come back here and pick up his trail."

"That friend of yours you were lookin' for left outta here last evenin'," Malcolm Barnes said when he saw Cody walk into the stable. "Did you ever find him?"

"No," Cody replied, "but he sent me a message." He didn't elaborate. "He didn't say where he was headin', did he?"

"No, he didn't. Anyway, I see you got outta jail," Malcolm went on.

"Yeah, my lawyer got me out," Cody replied, and nodded toward Jug, who grinned wide in response. "I'm leavin' now myself. How much do I owe you for the extra night?"

While Cody settled up with Barnes, Jug remained by the front door of the stable, keeping an eye on the street running up the gulch. In a few minutes' time, Buttermilk was saddled and Cody led him out to join Jug. "We'd best stay in the alley goin' back," he said. "That fool sheriff might be back by now."

Returning to the point where Yeager had left the alley, the two brothers stepped up in the saddle and prepared to follow. Cody reined the Appaloosa to a halt between the stores and pointed at two riders in the street. "Sheriff Price and Lonnie," he said. "Looks like they're headin' to the stables. I expect we'd better get movin'."

The trail was not difficult to follow. Yeager had taken no pains to hide his tracks in his efforts to get away as fast as possible, riding east for about fifteen miles before turning south. "He's goin' to Three Forks," Cody said. The tracks led along the valley, skirting the mountains for a few miles before veering slightly southeast to strike the common trail to Three Forks. The question left unanswered, however, was where he would go from there, for there was nothing in that small settlement to hold a man like Yeager, a paid assassin. They could not count on being able to track him indefinitely, and would have to make a decision once they reached Three Forks. He could continue south to Virginia City, or turn to the east and follow the Yellowstone to Bozeman, or maybe Coulson. "Yeah," Jug said, "and he just might head back west to Butte." The more they speculated upon it, the smaller their chance of catching Yeager seemed.

"All we can do is follow his tracks as long as we can find 'em," Cody replied, "and hope for a helluva lot of luck after we can't."

They were able to make good time in following Yeager's escape route until they reached the common road. A little time was lost there until Cody was able to confirm his speculation that Yeager was intent upon

heading to Three Forks. A pair of deep ruts told them
that a heavily loaded wagon had recently passed along
the road. With a team of four horses pulling, the result
was a conglomeration of hoofprints, calling for close
inspection of the ground until Cody found one with
two notches filed in it. "Yep," he announced. "That's
where he's headin'." By this time, they had used up most
of the daylight, so they started looking for a place to
camp. They picked a spot by a small stream where it
emptied into the river.

As best he could recall, he was thirty or so miles from
Bozeman. If he continued at the same pace he had maintained to reach Three Forks, he could make it in less
than a day, although he no longer felt the urgency to
push the horses as he had been, alternating from his
horse to the bay, so as not to have to rest them so often.
He figured he was past the necessity to worry about
pursuit, feeling fairly confident that the sheriff wasn't
going to chase him this far from Helena. And as far as
the other McCloud brother was concerned, he was in
the Helena jail and the least of his worries. When he
considered these facts, it was easy to return to his old
swagger. "It'll take more than that to clip ol' Bob Yeager's
tail feathers," he announced to the blue roan he rode.
"I coulda used that extra fifty dollars, though." No
longer in a hurry, he decided to stop at a shabby little
trading post on the chance the owner might have some
strong spirits. It was a short visit, for the old man who
owned it could offer nothing more than some apple
cider. He might have considered staying the night there,
had there been something more. So he gave the horse

a little kick, and under an overcast sky, set out for Bozeman, Cullen McCloud's light bay following behind.

A little before dark, a gentle rain began to fall. It
was just enough to make riding miserable, so he decided to keep an eye out for a campsite that might offer some protection from the wet. He decided to swing
off the trail and ride closer to the bluffs of the Yellowstone, hoping to find a spot where the bank offered
some shelter. After he crossed a series of gullies that
led down to the water's edge, he suddenly pulled his
horse up short. Peering into the increasing darkness,
he was sure he had seen the faint glow of a fire. Not
certain, he dismounted and left his horses tied to a
bush, then made his way a little closer on foot. Strain-
ing to see through the misty darkness, he was distracted by a movement in the trees by the river where
the bank jutted out to form the roof of an open cave.
He dropped at once to his knee and brought his rifle
up ready to fire before he realized that the movement
he had seen was the shuffling of three horses tied in
the trees. Someone was camped under the bank of the
river, and their horses had no doubt been alerted to
the approach of Yeager's two. *I'll just get a little closer to
see what I've run up on*, he thought, cautious that he
might have stumbled upon an Indian hunting party.
On the other hand, it could be an opportunity to way-
lay an unsuspecting traveler on his way home.

The challenge was to try to move to a position that
would let him see how many were around that fire
under the bank. They were not making any noise, so it
might be only one, which would make his job that much
easier. He decided he could risk climbing down to the

water's edge, which would permit him to get a better angle to see inside the opening. After a few minutes of careful maneuvering, he gained the position he sought. There appeared to be two people in the camp, one standing between him and the fire, another seated on the other side of the fire. *Like sitting ducks*, he thought, and raised his rifle to aim at the man standing, confident that he could hit him, cock his rifle, and shoot the one sitting before he had a chance to react. There was never a thought about the senseless slaying of two innocent human beings. They might not be carrying anything of value, but the acquisition of the three horses was enough to justify his actions. *It ain't even a sin if nobody sees you do it*, he thought, and chuckled to himself. Steadying his rifle to take dead aim, he hesitated before squeezing the trigger. Something about the man beside the fire looked familiar. Then he almost chuckled aloud as the irony of the situation struck him. *Jack Sykes!*

The realization that he had lucked upon Sykes struck him as extremely fortunate, and humorous as well. *Fifty dollars*, he thought. *You son of a bitch. You weren't planning to be around to pay me after I killed that McCloud fellow.* He brought the front sights of his rifle to bear on Sykes again, but paused to consider his options. Was he missing a bigger payday by killing Sykes? For he now realized that the figure seated at the fire was a woman, the mysterious woman that Jack had steadfastly denied. Yeager's was not a complex mind, but he figured that the woman was the source of Jack's money, and maybe he might be killing an opportunity to gain a share of whatever their scheme might be.

Besides, he thought, *it would be downright entertaining to walk in on them.* He lowered his rifle and stood up.

Holding the weapon at the ready in case Jack's reactions were deadly, he slowly approached the campfire. Sykes, with his back to the riverbank, was not aware of the man casually walking up behind him until Yeager spoke. "Evenin', Jack." Startled to the point that he almost stumbled into the fire, Sykes reached for his pistol. "That'd be a mistake," Yeager warned, leveling his rifle at Jack's waist. "Ain't no way to greet a partner, anyway." Grinning broadly, he walked into the camp. Glancing at Roberta, who was still seated, he tipped his hat and said, "Evenin', ma'am. I've been wantin' to meet up with you."

"Yeager!" Sykes exclaimed, shocked to see the man, and at a loss for something to say. "Did you get Cody McCloud?" he finally thought to ask.

"Why, sure I did," Yeager lied, seeing no sense in admitting failure when fifty dollars was on the line. "I'm just a little put out to have to track you down to get paid for the job, though." He figured it was better to let Sykes sweat a little over the fact that he found him, so he declined to confess that the meeting was purely accidental.

"Hell, Bob," Jack quickly responded, "you know I wouldn't cheat you. I was plannin' on coming back to Helena to find you." He looked at his sister, who was watching the confrontation warily, her hand on the handle of the revolver under the edge of her skirt. "Ain't that right, Roberta? We was talkin' about that very thing this mornin', 'bout how I'd have to get back to see that the job was paid for."

"Is that a fact?" Yeager replied, and stepped over beside Roberta. She did not recoil when he stuck his heavy bush of a beard practically in her face. Instead, her eyes locked on his with a gaze as hard as steel. It was not lost on Yeager. "Damn, you're a tough-lookin' woman behind that pretty face, ain't you?"

"How do we know Cody McCloud is dead?" Roberta asked, her words clear and without fear, as she sized up their paid assassin.

Yeager jerked back in mock surprise. "Why, because I just said he was, darlin'. Now let's talk about where you're gettin' all that money ol' Jack's been flashin' around, 'cause this is your lucky day. I'm your new partner."

"Is that so?" Roberta replied, still with no show of alarm. "Partner in what?"

"Whatever you got goin' for yourselves," Yeager said, glancing back and forth between the woman and her brother. "Maybe we'd best take a look at what you're carryin' in them packs yonder."

Roberta laughed contemptuously. "Is that what you've sneaked up on our camp for? To rob us of some cooking utensils and women's clothes? Do you think we're stupid enough to travel with any valuables when there's just the two of us to watch for slimy idiots like you?" She looked him straight in the eye, all the while knowing that the packs held a substantial sum of cash money as well as a sack of gold dust that Jack wasn't even aware of. "Maybe you're after my brother's extra suit of underwear, or that sack of flour."

Aware then of his sister's bluff, Jack joined in the charade. "Yeah, maybe you're after my dry socks. Hell,

I'll pay you for doin' the job on McCloud, but we have to get to where the money is. We ain't got it with us."

Yeager glanced from one of them to the other, this time in uncertainty. His simple mind was easily convinced that there was the possibility they were telling the truth. "Well, I'll just ride along with you to where you got the money," he said, his attitude on a completely different tack. "All I want is to get paid for the job I done." Aiming his proposal at Roberta then, he continued. "We're all goin' in the same direction. We might as well ride along together. This is kinda dangerous country for a man and a woman travelin' alone, and I'm handy with a gun. You already know that. So whaddaya say we join up till we get to wherever that is you've got your money?"

"Maybe you're right," Roberta said, much to Jack's surprise. She was not at all convinced that Yeager had taken care of Cody McCloud. "Maybe we could use some extra protection. Jack said you had Cullen's horse and gun belt to prove you shot him. I don't suppose you have anything of Cody's to prove he's dead." She studied his reaction to her comments closely.

"No, I don't reckon I do," Yeager replied, a slow grin forming on his bushy face. "I shot him through the bars of the jailhouse window, so there wasn't no way I could take no souvenirs."

"You know something, Mr. Yeager," she remarked calmly. "You're a rotten liar. You didn't get Cody McCloud, and now you've caused me extra trouble because you might have led him right to me."

Stunned by the woman's frank and fearless damnation of his lie, Yeager was without an immediate response, causing him to stammer for a second in search of a reply. "That ain't so," he finally blurted. "I got him, just like I said."

"There you go again," Roberta scolded. "You're just compounding one lie after another, and you're about the worst liar I've ever seen. Now, you say you want to be a partner in whatever Jack and I have going. Well, you're right. We are onto something big enough to make us all rich, but I'm not going to stand for any more lying if you're going to work with us. Do I make my-self clear?"

"Yes, ma'am," Yeager replied, properly flustered by the unexpected dressing down, but encouraged by her mention of the possible partnership. "It wasn't all a lie," he confessed. "I did shoot at him through the jail-house window." Then he was quick to add, "But I didn't lead him to you, 'cause he's still in the jail."

His confession was the confirmation she sought. Cody McCloud was still coming after her. "All right, Bob," she said, affecting a calmer tone. "Cody McCloud will be on our trail again, and probably sooner than you think. With me gone from Helena, they would hardly hold him much longer. There are no charges against him. We can use a man who's handy with a gun, so if you still want to be a partner in our plan, your job is to go back and make sure he doesn't follow me. If you can stop him, and bring me proof that he's dead, then we'll take you in as a partner. What do you say, Bob?"

Jack watched in awe as his sister defused Bob Yeager's swagger, and took total control of the fearsome killer, hesitating to open his mouth while Roberta took Yeager to task. Consequently, he was not surprised by the out-law's answer.

"I reckon that suits me just fine," Yeager decided. "Now, how about tellin' me what the plan is and how much is my share?"

"There's plenty of time for that when you get Cody McCloud off my back," Roberta said. "Just know that it'll certainly be worth your while."

"I'll start out at first light in the mornin'," Yeager said, thinking it best not to push her for details. "I'll get him and I'll bring his scalp back to prove it."

"Good, we've got a deal, then," Roberta said, and offered her hand to seal it.

"We've got a deal," Yeager echoed. "I'll go fetch my horses and tie 'em up in the trees yonder with yours."

"We'll wait for you in Bozeman," she said.

When he had gone, Jack took the opportunity to voice his doubts. "I don't know if I like the idea of splittin' our take three ways."

"Don't be a fool," Roberta replied. "I'm not cutting that imbecile in for a penny. But make no mistake about it, Cody McCloud will be coming after us. And maybe, with more incentive, Yeager might stop him this time, so he might be doing us a favor after all."

"If he does kill him, and comes lookin' for a share, what then?" Jack asked.

"Do I have to tell you?" Roberta responded, her tone condescending. "You shoot the son of a bitch."

Chapter 12

"If I remember correctly," Jug commented, "there's a little tradin' post on this side of the river that might have some beans and bacon for sale. That damn jerky we had for breakfast is long gone."

Cody chuckled. It had been a long time in the saddle since they had last eaten, and he was surprised that there had been nothing out of Jug before this. They had managed to follow Bob Yeager's trail to the banks of the Gallatin River, thanks to the outlaw's careless flight. "I reckon we'd better feed you before you dry up and blow away," he said. "Might be the feller that runs that tradin' post has seen Yeager. He coulda stopped there if he's as big an eater as you are," he teased. "If that store is even there. It wasn't much before." He truly hoped that Yeager had stopped there, and possibly given some hint as to where he was heading when he left there. It had become more and more difficult to find the impression of the right front shoe on Cullen's horse as the trail became older. He had to

count it as luck when he found one clear print in a
stretch of soft sand on the riverbank. By the direction
the hoof was pointed, Yeager was still heading south.
Did this mean Virginia City was his destination? It
was hard to say, for there was still a mile or so to strike
the east-west trail that could lead to Bozeman or Butte.

Much to Jug's relief, the simple trading post was
still there, run by the same old man. Smiley Watson stood
in the open doorway of the log building that served as
his domicile and trading post. The structure was actually a chain of four cabins, built at separate times as
Smiley's business expanded over the years to accommodate the fur trade, the Indians, the gold rush, and
the army. No one was sure how old Smiley was, some
said not even Smiley. But he was a young man when
Lewis and Clark named the three rivers that formed
the origin of the Missouri River. He had traded with the
Blackfoot, Shoshoni, Flatfoot, and Crow before Lewis
and Clark, but his business had fallen on lean times for
the past dozen years, the world having moved around
him, so it was with a natural curiosity that he stood
watching when he saw riders approaching. Most new
customers were actually lost when they stumbled upon
his business. If he was lucky, they would buy or trade
something before they left.

"Hey, old man," Jug called to him as he and Cody
reined up before the store, "I see you're still here."

"Hell yeah," Smiley replied. "The Lord ain't sent for
me yet. I reckon He'll let me know when he needs
me." Although there were plenty of signs of age in his
white beard and bent body, there was nothing wrong
with his memory. "Last time you was in here, you bought

a half side of bacon and some of them dried apples I had. If I recollect, you and your brother was partial to some cider I got from Benny Denson, too." He took a hard look at Cody. "This ain't the feller you was with."

Jug grinned, amazed by the old man's ability to recall details of incidents that had happened years earlier. "No, sir, that was my brother Cullen. This is my other brother Cody." He turned to Cody then to explain. "When me and Cullen went to Bozeman three years ago this winter," he said. Looking back at Smiley, he said, "We're needin' some more bacon and some dried beans if you've got 'em."

"It's a little early yet to kill hogs, but I've got some meat left in the smokehouse," Smiley said.

"Cut me off a quarter of that side meat," Jug said, as he glanced around the store in case something else caught his eye.

"We're also lookin' for a feller," Cody said, since Jug showed no indication of leaving the topic of food, "may have passed your place a day or so ago."

"Bushy-faced feller with a scar down the side of his face?" Smiley replied. Surprised, Cody nodded and Smiley continued. "Yesterday, late in the afternoon, came in lookin' for whiskey. I didn't have none, so he moved on. Didn't buy nothin'." He paused to examine the expressions on both their faces. "I take it he warn't no friend of yours."

"No," Cody said. "He ain't a friend of ours."

"He shot my other brother, the one with me last time," Jug said. "That bay horse he had with him is Cullen's horse."

"I knew he had a mean look about him," Smiley

said. "Your brother dead?" When Jug replied that Cullen had survived, Smiley said, "Well, I reckon you're about a day behind that feller."

"I expect we'd better not tarry, then," Cody said. "He didn't happen to say where he was headed, did he?"

"Nope, and I didn't ask."

Taking no more time than necessary to load their new supplies, the two brothers prepared to continue their search. Smiley stood by, watching them load their food. Then he handed Jug the quarter of side meat when the big man had arranged a place for it. Grinning appreciatively, Jug lifted it up to tie on behind his saddle. In the next moment it was almost wrenched from his hand by a bullet. An instant later, the sound of the rifle that had fired the shot rang out, sending all three of them scrambling for cover. Jug and Smiley dived behind a large cottonwood while Cody hustled behind a corner of the front porch. Several more shots kicked up dirt in the yard before silence followed.

"He's up yonder in the bluffs," Cody called out, "in that bunch of bushes. Looks like we ain't chasin' him no more. He's chasin' us."

"Well, he's got us pinned down pretty damn good," Jug called back. He didn't have to point out that both their rifles were on their saddles and the yard was too open to risk making a dash for them. At a range of approximately a hundred yards to the berry bushes from where the shots had come, pistols were of little use. "Wonder why he don't shoot the horses."

Cody had already wondered about that. The horses

were surely easy targets. "'Cause he ain't out to stop us from followin' him. He's of a mind to kill us, and then I reckon he figures he'll take the horses."

"The sorry son of a bitch coulda waited till you left my place," Smiley complained, edging around closer to Jug with a notion to position himself behind the huge bulk that was Jug's body.

"I hope that bullet didn't do too much damage to that bacon," Jug muttered, primarily to himself. "If we had our rifles, we might could smoke him outta them bushes."

Smiley glanced behind him at his store and the cover possible between the building and the cottonwood tree. "I might be able to get you a rifle," he said, "if you think you can rout him outta there." Then not waiting for Jug's answer, he crawled away from the tree and made his way on hands and knees along the side of his house. A couple of shots from the bluffs kicked up the dirt behind him, but he was soon safely behind the first unit in his chain of cabins.

"Give it to Cody," Jug yelled. "He's the best shot."

A few minutes later, the shutters on a front window opened and an 1866 Winchester rifle slid across the porch floor to the corner where Cody quickly reached up and snatched it. A few seconds later, a cartridge belt followed. Ready to do some business with their unseen assailant now, Cody pumped a full magazine into the clump of bushes. He was in the process of re-loading when he involuntarily jumped in reaction to what sounded like a cannon over his head. "By God!" Smiley shouted. "That'll give him somethin' to think about," as he reloaded the Sharps Model 1874 buffalo rifle with a .50-70 cartridge, and steadied it on the windowsill for another shot.

There was a temporary lull in the shooting from the bushes after Smiley's blast cut a sizable branch in two. Knowing he would not likely get another chance, and gambling that Yeager had been as startled as he, Cody darted out from the edge of the porch and jerked his rifle from the saddle sling. Amid a volley of shots from the bluffs, he hit the ground and rolled over and over to come up beside Jug behind the tree. He gave Smiley's '66 Winchester to Jug. "Keep him busy," he said. "I'm gonna slip down the river and see if I can get behind him." Jug nodded and started firing at once. In a matter of seconds, Cody crawled to the riverbank and dropped out of sight.

"Damn the luck," Bob Yeager complained as he reloaded yet again. Things were not going as he had planned, and he cursed the unlucky shot with which he had opened the assault. Now he was in a shoot-out, a situation he had hoped to avoid, and the first shot from the buffalo gun had come uncomfortably close to his head. *That old fool*, he thought, for he knew the shot had not come from either of the other two. He realized that he was now facing a standoff and he was outnumbered three to one. When he was faced with tight spots like this, Yeager's natural tendency was to run, and he decided this might be the better choice at this time. He would just have to wait for another opportunity. His decision made, he pumped another flurry of shots at the trading post before carefully backing away from the sandy mound in the bushes that had been his protection. Wary now that he would have two after him, he wasted no time in an effort to get back to the gully in the bluffs where he had left his horses.

Reaching the steep edge of the deep defile that led to the water, he sat down and slid on the seat of his pants to the bottom. He scrambled to his feet only to find himself gazing at the business end of a Winchester '73 in the hands of Cody McCloud. His reaction was automatic as he raised his rifle, but had no chance when competing with a bullet already on its way. Cody's shot caught him in the chest, staggering him. The second shot spun him around and dropped him to the ground. Cody then calmly walked up to him and said, "Say hello to the devil for me. Tell him Cullen McCloud sent you." Then to avoid repeating the mistake that Yeager had made when he left Cullen for dead, he placed the third shot in the back of Yeager's head. The job done, he yelled for Jug and Smiley.

With Cullen's assailant lying dead on the ground, there was a feeling of uncertainty hovering over both brothers. While there was a sense of completion in regard to all those who had physically wounded the three brothers, there was also the feeling that something else was left to be done. That something was Roberta Morris. True, hers was not the finger on the trigger that left Cullen for dead, or ripped a hole in Jug's side, or wounded Cody's shoulder. But there was little doubt that she was the cause of it all. The question before the two brothers now was what, if anything, they could do about it. They had no idea as to where she might have fled. They only knew that she had left Helena, and it would only be a guess as to what direction she had gone. In the end, they decided that it would be a waste of time and effort to search blindly for the scheming vixen. She had won. She got away with the gold she sought. That much was a shame and a sin. On the other hand, it appeared that the McCloud family would all recover, and they had lost nothing to the beguiling woman. So they decided to head back to Garrison to pick up Cullen. Then they could just go home and try to forget that they had ever met Roberta Morris, or Lawrence, whatever her name was. As best they could estimate, it would be about four to four and a half days to the swing station on Clark Fork where Cullen waited. Since there was no longer a sense of urgency, they decided to wait until morning before starting out for Butte.

To settle up with Smiley for his part in the shoot-out, they gave him the blue roan that Yeager had ridden, plus his saddle and weapons. Smiley was grateful and offered Jug the rest of that side of bacon, since they now had Cullen's horse to carry it. "I reckon you mighta took that bullet if you hadn't been holdin' up that bacon," Smiley said.

Cody chuckled. "Yeah, instead of you savin' our bacon, I guess our bacon saved you."

The next morning found both brothers in an almost carefree mood. "I thought you might wanna ride on back through Helena and visit your friend Lonnie," Cody joshed as they were soaking up the last of the pot of coffee Smiley had made for their breakfast. "I bet him and that old maid sheriff would be happy to see you."

"I was thinkin' on takin' you back there—figured there might be some reward money for your capture—two, three, maybe even five dollars," Jug responded.

Cody laughed. He stepped up in the saddle then and said, "Let's go, Jug, and see how Cullen's gettin' along with that little Sullivan gal. What was her name?"

"Marcy," Jug replied.

It was a clear day in early fall, and they were heading home. However, there was a lingering cloud in Cody's mind, and he tried not to think about the fortune stolen from ol' Gabe's brother, for there was really nothing he and Jug could do about it. They had already been away from the M Bar C for too long. The summer was gone. It was already August. There was a lot of work to be done and their father was left shorthanded. Roberta and her male companion, who the Sullivans said was introduced as her brother, most likely headed back east to spend their ill-gotten gains. There was no use in crying about it. That was just the way things worked in this country. *Sometimes you eat the bear, sometimes the bear eats you,* as the saying went.

Cullen looked up when he heard the door opened ajar. "It's all right, Marcy," he said. "I'm up already." He thought he could smell the coffee he knew she would be bringing. It had become a ritual. She would bring him a cup of fresh coffee every morning before breakfast, although he had insisted that it was no longer necessary, for he was perfectly capable of coming to the kitchen to get his coffee himself. He found himself looking forward to the early visit from his cheerful nurse, so much so that he had to warn himself to remember the first time he had let himself be attracted to a pretty face. Of course, there was no comparison between the two women. His concern was for Marcy, not himself, for he was almost ten years her senior. He had convinced himself that her attention to him was strictly out of sympathy for his misfortune, and as soon as he was healed, that mild infatuation would disappear. *Well, I'm healed*, he thought, *at least well enough to return home.*

"Good morning," Marcy sang out in her typical sunshiny manner. "How's my patient this morning?"

"Good morning, Marcy," he returned. "I guess your patient is about ready to stop lyin' around bein' waited on, and see about gettin' back to the M Bar C." His remark brought a frown to the pretty face beaming up at him.

"You know what Dr. Hicks told you," she scolded. "Don't go thinking you're well too soon, or you'll just cause those wounds to open up again."

"I think those wounds are healin' up pretty well," he replied. "And the stiffness I had in my shoulder and back is almost gone." He took a sip of the hot, black coffee and smiled at her. "I don't think I would've made it without your help, though. I'm pretty sure your mama and papa would love to see me ride outta here, though. I'm gonna have to pay them for all the grub I've eaten."

"They're not worried about that at all," she protested. "If they were, I would have known it." A wide smile lit up her face then. "Besides, you can't ride away from here. You don't have a horse."

"That is a problem, ain't it?" He had forgotten that,

but he only hesitated for a moment. "I expect Jimmy might loan me his horse until I could bring it back."

"I expect he might," she said, pretending to pout. "I believe he'd give you anything of his you fancied." Cullen laughed. She wasn't far from wrong. He was well aware of her young brother's fascination with him. Then for a moment another frown chased her pout away, and she said, "I don't want you to go." Like a bullet fired, she could not call it back. Realizing it might have sounded a bit forward, she quickly followed the remark. "I promised Dr. Hicks I'd see that you didn't get back on a horse too soon."

Caught in the awkwardness of the moment, they both gazed at each other while the room around them seemed to fall into total silence with neither knowing what to say. They were saved when Jimmy stuck his head in the door. "Mama said breakfast is ready." Cullen and Marcy exchanged brief smiles of embarrassment and followed Jimmy into the dining room.

"You're lookin' stronger every day," Fred Sullivan said as Cullen walked in.

"I'm feelin' stronger," Cullen replied, and made his decision right then. "Matter of fact, I think it's about time I got on my way. I've put you folks out enough as it is." He directed his next comment toward Marcy's younger brother then. "I was hopin' I could work out some kinda deal with you, Jimmy—maybe borrow your horse for a spell. When I get home, I'll see that you get him back." His statement caught all of them by surprise. The evidence was plain in their faces.

"Sure," Jimmy immediately responded, to no one's surprise. "You know you're welcome to my horse."

"Well, now, Cullen," Fred commented, "we don't want you to push yourself too soon."

Myra was quick to second her husband's remark. "No, indeed. I certainly hope you're not leaving because you think you're too much bother. We're happy to have you stay as long as you like." She was sincere in her statement, for she had developed a strong fondness for the quiet young man, as well as a large measure of respect. "We're all glad to see you recovering so well, but we're in no hurry to see you go." She glanced then at her daughter, interested to test her reaction to the news. As she had feared, there was a deep disappointment on Marcy's face, and Myra was struck with compassion for the young girl's feelings. She had been afraid that her young daughter had been riding for a fall.

"It's time I was leavin'," Cullen repeated. "I'll bring your horse back as soon as I can," he told Jimmy; then, turning back to Fred, he said, "And I'll pay my bill then for all the food and care. I don't think I've got enough money at home to pay for the nursin' care, though." He aimed a wide grin in Marcy's direction. She made no reply, but managed to affect a gentle smile for his benefit.

As soon as breakfast was finished, Cullen collected his belongings, what little was left on him after Yeager bushwhacked him, and loaded them on Jimmy's horse. They all stood around and watched him get ready to leave. Fred handed him his double-barrel shotgun and a sack full of shells. "You can bring it back with Jimmy's horse," he said. Then he shook his hand. "You watch yourself." Cullen nodded.

"I declare," Myra admitted, "we're gonna miss you around here. You take care of yourself." She handed him a cotton sack with some cooking utensils she had rounded up for him.

"I will," Cullen replied. "Thank you, ma'am."

Marcy stood off to one side during the good-byes, not sure of her feelings. When the moment came and Cullen started to step up in the stirrup, her emotions took control, and she suddenly ran quickly up to him and kissed him on the cheek. Then just as quickly, she backed away again to leave him confused and uncertain. Unable to think of anything to say beyond a simple "Thank you," he stepped up in the saddle and turned the roan's head toward the river.

After crossing the river, he continued west, planning to take as direct a route as possible to the Bitterroot Valley. As best he could figure, he had a full two days' ride if he was in fit condition. Since he was still weak from his wounds, he decided to take it a little easy and make the journey in three days. It was not an easy ride for a man with three bullet holes in him, riding directly over the Sapphire Mountains before reaching the M Bar C. The first twenty miles were relatively comfortable and he went into camp on Flint Creek with few complaints of soreness or discomfort.

There were a good many things on his mind as he fried some bacon in the frying pan Myra had loaned him. He still didn't have much of an appetite, so the bacon would be enough to satisfy him, and would go well with the coffee he was brewing in the old pot that was also a loan from Myra. *I'm going to need a packhorse to return everything I've borrowed,* he thought. He had lost everything when Bob Yeager had bushwhacked him. *It's a good thing I've got some money saved up.* He let his mind wander back to that morning and the image of Marcy peeking around the bedroom door, holding a fresh cup of coffee for him. Every detail of her face was still clear in his mind as he recalled the moment before Jimmy had come in to summon them to the table. It was that moment when she had uttered, *I don't want you to go.* Was he sensing more than she intended? "I wish to hell I knew!" he exclaimed, and decided to think of something else before his mind created something that wasn't there. After his supper, he checked the load in Fred's shotgun and laid it beside his blanket. *I feel downright naked without my rifle.* That was his last thought before drifting off to sleep.

He was surprised to find that he was not as stiff and sore as he had expected to be when he awoke the next morning. *Maybe I'm healing faster than I thought,* he speculated. The notion was encouraging, for he had not really felt ready to ride the day before. His decision to leave had been dictated by the fear that he was becoming too fond of Marcy Sullivan, and he had thought it best to go. The fact that he was feeling stronger on this morning was sufficient to raise his spirits from the lows of the night before. After checking the condition of Jimmy's roan, he saddled up and set out for the Sapphire Mountains and a trail he had ridden when hunting in these hills. With his new optimism, he revised his original estimate and planned to try to reach home late that night.

"Now, mister, you can just roll your ass outta that stall with your hands where I can see 'em."

There was a lengthy pause before a response came

forth from the figure huddled in the hay of the first stall in the barn. "Well, that's a helluva welcome home."

"Cullen! Is that you?"

"Yeah, it's me."

"When did you . . ." Donovan stammered, completely flustered. "What the hell are you doin' in the barn? Why didn't you come in the house? Where are your brothers? Didn't they find you? Damn, boy . . ."

"Just hold on a minute," Cullen said, "and I'll try to answer all your questions."

Donovan could not find the patience to wait. "But what the hell are you doin' in the barn? I saw that strange roan horse just standin' at the gate this mornin'. I mean, Smoke saw it when he came out to the pump to draw water for breakfast, and told me we had a stray horse at the barn. Where's your horse?"

"It was so late when I got here last night, I didn't wanna wake you up. I was afraid you'd shoot me if I tried to sneak in the house in the middle of the night," Cullen replied. He rolled over on his hands and knees, and used the side of the stall to help him to his feet. "I hope Smoke's got some coffee made. I could sure use a cup."

Donovan watched, astonished, as his eldest held on to the side of the stall for support while he brushed some clinging pieces of hay from his clothes. The rays of the early-morning sun found their way through the open barn door to reveal the effects of his son's recovery from his wounds, for Cullen's face and neck were obviously leaner, a result of his substantial weight loss. Donovan was stunned. "Son, what in hell happened to you?"

"Let's go in the house for some coffee and some-thin' to eat and I'll tell you what happened, but I warn you, it's a helluva story." He glanced at the roan stand-ing there watching them. "We might take the saddle off Jimmy's horse first."

"Who's Jimmy?"

"Part of the story," Cullen answered. "Let's go in the house, so I don't have to tell it twice."

Smoke looked up when they came in the door. "Well, I'll be go to hell," he muttered. "Look what the cat drug in." He retreated a couple of steps, reared his head back, and took a long, hard look, then added, "And I mean *drug in*. You look like hell, boy."

The three of them sat down at the kitchen table and drank coffee while Cullen told them all that had hap-pened since Cody brought Jug home from Blodgett Canyon. Donovan and Smoke were amazed to hear of Roberta's treachery. Like everyone else the vicious woman came in contact with, they had both been charmed blind. Obviously disturbed when he realized that the apparent fragile appearance of his typically robust son was due to Cullen's having been shot three times, Donovan was naturally concerned about the welfare of Jug and Cody. Cullen apologized for not going to find his brothers instead of returning home, but he knew that he would be of very little help to them until he had regained some measure of his strength. Donovan quickly assured him that there was no call for an apology. He had done the right thing. "I know they can take care of themselves," Cullen said, "but it's a dangerous man they're dealin' with, and I'll be goin' after them as soon as I can feel like I can stand on my own two feet."

"You'll be back in no time," Smoke said. "You just need to get some of my cookin'—get some red meat in you to get your blood built back up."

"That's what I'm thinkin'," Cullen replied, "startin' right now. This coffee's good, but I'm about ready to eat somethin' to soak it up."

"I reckon we are a little late on breakfast," Smoke said, realizing then that they had all been absorbed in the story. He got up and went to the stove, still interested in hearing details. "And Mule Sibley said ol' Gabe never had no wife?"

"That's right."

"Poor old Aunt Edna," Smoke remarked, recalling Roberta's lamenting. He grunted in obvious derision. "I could see that little vixen had all you boys fooled. You can't never trust a woman, 'specially one as pretty as she was." Donovan and Cullen exchanged amused glances.

Cullen's health improved daily during the next few days. Whether it was because of Smoke's cooking, as he steadfastly maintained, or Cullen's determination to get back in the saddle, he became stronger and stronger. His impatience to head back over the Sapphire Mountains was eased considerably when after one week Jug and Cody came riding into the M Bar C leading Cullen's bay gelding. A second homecoming celebration was enjoyed around the kitchen table as all the McCloud men were finally home. Overjoyed by the return of his horse, Cullen also recovered his rifle and handgun, as well as his cooking gear and supplies. "I reckon I can take Jimmy Sullivan's horse back to him," he remarked, "and Mrs. Sullivan's pots and pans, too."

"Yeah, that's right," Cody said. "And you can get a checkup from that little nurse of yours, too." He winked at Jug. "What was her name, Jug?"

"Marcy," Jug replied with a mischievous grin pasted across his broad face.

"Right, Marcy," Cody said, knowing full well what the girl's name was. "Well, little Marcy sure seemed to ask a powerful lot of questions about ol' Cullen when we stopped by there on the way back." He winked at Jug again. "What kinda spell did you put on her, Cullen? I swear, the rest of us ain't got a chance with you around. First it was Roberta that had her eyes all over you. Now it's Marcy. How 'bout lettin' me and Jug in on your secret power over women?"

"You go to hell," Cullen replied, embarrassed.

Chapter 13

Raymond Tower walked into the Billings Gentleman's Club, looking for his partner. It was the first time Tower had been to his establishment, which was really a saloon, in over a week. The past week was also the first time he had taken a vacation in the twenty years he had been in business. The Gentleman's Club was only a few months old, and had been the source of considerable worry for him, but he felt he had no choice in the move. His prior saloon, Tower's Place in Coulson, was losing business as the town dried up around him when the railroad opted to build in Billings instead of Coulson. There was nothing for him but to move with the railroad if he was to keep his business alive. He invested everything he had on the construction of his new saloon, and the question soon arose as to whether or not he had enough capital to keep it afloat until he picked up the required patronage. He felt he had to count his lucky stars when an investor with ready cash came along to keep the club alive. Behind the pretty face, his new partner was smart and progressive. She had ideas for attracting new business as well as maintaining steady customers. She started by suggesting the sophisticated name for the saloon, something he would never have come up with. It hadn't caught on yet. Most folks just referred to it as the new saloon. However, he felt confident that for the first time in his business life, he was being guided by someone who knew success.

"Jack," Tower called out upon seeing his partner's brother carrying an armload of wood inside for the fireplace at the end of the large barroom. "I'm looking for my partner."

Sykes cocked his head to the side to gawk at him. "She's in the back room. I'll tell her you're lookin' for her."

"I appreciate it," Tower said. He made an effort to be civil to the irritating man with the constant scowl even though he found him an unpleasant sort. While he waited, he sat down at a table and ordered a drink.

Sykes walked into the back room, where he found his sister looking through some papers she had prepared for Tower to sign. "Hey, Roberta," he started, then corrected himself. "I mean, Rebecca. Your partner's at the bar. Sez he wants to talk to you."

"Damn it, Jack, when are you gonna learn? My name's Rebecca," she scolded, "Rebecca St. James."

"Sorry, Your Highness," Sykes replied sarcastically. "Anyway, that whiny old bastard you call your partner is at the bar." Jack wasn't totally comfortable with Roberta's assumed identity. He understood the logic behind changing their names, especially with the trail she had left behind her. They had to figure that some-one would be looking for them, either Bob Yeager or Cody McCloud. Yeager had not caught up with them. Maybe it was because he hadn't figured out that they had headed to Billings, or maybe it was because Cody McCloud got him, instead of the other way around. Roberta had also explained why it was better if she was the partner in this deal, instead of the two of them. She said that Tower might have felt threatened by him, while he would feel more comfortable with her.

He was sincere in his admiration for her, however, and her ability to bounce back from disappointment. Her plan to buy up the land around Billings seemed especially shrewd, but they were too late to cash in. They arrived in town to find that the president of the Northern Pacific Railroad, Frederick H. Billings, and some of the other railroad executives had long ago picked that plum—and sold the land back to the rail-road. That would have been enough to send Jack to the saloon to drink the money away. Roberta hardly blinked, and in two days' time, she was wooing Ray-mond Tower for half ownership in a new saloon. He appreciated how lucky he was to have her managing their money. He was bound to end up a wealthy man, and he knew it was all because of his sister. Because of that, he supposed he could live with his role as his sister's lackey for a brief period until the untimely death of Raymond Tower, which wouldn't be very long after Roberta got all the necessary papers signed that would ensure that the business went to her. Then, she prom-ised, he would become her equal partner. Had he been possessed of a slightly sharper brain, he might have wondered how far in the future his partnership would last—sister or not.

"Raymond!" she sang out cheerfully as she swept into the barroom. His face reflected the effect of her theatrical entrance, lighting up his graying features, and he quickly rose to his feet to hold a chair for her. Her arm extended, she gestured in a sweeping motion that covered the entire room. "What do you think? Do you like it?"

"Indeed I do," was his enthusiastic response. "You've done wonders with the place, and in only one week's time."

She sat down then. "Thank you, sir," she replied sweetly. "I'm so glad you like it." She placed a hand on his forearm and gave him a gentle squeeze. "That is my intent, to please you." She paused before adding, "In every way."

Watching from the far end of the bar, Jack chuckled to himself as he watched his sister work. *That old fool,* he thought. *She'll have him following her around like a puppy dog.* "Careful now," he heard Tower say, "you might wanna be careful what you say to an elderly man like me." Jack snorted, amused. Even he was sharp enough to recognize Tower's remark as a cautious probe from a hopeful old man. *Sic him, Roberta!* She did.

"Why, Raymond," she replied, "you're hardly what I would call elderly." She cocked an eyebrow and bestowed a smile dripping in honey upon him. "Besides, I find older men much more attractive than younger inexperienced boys. Don't you find that most women do?"

Am I seeing something that isn't really there? Tower asked himself. *She's just toying with a gullible old man.* But he could not deny that she was stirring feelings inside him that had long ago deteriorated. It was not exactly her words that fanned the dying embers in his brain. It was more the tone and inflection of her voice that led him to question her meaning. He was about to decide that he had led himself into wishful thinking—until her next suggestion.

"Are you staying in the hotel tonight?" she asked. When he said that he was, she continued. "I've got some papers that I want you to sign, but they're not quite ready. They just say that I'm authorized to act on behalf of us both." She placed her hand on his arm again. "Some men don't think a woman can order supplies or whiskey. This will just make my job easier." When he nodded his understanding, she said, "Why don't I bring them over to the hotel tonight? They should be ready to sign by then."

"Fine!" he blurted in excitement. "Fine! That would be fine! What time?"

"Why don't we meet for dinner? Say, seven o'clock. Then we can go up to your room to take care of our little business."

"Excellent!" he replied at once. Never before had those three little words, *our little business*, held such sensual emotions. "I look forward to it."

"Good," she said, getting up from her chair. "Now, I'm afraid I've got things to do to get this place ready for our customers. Are you staying to supervise?"

"No," he answered quickly. "I've got some things to take care of myself here in town. I'll meet you in the dining room of the hotel at seven." The pressing business that he had to take care of, and the only thing on his mind at the moment, was to buy some new underwear to replace the ragged long johns he was wearing.

She took his arm and walked him to the door. When he had gone, she turned to find her brother walking toward her, grinning like a dog that had gotten the last bone. Before he could comment, she said, "I want you to be where I can find you later on. I'm gonna need you to help me tonight."

"It'd be my pleasure," he replied grandly.

"Don't do it right away," she said. "Wait till later this afternoon."

"All right, boss." He emphasized the word *boss* with a bit of sarcasm. It didn't occur to him that by Roberta having him ask about Tower's room, if it became an issue later on, she would not be the one who had inquired.

At a few minutes before seven, Roberta gave Jack instructions to wait on the porch until she came out to let him know she and Tower were going up to his room. "I'll make sure the door is unlocked so you can slip in. And make sure nobody sees you. I might be able to get the job done myself, but I don't want to take any chances. The old fart might be stronger than he looks." When she was sure he knew his part, she left him and went to meet Tower in the dining room.

Raymond was already seated at a small table in the corner of the room. He rose to his feet when he saw her come in. *Probably been here half an hour,* she thought as she affected a smile for him. Although he was wearing the same coat and trousers, she noticed that he wore a new shirt. The thought brought a smile to her face. "I hope I'm not late," she said.

"No, no, not at all," he was quick to reply. After she was seated, he said, "I saw your brother sitting in one of the rockers on the porch. Do you want me to ask him to join us?" He hoped with all his heart that she did not.

"No," she said, giving his arm that little squeeze that had set his mind off on thoughts of fantasy before. "It's nicer if it's just the two of us." He was thoroughly caught in her web.

Dinner would have been more pleasant for Raymond Tower had it not been for the fact that his nerves had killed his appetite. That and an irritating itch from the new underwear he had purchased, along with the shirt, caused him to squirm perceptively in his chair. All the while he could not bring his mind away from the notion that he was too old to be entertaining thoughts of romantic conquests. She pretended not to notice his nervousness, keeping the conversation light and cheerful while painting a picture for him of the future of their successful union. When the meal was finished, she brought out her sheaf of papers, but looked around her as if annoyed. "Let's go up to your room to take care of this," she suggested. "I don't like to do business in a public dining room." He of course immediately agreed. "Why don't you go on up ahead of me?" she said then. "We don't want to cause any gossip." He was glad to do as she asked. He told her his room number and left immediately. She waited until he had disappeared up the stairs, then walked out the front door to the porch where Jack was waiting. "Give me about twenty minutes," she said. "He's in room 220."

"I thought it might be a bit chilly this evening," she said when she entered Raymond's room, "but I clearly didn't need this jacket." She slowly removed the garment, giving special attention to each button. It might as well have been a striptease for Raymond, as his excitement increased as each one came free. Gazing at her in the tight blouse, the old gentleman was already too far gone to worry about details in the agreement she brought with her. "Let's go ahead and get this silly business out of the way, so we can relax. It amounts to nothing more than authorization for me to purchase supplies for the bar without your signature." She placed the papers before him and handed him a pen, standing so close over him that he could feel her breast brushing against his shoulder. "Good," she said after he hurriedly signed his share of the saloon over to her. "Now we can relax and get to know each other a little better."

Scarcely able to believe his good fortune, he watched her as she removed her skirt and blouse, then went to the door. "Let's make sure the door is locked," she said. "We don't want to be disturbed." He thought he had locked it when they came in, but he guessed that he must have been too nervous to be sure. Still in her petticoat, she moved close to him. "Don't you want to take off that coat? It's warm in here." She leaned forward and kissed him then. He was a dead man.

She had no trouble getting him stripped of all his clothing except his new underwear while she remained in her petticoat. At her suggestion, he got into the bed and lay on his back as she playfully kissed his weathered face and permitted him to grope a little, all the while wondering when Jack was going to bolt through the door. Finally she felt she could tolerate the old man's childlike attempts to make love to her no longer and decided to make her move without her brother's assistance. As her victim lay there gasping for air in his excitement, she suddenly grabbed the pillow and pressed it violently over his face. Confused, he did not resist for a few seconds until he realized that he couldn't breathe. In a moment of panic then, he tried to fight for his life. The harder he struggled, the harder she pressed the pillow into his face. It was not as easy as she had envisioned. The old man had strength when the situation was desperate to the point of saving his life. He fought with everything he had, and he was at the point of turning the tide when Jack finally arrived. "Where the hell have you been?" Roberta demanded. "This old bastard is a tough old bird."

"I didn't wanna spoil your fun," Jack replied. Tower was no match for the two of them, and after a little fight, he finally lay still. "I don't believe he wanted to go," Jack joked. Then he looked at his sister, standing beside the bed, still in her petticoat. "You didn't even let the old buzzard get a look."

Ignoring his attempts at humor, she said, "Let's get him looking comfortable."

After Jack helped her straighten the body, Roberta pulled the covers over him and tucked him in. When she was finished, she stepped back and took a hard look at the late Raymond Tower. Satisfied that when the hotel staff found him, he would appear to have passed away peacefully in his sleep, she gave Jack further instructions while she slipped back into her clothes. "Crack that door a little and see if there's anyone in the hall. We can't let anyone see us coming out of this room."

He gazed at his sister, his admiration for her growing by the minute. "I reckon we're the owners of a fine saloon," he said, beaming. "I might go straight from now on—be a big businessman—get myself a fine suit."

"That's right," she replied, favoring him with a grand smile. "It's all ours now." *But I don't expect you to last much longer than that old son of a bitch*, she thought. "Now I've got to get back to the saloon. I've got work to do."

Things were calm again at the M Bar C. Donovan had his sons back around him and Smoke was his old ornery self. In spite of the apparent calmness, however, there was still something short of normalcy that Donovan could not help noticing. Even Jug seemed more somber than usual, even to the point where Smoke commented on it. "What in the hell's eatin' at them sons of yours? Jug's off his feed, and I ain't never seen him like that except when he was lyin' in the bed half dead with a bullet hole in his side. Cody ain't much better—walks around all day like he's studyin' on somethin'. Cullen's just as bad, but I know what's botherin' him. He's thinkin' 'bout that little gal over on Clark Fork, and I betcha he's tryin' to make up his mind."

"You might be right," Donovan said. "I've been no-ticin' it, myself. Might be a good idea to call a little family meetin'."

He decided to address the subject at the supper table that night. "Me and Smoke have been noticin' all three of you mopin' around here like you ain't got a friend, ever since you got back. So what the hell's eatin' at you?"

None of the three volunteered to offer an opinion. In fact, they seemed surprised that there had been any noticeable change in their demeanor. Cullen shrugged and confessed that he was anxious to return Jimmy Sullivan's horse, but could not explain why he had waited until now. The conversation continued for a while until Jug finally opened a wound that all three shared. "I tell you the truth, I can't get it outta my craw that that woman got away free and clear after she caused all that misery to so many folks."

Cody picked up on Jug's confession at once. "I reckon that goes for me, too. It bothers my mind that we didn't run her and her partner to ground and put a stop to her shenanigans. There ain't no tellin' how many more innocent folks she'll cheat or kill before she's through. And the law ain't interested in goin' after her."

"It's a job left unfinished," Cullen said, agreeing with his brothers, "and that never has set well with any of us. If we had any idea where she went, we'd have ended it." He glanced at his father then. "And we can't leave you here without help while we search half the country, hopin' to chance on her." His comments pretty much summed up the general feeling among the three. They were unhappy with the situation, but they felt there was little they could do about it. "Anyway," he continued, changing the subject, "I made up my mind to head out in the mornin' to return Jimmy's horse and those other things I borrowed from the Sullivans."

His statement brought a twinkle to Cody's eye, and he winked at Jug. "Well, it took you long enough. Now, if you're too busy, me or Jug could take that horse back for you." The somber mood at the table disappeared, bringing a smile to all the faces except Cullen's.

"I reckon I can do it myself," Cullen replied. "You'd best just look after your own business." He got up, carried his plate to the hog bucket, where he scraped his leftovers, then went to his room.

Smoke leaned over to whisper in Donovan's ear. "I told you. That boy's made up his mind, all right, but it ain't just to return a damn horse. We'd best get ourselves ready for a weddin'."

Chapter 14

Leading Jimmy's roan as well as one of the Appaloosas he had traded from the Nez Perce, he had started out early the next morning to retrace his ride of a few weeks before. Smoke had been accurate in his assumption that a decision had been made, but Cullen knew that it didn't mean that Marcy was of a like mind. So it was with a slightly troubled mind that he rode back through the Sapphire Mountains.

It was early in the afternoon when he reached the western bank of the Clark Fork River. On the other side, he could see Fred Sullivan's house about fifty yards from the riverbank. He pulled the bay to a stop and sat there for a couple of minutes, looking at the barn to the right of the house, thinking about the days he had spent between life and death in the back stall. He remembered the feeling of indifference when it came to whether he lived or died—and he remembered the angelic face that had smiled at him when he returned to complete consciousness. He had seen that face many times since, when he permitted his mind to wander. Without thinking, he reached up and felt his cheek where she had kissed him good-bye. *Well, are you going to just sit here daydreaming forever?* a voice inside him asked, bringing him back to the task he had set out to do. With his mind back on the business at hand, he turned the bay and rode upstream to the shallow ford where he had crossed several weeks before.

Fall had settled comfortably into the valley now and the days were shorter, the evenings cooler, already with heavy frost in the mornings. She had draped a shawl across her shoulders even though the sun was still above the mountains to the west when she came out to feed the chickens. As she watched them scrambling for the cracked corn, her mind was far away, beyond those mountains. Suddenly, she thought she felt an unexpected warming of the chilly breeze for only a second, causing her to turn to look toward the river. She did not hear her empty bucket when it landed on the ground at her feet, nor the startled chickens that scurried away as a result. She was aware of nothing beyond the solitary rider coming up from the river, leading two horses as he approached the barn. She knew he would come back. *He had to.* Her father and her brother had joked about it. Her father teased Jimmy that he had lost his horse, that he'd never see the roan again. She knew her father didn't really believe that, but she had known for certain that Cullen McCloud would return because she wanted him to so badly. She left the bucket lying where it had dropped and hurried toward the barn where her father and Jimmy had been cleaning out the stalls.

"Well, look who's here," Fred called out cheerfully as he and Jimmy walked out of the barn, heading for the house. They stopped and waited when Cullen rode up to them and stepped down from the saddle. "Young fellow, you're lookin' a helluva lot better than the last time I saw you." He stepped forward to shake hands.

"I reckon I'm *feelin'* a helluva lot better," Cullen replied. He handed the lead rope on the two extra horses to Jimmy. "Reckon you can take care of these horses. I thank you for the loan of yours. I don't think he's any worse for the weather."

"Yes, sir," Jimmy replied, and took the rope, his eyes on the Appaloosa. "That one looks like Buttermilk."

"I guess he does at that," Cullen agreed. "He's his brother—come from the same mare a year apart." He let Jimmy admire the horse for a minute before saying, "He's yours, payment for lettin' me borrow the roan."

Jimmy was rendered speechless for a few moments, but a voice behind Cullen commented, "That was a special thing to do. I'm sure Jimmy will say so as soon as he comes back to earth."

"I sure will!" Jimmy exclaimed, and Cullen turned to find Marcy coming from the chicken coop on the other side of the house.

"Hello, Marcy," Cullen said softly. "I thought you might wanna see if your patient was still livin'." Fred was rambling on about something to do with the stage line, but Cullen heard not a word, his mind captured by the radiant face gazing up at him.

"You're looking real good," she said, also oblivious of the others there. "I think I did a good job."

"What?" Cullen blurted, just then aware that Fred had asked a question and was waiting for the answer.

"I said are you stayin' for supper, and maybe a while longer?"

"I reckon, if your missus doesn't mind," he murmured. Then momentarily released from the spell that held him locked in a gaze with Marcy, he answered more forcefully, "Yes, sir, I'd like to stay overnight if it's all right." Then remembering, he continued. "I brought some money to pay for what I owe for all the food and care I got when I was laid up."

"Son, you don't owe us anythin' for that," Fred responded. "We were just glad we were able to take care of you. Why, we felt like you was family."

Marcy gave him a little smile after her father's comment. "That's right," she said. "I'll go in the house and let Mama know one of our family will be here for supper." She turned and left them to argue over whether or not Fred would accept money for Cullen's care.

Myra Sullivan was all smiles when the men came in from the barn. She met them at the door and gave Cullen a little hug. "I'm so glad you came back," she said, beaming at him. "We were awfully worried about you, young man. You didn't look too well when you left here."

"I started missin' your cookin' too much," Cullen joked. "Besides, I owe you folks some money for all the grub I ate, and for the room and doctorin'."

"Now, we've already settled that," Fred insisted. "That Appaloosa horse you gave Jimmy more'n made up for anythin' you mighta owed us."

"Fred's right," Myra said. "You don't owe us anything."

The debate continued for a few minutes until Cullen finally gave in and thanked them all for their care and hospitality. Through it all, Marcy said nothing. Her mother noticed that she had gotten strangely quiet, and she could pretty well guess why. She knew that Marcy had made her decision, and she was wise enough to wait for Cullen to make his. Myra's concern was naturally for her daughter and she prayed that Marcy's heart would not be broken if Cullen turned out to be wed to the mountains and rivers, born to be a wanderer. If things turned out the way Marcy wanted, it would be both a happy and sad occasion for Myra, for Marcy was still a baby in her mother's eyes. Things generally happened for the best, she finally told herself, and brought her attention back to preparing a meal for her family and their guest. "Your old room is ready for you," she said when there was a lull in the conversation.

"Uh, thank you just the same, ma'am," Cullen replied, "but I reckon I'll just throw my blanket down in the barn if it's all right with you. There's no need to mess up your room."

"Nonsense," Myra replied. "It's no trouble. You don't have to sleep in the barn, for goodness' sake." She quickly glanced at Marcy, who had paused in the process of patting out the biscuit dough, waiting to hear his answer. "Of course it's up to you. You might feel more comfortable in the barn."

"I appreciate your invitation, but the barn suits me just fine, and out there I don't feel like I'm in anybody's way."

"Well, if you change your mind, just say the word,"

Myra said. Marcy turned her attention back to the biscuit dough.

After supper, Cullen went out to help Jimmy get
acquainted with his new horse. "I worked with him
some," he said. "He's got spirit. I think he's gonna be a
good one. He's saddle broke, so you can throw a saddle on him." He climbed up to sit on the top rail of the
corral and watch the boy hem the Appaloosa in the
far corner. "Let him get used to your smell a little bit,"
he called out. Jimmy stroked the horse's face and neck
for a few minutes, then slipped the bridle on him with
no resistance from the horse. Fred climbed up beside
Cullen on the top rail while Jimmy saddled his new
horse. When the Appaloosa was cinched up and ready to
mount, Jimmy climbed up in the saddle. Cullen hopped
down and opened the gate for him, and Jimmy rode out
the lane toward the road, the horse stepping smartly in a
fast walk.

"You think he'll be all right?" Fred asked when
Jimmy disappeared down the road toward Butte.

"Yeah," Cullen replied. "That little geldin' is as gentle as a lamb."

In spite of Cullen's assurance, Fred began to worry
when Jimmy had not returned when it was almost bedtime. He was of a mind to suggest that they go look
for him when Jimmy appeared at the top of the lane
and rode into the yard at a comfortable lope. "Boy, he's
a beauty!" Jimmy exclaimed when he climbed down
from the saddle. "Thanks, Cullen. He's the best horse
I've ever seen."

"Well, you've got two horses in your string now,"

Cullen said. "Make sure you take care of both of 'em."
Watching the boy leading the Appaloosa back into the
corral, he was reminded of a young Indian named Yel-
low Hand, and he recalled how proud the Nez Perce
warrior had been to show off the horse's good points.
He couldn't help wondering if there would be any
future opportunities to trade with the Nez Perce if they
were successful in escaping the soldiers.

After Jimmy's horse was put away for the night,
Cullen walked back to the house with Fred and his
son to express his thanks to Myra and Marcy for the
supper. After a promise from Myra for a big breakfast
in the morning, he said good night. Myra quickly
switched her gaze to her daughter's face, but Marcy
remained silent, giving no indication of particular concern. After the dishes had been washed; however, Marcy
wrapped a couple of the leftover biscuits in a cloth and
said she was going to take them out to the barn for
Cullen.

Trying not to appear obvious in her concern, Myra
commented, "Jimmy can run over there with them."

"No," Marcy said. "I'll take them. I could use some
air, anyway."

Myra walked to the kitchen door and stood watching Marcy's back until she could no longer see her in
the fading light. She hoped she had done a decent job
of raising her daughter. She firmly believed that she
had done her best to instill the proper principles in her
upbringing. But now that it had come to the day she
knew would someday arrive, she had to trust that Marcy
would make the right choices. There was little good in

worrying about it, she told herself. And it would be totally useless to lecture Marcy about running after a man far more experienced in the world than she.

"What's the matter?" Fred asked when he walked in and found Myra still standing in the door.

"Nothing that you need be concerned about," Myra said with a weary sigh, and returned to dry the rest of the dishes.

"Are you decent?" Marcy sang out when she entered the barn.

"Yes, ma'am," Cullen returned. "Is that you, Marcy?"

"I brought you a couple of leftover biscuits in case you get hungry before breakfast," she said. He thanked her and placed the biscuits on a corner of his blanket. She gazed around the stall as if seeing it for the first time. "Looks like you'll be cozy here, but it'll be pretty chilly tonight. Have you got enough covers?"

He assured her that he did. "It'll be like a feather bed here in the hay. I was sleepin' on the ground last night."

"It seems strange seeing you in this stall again. I would think you'd want to sleep somewhere far away from the place you were wounded so badly from that murderer's attack."

"I suppose it depends on how you look at things," Cullen replied. "Bob Yeager ain't gonna cause anybody any trouble again, except maybe the devil." He paused to consider his words before continuing. "I figure I owe Yeager." When her face registered surprise for his comment, he said, "If he hadn't shot me, I wouldn't have got to know you."

She did not blush. Her thoughts were too serious

for that. She studied his face carefully in search of any hint of playful teasing. There was none. His eyes locked on hers, he was watching for her reaction, worrying that he might be embarking on a fool's highway. A silence followed, broken only by an occasional stomping of a horse's hoof in one of the stalls. Though only a moment, it seemed an eternity before she spoke. "I'm glad you came back, Cullen. I was praying that I would see you again soon."

"Marcy, I had to come back. I couldn't stop thinkin' about you." He hesitated, then said, "There, I reckon I've made a big enough fool of myself. I hope I haven't offended you."

Her solemn expression melted swiftly away and she permitted a smile to warm her face. "If you're a fool, then I guess I'm a fool, too, because I haven't been able to stop thinking about you."

She came to him then, for there were no further words necessary at that moment. He opened his arms to her and she stepped inside his embrace to press her face against his chest, content to remain in his arms forever, and wishing with all her heart that the moment could last that long. Equally content, he felt at peace, knowing he was at home. Finally, they parted long enough for her to turn her face up to his to receive his kiss. When they parted again, she whispered, "I love you, Cullen McCloud."

He answered, "I love you, Marcy Sullivan."

Having made the commitment, both parties were uncertain what the next step should be. "I don't know what your thinking is now," she said. "Where does this lead us?"

He was certain of his thinking. "I hope, if you're feelin' the same way I do, it leads to the preacher. I want to marry you. Will you?"

All reserve vanished then, replaced by a wide, happy smile, and she nodded her head rapidly while answering his proposal. "I will! When?"

"Maybe we can find a preacher to tie the knot right away. What do you think your folks will say? They might not approve of it."

"I think they'll approve of it," she replied confidently. "They did a lot of talking about what a decent man you are." She shrugged and smiled when she added, "But if they don't, we're getting married anyway."

They spent the next half hour making their plans to accomplish the marriage with the least trouble for all. Marcy recalled that there was a church in Deer Lodge where they might have the ceremony. "Maybe the preacher might even ride down here to get us married," Cullen said. "That way your folks wouldn't have to leave the station here."

"Maybe we could send Cody after him," Marcy remarked. "He seems very talented at persuading people." They both laughed at that suggestion; then Marcy asked, "What about your folks? We should send word to them about the wedding."

"There isn't anybody but my pa and my brothers . . . and Smoke. They'll find out when I show up with you by my side," Cullen said.

Marcy tilted her head to one side, thinking of his response. "Oh, Cullen, I think your father and your brothers might be hurt if you didn't invite them to the wedding. We could wait long enough to give them time to ride over here." She smiled then. "We'll talk about it later."

He laughed. "You're talkin' like a wife already."

Myra stood at the kitchen window, gazing into the darkness that now hindered her view of the barn. Suddenly, Marcy appeared, walking briskly toward the back door. Myra strained to see her more closely, and was immediately relieved to note no suggestion of disarray in her daughter's clothing. *Thank you, Lord,* she thought, and reminded herself of the faith she had in Marcy's sensibilities. She walked over to the table, so as not to be seen looking out the window, although she could fairly well guess that Marcy had already seen her at the window. "Was Cullen glad to get the biscuits?" she asked, unable to think of anything else.

"Yes," Marcy replied. "Has Papa gone to bed?"

"He was getting ready to, but I don't think he's in bed yet."

"Cullen will be coming over in a few minutes. We have something to tell you and Papa."

When they announced their intention to wed, there ensued a discussion that lasted late into the night. Of the three astonished members of Marcy's family, Jimmy was by far the most excited, Fred was generally pleased by Marcy's choice, and Myra resigned herself to the idea that it was bound to happen sometime; she only wished that it could have been a few years in the future. All things considered, they took the news as a positive step in Marcy's young life.

Chapter 15

It had been too long since Cody had the opportunity to pay a visit to Mule Sibley's establishment to see Mule's daughter, Brenda. Cullen had left that morning to visit his lady friend, although he maintained it was to return a horse, so Cody decided to scratch an itch himself. When he turned down the narrow lane leading to the trading post, he noticed a horse tied at the corner of the porch. Dismounting, he looped Buttermilk's reins loosely around the hitching rail and walked in to find Mule and Rena talking to a stranger at the saloon side of the room. "Howdy, Cody," Mule called out. "Where you been hidin'? Ain't seen you in a while."

"Howdy, Mule, Miz Sibley," Cody replied. "I've been kinda busy."

"Say howdy to Pete Scoggin," Mule said. "He's just rode all the way from Miles City, guidin' a feller and his two sons to Missoula."

"Four of us and two extra horses," Pete volunteered, "close to five hundred miles, and we made it in less than two and a half weeks."

Cody took a moment to look at the stranger. Gray-haired, with a full gray beard, dressed in buckskins, he looked as though he might have been an army scout in his younger years. "That's a long time in the saddle, but you made mighty good time," he said.

"Woulda made better time than that if we hadn't run into a blame war. I was just tellin' Mule here. Little town west of Coulson, name of Billin's—we hit there right after ol' Chief Joseph crossed the Yellowstone with his band of Injuns. They had a dandy of a fight with the soldiers there at Canyon Creek. So we had to stay in Billin's for a couple of days and wait for 'em to clear outta the way. You could hear the shootin' from the main street in town." He paused to finish his glass of beer. "That's mighty good," he continued. "All this jawin' has made my mouth dry. I'd best have another glass."

Cody looked beyond Rena in hopes Brenda might have heard him come in, but she was evidently doing something in the back of the house. He turned his attention back to Pete's rambling account of his trip.

"Say," Pete started up again while he watched Mule draw another beer, "you oughta see this fancy saloon they got in Billin's. The Gentleman's Club they call it. Hell, I went in anyway. It's all decorated up with paintin's on the wall and a mirror as long as this bar here. Feller there told me that was a woman's touch. Said this highfalutin woman with a lot of money just showed up in town one day and bought half interest in the saloon. I saw her. She's a looker."

"Where'd she come from?" Sibley asked.

"Don't know. This feller thought she came from Chicago, but he warn't sure."

Like a bolt of lightning jolting his spinal cord, it suddenly hit Cody, and he blurted, "What did she look like?"

"Like I said," Pete replied, "she's a looker."

"Kinda tall for a woman, long dark hair?"

"Yeah, I reckon. You know her?"

"I might," Cody replied. "I just might. I gotta go." He looked at Rena, who was eyeing him, plainly astonished.

"Well, you didn't stay very long," she said with a chuckle.

"I know," Cody said, already walking briskly toward the door. "I gotta go. Tell Brenda I'm sorry I missed her, but I still love her."

Donovan and Jug agreed, it was too much to be a coincidence. The odds were very high that the mysterious saloon owner in Billings could be Roberta Morris. Donovan could see the tension already developing between his two sons. He understood their eagerness. He felt the same way. He didn't bother with asking if they were going; he simply told them to get their horses saddled while Smoke gathered up some supplies for the trip. "You'll be goin' by way of that stage station to pick up Cullen. Right?"

"Yes, sir," Jug answered as he followed Cody out

the door. "He'd be kinda put out with us if we didn't." They were off within the hour.

"I believe if we pick it up a little, we can make it there in time for supper," Jug urged. "That woman can flat cook up a meal."

Cody couldn't resist the chance to tease him. "I don't know, Jug," he said. "We've been ridin' these horses pretty hard. Maybe we oughta stop and give 'em a rest. Besides, we've got plenty of bacon and some jerky. We can just go ahead and eat our supper now."

Assuming Cody was japing him, but afraid that he was not, Jug replied, "My horse ain't tired a bit, and he's carryin' a bigger load than that Appaloosa you're so proud of. So you stop if you want. I'll wait for you at the station." He shook his head and said, "That woman serves potatoes and beans at the same time, don't matter the meat." Much to Jug's delight, they arrived at Fred Sullivan's house while supper was still in progress, and as usual, Myra had enough to feed two extra mouths.

"What are you two doin' here?" Cullen asked, still seated at the table beside Marcy. He glanced at her and winked. "The news couldn't have traveled that fast."

While Myra scurried around to get plates and utensils for them, Cody and Jug sat down at the table. "We came lookin' for you," Cody said, "but we'd best talk about it after supper."

Cullen didn't understand. "Why?" he questioned upon observing both brothers' suddenly somber expressions. "What's wrong?"

"Well," Cody stalled, "nothin's wrong. Let's just let it wait, all right?"

Myra came back from the kitchen then and interrupted. "Has Cullen told you the news yet?"

One look at Cullen's face and Cody guessed what she was going to say. "No," he answered, a great big grin lighting up his face, "he hasn't told us the news." With no apparent interest in the news, whatever it was, Jug dived into a plate heaped high with food, oblivious of the conversation around him.

"There's gonna be a wedding here at the Sullivan house," Myra said, beaming her pleasure in the announcement.

"Why, that's first-rate," Cody remarked, delighted by the embarrassed expression on Cullen's face. "Anybody we know?"

Amid wide smiles all around, Cullen cringed. He wished then that he had simply ridden in one dark night, carried Marcy off, and married her. Even Jug paused between bites to give his brother a big grin. After the wedding announcement, all talk of a more serious nature was forgotten in the conversation that followed. It continued until the dishes were cleared away and Cullen had suffered through a generous portion of teasing from his brothers. Finally, Cody became serious and welcomed Marcy into the family with a strong brotherly hug, assuring her that she was getting the best for a husband. "If he doesn't treat you right," he promised, "Jug and I'll whip some sense into him." Serious again, he asked, "When are you figurin' on havin' the weddin'?"

Myra answered, "We want to wait at least a week,

maybe longer, so your family has time to come." Cody nodded, but he didn't comment.

Supper and after-supper coffee finished, Jug announced that it was time to turn in, since they were planning an early start in the morning. Never having received an answer to his earlier question, Cullen wanted to know where they were going. "Come on while we get settled in the barn," Cody said, "and we'll talk about it." When they walked into the barn and he saw Cullen's saddle and blankets already spread in one of the stalls, he couldn't help commenting, "Damn, ain't they ever gonna allow you in the house?"

While Jug and Cody made their beds, they related the story told by Pete Scoggin in Mule Sibley's saloon. Just as it had struck them, Cullen was taken aback by the news, and shared the feeling of responsibility to act on it. "If we'd known about the weddin'," Jug said, "we'da gone on without you." Cody nodded his agreement.

"Why?" Cullen asked, astonished. "It was right to come get me. I'm as responsible as anybody. We need to do this thing together. We don't know anything about this other person she's hooked up with, or how many more she's picked up. No, we have to do this together."

Jug grinned. "I knew you wouldn't let us go without you."

"I will have to explain to Marcy, though," Cullen said. The words had no sooner left his mouth than they heard her call from outside the barn.

"Hello in there," she yelled. "Is everybody decent?"

"Well, no," Cody answered, "but we've all got our clothes on."

"I just wanted to say good night to my fiancé and my new brothers," Marcy said when she joined them.

"Fiancé," Jug repeated, and snickered, thinking the word a funny one to call Cullen.

Cullen ignored him and took Marcy by the arm, leading her back out of the barn. "I need to talk to you," he said.

As soon as they were outside, she turned, put her arms around his neck, and pulled his head down to receive her kiss. "I can't believe I'm going to kiss you every night for the rest of my life," she said, smiling up at him.

"You might get tired of it before you know it," he replied, and they both laughed. "There's somethin' I've got to do before the weddin'," he said, and told her of the obligation he felt to accompany his brothers on this one final quest to put a stop to one woman's evil deeds. She couldn't understand at first why he felt he had to go with them until he explained that they could not be sure what they faced if, indeed, this was the woman they thought her to be. "Marcy," he promised, "I'll be back for you. That's the one thing you can count on."

She put her arms around him and pressed her face tight against his chest. "I'll be waiting here for you."

"I'll be gone when you wake up in the morning," he said.

Chapter 16

They were saddled up and pulled out before daylight the next morning, before anyone in the house was awake except one. Standing at a parlor window, Marcy stood, still in her gown, and watched them until they faded into the darkness. "God, please bring him back to me," she whispered.

They spent long days in the saddle, pounding out as many miles as possible, past Butte, Three Forks, Bozeman, and Big Timber, stopping to rest only when the horses needed it. The weather turned from chilly to bitter cold as they continued east, following the Yellowstone. By the time they reached Billings, they had been in the saddle a week.

It was close to sundown when the three brothers rode into the busy settlement. "Well, they sure weren't lyin' when they said this town sprung up overnight," Jug commented upon first glimpse of the new buildings in various stages of construction.

"There it is," Cullen said, pointing to a two-story

building near the end of the thoroughfare. It was not difficult to identify the Gentleman's Club. It was the only one with a three-colored sign mounted over a pair of swinging doors.

"That's a mighty fancy name for a saloon," Cody remarked. "But I reckon it's just the place gentlemen like us need to get a drink of whiskey." Then he looked over at Jug and pretended to grimace. "I reckon you'll have to wait outside while me and Cullen go in." He grinned at his eldest brother, but Cullen's expression told him that he had no time now for playful banter. If what they had been told was fact, the woman responsible for a world of grief might be inside the rough building with the gaudy sign, and this might be the end of a long, hard road.

There were only a couple of horses tied at the hitching post in front of the saloon when they dismounted. "I think it'd be a good idea to split up when we go inside," Cullen said, "since we don't have any notion what this fellow with her looks like. That way maybe we can all keep an eye on each other and see who's behind our backs."

Pausing to look inside before pushing through the swinging doors, Cullen scanned the barroom from end to end. There was no sign of the woman they had come to find. Once inside, they paused to survey the evening crowd, which was sizable considering there were only two horses out front when they rode up—an indication that the saloon was obviously popular with the local citizens. "It is pretty fancy—that's for sure," Cody commented as he glanced at the paintings on the walls. Jug grunted his concurrence. They walked over to the bar and ordered a drink. "That table in the corner looks like a good spot to watch the stairs," Cody said.

Cullen agreed. "You and Jug go ahead," he said. "I think I'll stay here at the bar." He watched as they casually strolled over to the empty table in the corner. There had been no planning between them as to what they were going to do when and if they found Roberta and her companion. All three were relying upon their natural instincts and reactions to take care of whatever transpired, but generally, Cullen supposed they would turn the two of them over to the local law. None of them liked the idea of shooting a woman, no matter how vile, but they were dead set on stopping her, whatever it took to do it. He turned his attention to the bartender then. "I hear a woman owns this place," he said. "Is that a fact?"

"That's right," the bartender, Floyd, replied. "You fellers new in town?" When Cullen replied that they were, Floyd asked, "You boys with the railroad?"

"Nope, just passin' through on our way west," Cullen answered. "The woman who runs this place, is she from around here?"

"No, she's from Chicago. That's about all anybody around here knows about her except she comes from plenty of money."

"Is her name Roberta?" Cullen asked.

"Rebecca," Floyd corrected, "Rebecca St. James. Her brother, Jack, is here, too."

"Is he here in the saloon?"

Floyd paused to look around the room. "I don't see him right now."

Cullen nodded. "Rebecca St. James," he repeated. *Fancy*

name, fancy saloon, he thought. "I'd sure like to see Miss St. James. Does she come in the saloon?"

"Oh, sure," Floyd replied, "she's here most of the time." He glanced up at the open railing on the second floor. "She'll likely show up pretty soon. She's the reason most of these customers come in every night." He chuckled then. "There's a sight more men come in than there was when Raymond Tower owned it. I expect it's a good thing she showed up when she did. Old Mr. Tower died in his sleep right after she bought into the place. I mighta been out of a job." He was called away then by a customer at the other end of the bar, leaving Cullen to continue his surveillance of the barroom.

Leaving her new quarters on the second floor of the saloon, Roberta walked out into the open hallway. As was her custom, she paused at the top of the stairs to look over the busy barroom below her. There was already a good crowd in the room and it was early yet. *Before I'm through,* she thought, *I'll run every other saloon in town out of business.* The thought brought a smile of satisfaction to her face. Preparing for her usual grand entrance, she took several steps down the stairs and paused. Already several of the patrons had spotted her and interrupted their banter to witness her arrival. She favored them with a sweeping gaze and a smiling face. Her gaze fell on two men seated at a corner table, and her smile froze, stunned, not certain her eyes weren't playing tricks on her. She suddenly needed to grasp the stair rail to steady herself. It was no illusion. Cody and Jug McCloud were sitting at one of her tables. They had not spotted her yet, for neither looked her way. Maybe it was merely coincidence that they had stopped in her saloon. How could they know to look for her here?

With that hope in mind, she carefully took one step back up, pausing to see if they had noticed. When there was no sign that they had, she took a moment to scan the room again to see if Jack was around, but he was nowhere to be seen. Glancing at the bar, she was stopped cold by the tall, dark-haired man gazing back at her. The icy hand that gripped her heart almost caused her to cry out when Cullen raised his empty glass toward her in a deadly toast. Her reaction was automatic. She turned and fled up the stairs to her rooms.

"Upstairs!" Cullen shouted, and Jug and Cody scrambled after him as he ran toward the steps. Taking them two at a time, he stopped at the top with his brothers right behind him. They were forced to take a minute to decide which of the doors she had escaped behind.

"Was it her?" Cody exclaimed.

"It was her," Cullen confirmed, his gun in hand, as he watched the closed doors cautiously. "She's in one of these rooms and you can bet she's waitin' with that .44 of hers."

"Whaddaya wanna do?" Jug asked, knowing it was more than a little risky to go charging through the door to be met by a blazing .44 revolver.

Cullen exchanged glances with Cody. Cody shrugged and said, "We rode a helluva long way to let a wooden door stop us."

"All right, then," Cullen replied. "Let's take 'em one at a time, but, damn it, be careful."

They approached the first door then. With Cullen and Cody on each side, guns ready, Jug slammed the door open with one solid kick, then dived to the side for cover. His brothers braced for return fire as they quickly scanned the room from both sides of the door before entering. The room was empty. While they moved to the next door to repeat the assault, the barroom downstairs was turned into a turmoil of confusion. With an absence of gunfire from upstairs, none of the patrons was frightened to the point of fleeing, but the crashing of doors and the drawn pistols of the three who ran up the stairs was enough to send for the sheriff.

Upstairs, the last door at the end of the hall splintered as Jug's big boot tore it from the doorjamb. As was the case with the others, the room was empty, but they discovered another door to the outside and a back stair to the alley. "Damn!" Cody exclaimed. "We shoulda thought of that." They wasted little time descending the steps. At the bottom they decided to split up, Jug around the other side of the saloon, Cody to the street out front, and Cullen following the alley.

Searching hurriedly as he passed behind several stores, Cullen ran down the narrow alley that ended a few dozen yards from the stables behind a blacksmith's shop. Determined that she was not going to escape yet again, he raced across the open ground to the stable door, unaware of the man coming from the blacksmith's to intercept him. When he learned of the commotion at the saloon, and was told that three men were obviously chasing Rebecca, Jack Sykes was consumed by one thought, to save his sister, whom he adored.

At the door of the stable, Cullen adopted a more cautious approach, hesitating to charge in before taking a careful look around the door. He was surprised to discover no sign of Roberta. Instead he was met by Billy Johnson leading a saddled horse toward the door. Billy stopped when he saw Cullen, not sure what to make of the sight of the formidable man with a drawn gun. "Where is she?" Cullen demanded, but Billy was rendered mute by the sudden appearance of the desperate gunman.

"I'm right here, Cullen." She stepped out of the tack room door to stand before him. "Have you come to kill me? You're standing there with a gun in your hand."

He was not prepared for the gentle confrontation and he had to pause to consider. "No," he finally answered. "I've come to take you to tell your story to a judge."

She smiled patiently as she replied, "You know, I always thought you and I could be good together, maybe more than just a partnership. You were my favorite, and after all the accidents that happened after Blodgett Canyon, it was you that I missed the most." She carefully eased the Colt .44 up from behind her full skirt, determined to shoot before he could react. Her smile grew when she saw Jack slip into the stable behind Cullen.

Frozen in stunned silence to that point, a bewildered Billy Johnson reacted involuntarily when he saw Jack Sykes raise his pistol and take deadly aim at Cullen's back. "Look out!" he shouted. Without thinking, Cullen dropped to the ground a split second before Jack pulled the trigger. Rolling over against the side of a stall, he immediately returned fire, hitting Jack in the gut. Before Jack could fire again, Cullen put another round in his chest, and Sykes dropped his gun and fell to his knees. Remembering then, Cullen turned to counter an attack from Roberta, only to find her slumped against the tack room door, clutching her breast as she died from the bullet meant for Cullen.

"Gawdamighty!" Billy exclaimed when Sykes finally went facedown on the stable floor. "He shot his sister!"

Cullen remained on the floor for a few moments while his mind caught up with his reflexes, just then fully realizing what had just taken place. He was getting to his feet when the sheriff ran in, followed by Jug, Cody, and most of the crowd that had been in the saloon. "All right, damn it," the sheriff ordered, "just stand back till I find out what happened here." Jug and Cody ignored his directions and went directly to make sure Cullen was all right. All three then walked over to look down at Roberta as she stared up at them in death, shot through the heart.

"I saw the whole thing, Sheriff," Billy Johnson volunteered.

"You did, huh? Well, suppose you tell me what happened," the sheriff said. He pointed at Cullen. "You, young feller, suppose you just come on over here till we get this straightened out—them two with you, too."

After Billy related the incident as he saw it, the sheriff was still not certain that Cullen was innocent of a crime. "You're sure that's the way it happened?

This feller"—pointing to Jack—"was fixin' to shoot this feller"—pointing to Cullen—"in the back, but missed him and shot Miss St. James. Then this feller"—pointing to Cullen again—"rolled over and shot him. And that's the straight of it?" Billy nodded enthusiastically. "You'd go before a judge and swear to it?"

"Yes, sir," Billy replied.

"So Jack, there, shot Miss St. James, and this feller shot Jack," the sheriff summed up. "Helluva thing, ain't it? Raymond Tower died last week and left the saloon to the lady and here she gets shot today. And she ain't been in town long enough for anybody to know anythin' about her."

At that point, Cullen was in the clear. He could have kept his mouth shut and gone on his way, but he decided it needed to be said. "Her name ain't St. James," he said, "and she didn't come from Chicago. Her name's Roberta Morris and I don't know for sure, but I'd bet she came from Coulson, right up the river, since that's where Gabe Morris came from. All the money she had came from the gold she stole from Gabe. It was supposed to go to Gabe's brother, Jonah, so if you wanna be square about it, I reckon Jonah Morris owns this saloon now. I don't know the man. I'm just sayin'."

"Now, how the hell do you know all that?" the sheriff wanted to know.

"Because she just came from the Bitterroot Valley, where she called herself Roberta Morris," Cullen said.

"Damn!" the sheriff muttered. "I'm gonna need you to stick around till we get all this straightened out. "I don't want you to leave town."

"Whatever you say, Sheriff," Cullen said. He nodded to his brothers and they followed him out the door. Then while the sheriff was getting the others to help pick up the bodies, they returned to the saloon, stepped up in their saddles, and headed west. It was settled as far as they were concerned.

Myra Sullivan stopped to study her daughter as Marcy stood in the open doorway, gazing into the fading light. Another day and Cullen had not returned. In her mind, it was a foolish errand he had set out to do. Myra was fond of Cullen, and by all indications, he was a decent, honorable man. But he was a man, and as he was such, it was possible that his passions had cooled and he'd had second thoughts about giving up his freedom. She hoped this was not the case, but it had been a little longer than the two weeks Marcy anticipated he'd be gone. She dared not mention her concerns to Marcy, for her daughter maintained that Cullen would return to marry her because he had promised to. But Myra could read the uncertainty in her daughter's eyes when she thought no one was watching her. For that reason, Myra quickly shifted her gaze when Marcy stepped back and closed the door.

"Well, the kitchen's all cleaned up," Myra said, her tone casual, "so I guess I'll get ready for bed. Your pa and Jimmy turned in an hour ago." She went over and put her arm around her daughter. "I guess you'd best get to bed, too. You're looking tired lately."

"I'm all right, Mama. I'm going to bed in a few minutes." She said good night to her mother, but decided to sit down in the darkened parlor for a while in case he might yet arrive before she had to mark off another day. Every night seemed the same now, with so many thoughts swirling in her mind, robbing her of her sleep as she tried to picture him on his way back to her. Surely he would come tonight, she thought. She literally ached for his return. But he did not, and when the brass grandfather clock in the hallway officially announced the completion of another day, she wearily got to her feet and tiptoed off to her room. Hearing the creak of the floorboards as Marcy passed her bedroom door, Myra said a silent prayer for her daughter.

The morning broke clear and chilly, and Myra lingered a few minutes longer under the heavy quilts. She could hear the sounds of Fred starting a fire in her kitchen stove and she decided to give it a few minutes more to let it warm up a little before she placed her feet on the cold floor and hurried in to stand by the stove. She heard Marcy's voice, saying something to her father, and shook her head when she thought of the late hour when her daughter finally went to bed. With a sigh of resignation then, she threw back her covers and willed herself out of the bed.

"Good morning," she said cheerlessly when she walked into the kitchen. "Is Jimmy up?"

"He's already gone to milk the cow," Fred replied. "You're the last one up, lazybones."

At that moment, they heard Jimmy's step on the back porch and the kitchen door opened. "Look what I found in the barn," he announced with a grin from ear to ear. All eyes turned to discover Cullen following him into the kitchen.

"Well, I'll be . . ." Fred uttered. Marcy barely beat her mother in a race across the kitchen to greet him. It seemed a draw to Fred as to which one of the women was the most relieved to see the beaming young man. It was a while, though, before Marcy released him.

"I went out to milk the cow and there they were, all of 'em sound asleep."

"Why on earth—" Marcy started to ask, but Cullen interrupted.

"I wanted to make it in last night, so we just kept on ridin'. It was close to first light by the time we got here, and I didn't wanna wake everybody up at that hour. So we just went in the barn and went to bed," Cullen said with a sheepish grin. "I reckon I'd still be sleepin' away if somebody hadn't woke me up." He winked at Jimmy.

"I declare," Marcy said, pretending to frown, "I guess after we're married, you're gonna want to set up housekeeping in that back stall in the barn."

He laughed, then said, "Well, I do feel at home there." She took a step back to give him a good, intense look, shook her head as if exasperated with him, then stepped back, put her arms around his neck, and kissed him long and hard. She didn't care who saw it.

"I guess we've got a wedding to plan," Myra remarked happily. "I better get some breakfast cooking, 'cause I'm sure Jug hasn't lost his appetite."

Read on for a special sneak peek
at the next thrilling
Western adventure from Charles G. West,

Left Hand of the Law

Coming from Signet in July 2011.

Ben Cutler looked up and smiled when his six-year-old son, Danny, appeared at the barn door, carrying a Mason jar half filled with cider. Ben knew that his wife, Mary Ellen, had no doubt put the thought in the boy's head to fetch the cider from the spring box in the creek and surprise his father with it. He wouldn't let on that he suspected as much, because Danny was very proud to be the bearer of the cool refreshment on this hot summer day in the southeast corner of Kansas.

"Well, bless my soul," Ben exclaimed. "I was just this minute wishin' I had a drink of cool cider. How'd you know that's what I was thinkin' about?" Danny's answer was a delighted giggle and he thrust the jar out for his father to take. "Why don't you have a little drink, yourself?" Ben suggested. It wasn't really hard cider. He hadn't let it ferment that long, so it wouldn't hurt the boy. Eager to accept the offer, Danny gulped a few swallows down, smacked his lips loudly, then extended the jar toward his father again. He stood back to watch as Ben took a long draw from the jar, and smacked his lips in turn to show his appreciation.

"Somebody's comin'," the boy suddenly announced, and Ben turned to follow his son's gaze to the head of the lane where he saw a lone rider coming toward the house.

Ben put aside the harness he was in the midst of repairing and got up to stand beside Danny. The rider looked familiar, and when he was halfway to the yard, Ben recognized Eli Gentry, a deputy sheriff from Crooked Fork. Ben could not say he knew the man very well, and what little bit he knew didn't impress him very much. He had what Ben would describe as a weasel face with dark eyes that seemed too close together on each side of a long, thin nose. The thing that set him apart was the cutoff sword he liked to wear on his side. In a scabbard like a long hunting knife, it had once been a cavalry sword until about a third of the blade had been broken off. Sheriff Jubal Creed's other deputy, Bob Rice, struck Ben as a much more mature lawman. He had to admit that he knew very few people in the settlement at the forks of the Neosho and Lightning rivers, some fifteen miles away from his place on the Neosho. Curious, he walked out to meet Gentry. "Howdy, Deputy," he called out in greeting. "What brings you out to this part of the county?"

Pulling his horse to a stop when he was hailed from the barn, Gentry turned to meet Ben and his son. "I swear, Ben Cutler," he replied with a genuine look of surprise. "Is this your place?" Ben responded with no more than a smile, since the answer seemed obvious. He was amazed that the deputy knew his name. Gentry continued. "You got a right tidy little place here, looks like. I didn't think you knew much about farmin'." He looked around him at the barn and the corral. "Looks like you're more into raisin' cattle."

Ben shrugged. "Well, I guess I do know a little more about horses and cows than I do about raisin' crops, but that's what happens to a man when he meets the little woman who's gonna run his life." He placed an affectionate hand on Danny's head. "Mary Ellen got tired of havin' me gone so much of the time, and wanted us to have a place of our own. Have to admit, she was right." He waited for the deputy to explain his appearance this far from Crooked Fork, but Eli continued to look around him as if evaluating the progress Ben had made. "Step down," Ben invited, "and get a cool drink of water, or some of this sweet cider. You didn't say how you happen to be out this far. Are you on sheriff's business?"

Gentry took another look toward the house before dismounting. "Yeah, that's right," he answered. "There's been some raidin' of some of the farms and ranches in the county, and Jubal sent me and Bob out to look around. He thinks it might be Injuns from down in the Nations."

"Is that a fact?" Ben responded. "Well, I haven't seen or heard of any trouble like that around here. If it's Indians, I doubt if it's any of the Cherokees. I talked to Jim White Feather a couple of days ago, and he didn't say anythin' about any raidin' around here."

"Huh," Eli snorted. "I doubt he'd say anythin' if there was. He mighta been one of 'em doin' the raidin'."

"I reckon I'd have to disagree with you there, Eli,"

Ben said. "Jim's a good man. He's been a friend to me ever since I started to build this place."

Gentry did not reply to Ben's statement. Instead, he affected a thin smile and abruptly changed the subject. "You are mighty close to the Nations. I expect you're about the only white family down the Neosho this far."

"Where are you headin' from here?" Ben asked.

"Back to town I reckon. I've got a long way to ride ahead of me, too long to get home tonight, and I'm short of supplies as it is. But I expect I'll make me a camp somewhere along the way."

Knowing common courtesy called for it, Ben said, "It is a long ride into Crooked Fork from here, and the afternoon's about played out. You'd be welcome to take supper with us, and you can sleep in the barn if you want. Then you can start back to town in the mornin'."

"Well, now, that's mighty neighborly of you, Cutler." Gentry was quick to accept the invitation. "That sure would make it a lot easier for me. You sure that pretty little wife of yours wouldn't mind?"

"I expect she'd most likely invite you herself," Ben replied, then turned to Danny. "Run to the house, son. Tell your mama we've got company for supper." Turning back to Gentry then, he said, "Come on. I'll help you put your horse in the barn." He led the way to one of four stalls in the barn, hoping that his irritation at piling this on Mary Ellen with no warning wasn't too evident.

"Yessir," Eli commented as he stood between the stalls and looked around him. "You fixed yourself up real fine here." He cocked his head back to look Ben in the eye and grinned. "Musta cost you a little money, from the looks of the barn and house."

"Well, I guess I had a little money put back from my cattle, but I built the house and barn myself, like everybody else in the county, I expect." It struck him as odd conversation to have with Eli Gentry, but he supposed that it was just the deputy's way of trying to make polite talk.

"If you've still got some of that money put aside, I hope you've put it away somewhere safe, like a root cellar or someplace where Injuns ain't likely to look."

Not wishing to pursue a subject that he considered his private business, Ben switched to another. "Like I said, you can sleep here in the barn. I can get you an extra blanket if you need it, but I doubt you will, hot as it's been." He waited for Gentry to pull his saddle off and spread his blanket on the hay. "We might as well go on up to the house and see how long it'll be before Mary Ellen has supper on the table."

"You know Deputy Gentry, don't you, Mary Ellen?" Ben asked when they walked into the kitchen.

"Evenin'," Eli offered while making no attempt to disguise his thorough study of Mary Ellen's body.

"Why, of course I know *of* the deputy," Mary Ellen said, with a forced smile, turning her attention to Gentry. "We've never met, but I'm pleased to meet you now. Welcome to our home." When Gentry shifted his gaze to see what was on the stove, she glanced at her husband and rolled her eyes, registering her annoyance. He shrugged and made a helpless gesture. When Gentry returned his gaze to concentrate on her again, she said, "Why don't you two go ahead and wash up for supper, and I'll have it on the table by then? You go along, too, Danny. I know your hands could use some scrubbing."

Feeling no compulsion to do likewise, Eli stood by while Ben and his son washed up at the pump on the back porch. "You know," he commented, "a drink of likker would go good before supper. You must have a bottle around here somewhere. Ain'tcha?"

"Sorry," Ben replied. "I ain't got anythin' stronger than cider, and it ain't even hard cider, but you're welcome to that." It was not the truth. He had a bottle of rye whiskey that he took a nip from every once in a while, but he figured supper was enough to waste on the likes of Eli Gentry. It could be, he thought, that he was judging Eli too harshly, but he had heard a few stories about the bullying tactics of the deputy. He guessed it boiled down to the fact that he just didn't like the man. It was a gut feeling.

Eli curled his lip in a show of disgust. "I reckon I'll pass on the cider."

Supper was a silent affair for the most part. Mary Ellen and Ben tried to engage in some polite conversation at first, but there was no response that amounted to more than a grunt from Gentry. His attention was focused strictly on his plate as he stuffed his face with food.

"Well, I reckon I've put you folks out enough," Gentry finally said. "I'd best get out to the barn and hit the hay." He looked at Mary Ellen, who was already clearing the table. "Thank you for the supper, ma'am. I ain't et that good in a while." Then he smiled at Ben and said, "You're a lucky man, Cutler."

Ben grinned. "I reckon I'm aware of that." He winked at Mary Ellen. "She won't let me forget it." He got up from the table then and walked Gentry to the door. "I don't know how early you're thinkin' about startin' out in the mornin', but you're welcome to some breakfast with us if you want."

"Just might do that," Eli replied, casting a quick gaze in Mary Ellen's direction. "Just might do that," he repeated, then stepped out the door.

"I'll send Danny out to get you when breakfast is ready," Ben called after him. He turned back to find Mary Ellen facing him.

"I'll be glad to see that man gone from here," she said. "He's got a look about him that makes my skin crawl."

"He ain't what you'd call housebroke is he?" Ben replied, shaking his head as he thought about the awkward mood around the supper table. "I reckon he's all right. I guess we can stand him for one night and breakfast in the mornin'." He clasped his hands together over his head and took a good long stretch. "I guess I'm ready to turn in. I've got a big day tomorrow if I'm gonna get the lower field plowed." He winked at his wife and shifted his eyes toward his son, who was emulating his father's stretching. Mary Ellen smiled and nodded her head.

Ben had already gone into the bedroom by the time Mary Ellen had finished cleaning up her kitchen. The evening had already faded from twilight to make way for the deep darkness that would soon follow when she paused at the back door before hurrying across the yard to the outhouse. Ben would probably laugh at her, but she didn't feel comfortable with Eli Gentry in the barn. Although she was sure he was not up and about, she still felt as if his eyes were somehow on her. As soon as her business in the outhouse was finished, she almost ran back to the house. Once inside, she quickly barred the door and made straight for the bedroom, never feeling at ease until she was snuggled up against her husband's back.

In spite of her sense of concern, the night passed as other nights before it, and she woke at first light and slipped out of bed. She would start the fire in the stove and put the coffee on to boil before waking Danny. Ben would already be awake. He was always aware when she left the bed. She rolled out her dough and formed her biscuits to be ready when the oven was hot enough. While they baked, she sent Danny to the henhouse to gather eggs while she cut strips of bacon. A thought occurred to her that it might not be a good idea to prepare such a big breakfast. It might encourage Eli Gentry to visit again. *But then he might tell everyone in Crooked Fork that Ben Cutler's wife was a sorry cook.*

Ben came in when she called to him from the kitchen. He poured himself a cup of coffee and sat down to await breakfast. He was into his second cup when Mary Ellen sent Danny out to tell Gentry breakfast was ready. Baked biscuits, a large bowl of scrambled eggs, and a plate piled high with bacon were all on the table and in danger of getting cold when Mary Ellen paused and looked toward the back door. "Where in the world is that boy?" she exclaimed. "How long does it take to walk to the barn?"

Ben chuckled. "Probably forgot why you sent him out there. I'll go get 'em."

Gentry was standing near the barn door when Ben walked in. "Mornin'," Ben said. When there was no sign of his son, he asked, "Where's Danny? He was supposed to tell you that breakfast is ready."

"He did," Gentry said. "He's over in that back stall."

"Danny!" Ben called. "What are you doin', boy?" When there was no answer, he walked back to the stall to see what the rambunctious boy might be up to. "What are you do—" he started to repeat, but was stopped cold by the sight of the boy lying facedown in the middle of the stall. "Danny!" he uttered fearfully and rushed to drop to his knees beside his son. Only then did he see the blood-soaked hay beneath Danny's head. "Danny!" he cried again, forgetting all else in his panic, his only thought was to save the boy's life. The horror of the discovery sent his mind reeling with a paralyzing jumble of thoughts. He turned Danny over and started to pick him up, but was staggered by the sight of his son's neck gaping from a bloody slit from ear to ear. Still, in an effort to save him, he struggled to his feet; his only thought then was to get to Mary Ellen, praying she could tell him what to do to save Danny's life. With Danny's body in his arms, he turned to be met with the full force of Gentry's half sword across his face. The blow rendered him unconscious. Dropping to his knees, and still clutching the still body of his son, he fell over on his side.

Charles G. West

**"RARELY HAS AN AUTHOR PAINTED THE
GREAT AMERICAN WEST IN STROKES SO
BOLD, VIVID AND TRUE."
—RALPH COMPTON**

The Blackfoot Trail

Mountain man Joe Fox reluctantly led a group of
settlers through the Rockies—and inadvertently into
the clutches of Max Starbeau. Max had traveled with
the party until he was able to commit theft and
murder—and kidnap Joe's girl.

Also Available
Ride the High Range
War Cry
Storm in Paradise Valley
Shoot-out at Broken Bow
Lawless Prairie

Available wherever books are sold or at
penguin.com

S805-111510

"A writer in the tradition of Louis L'Amour
and Zane Grey!"
—*Huntsville Times*

National Bestselling Author
RALPH COMPTON

**Available wherever books are sold or at
penguin.com**

S543-122310